THERE, THERE

". . . anyway, what
was the use of my
having come from
Oakland . . . there is
no there, there."

Gertrude Stein
Everybody's Autobiography

THERE, THERE

East San Francisco Bay
At Your Feet

MARGOT PATTERSON DOSS

Photographs by
John Whinham Doss, M.D.

Compiled and Revised from
San Francisco Chronicle Series,
"San Francisco at Your Feet"

PRESIDIO PRESS
San Rafael, California
London, England

Published by Presidio Press of San Rafael, California,
and London, England, with editorial offices at
1114 Irwin Street, San Rafael, California 94901

Library of Congress Cataloging in Publication Data

Doss, Margot Patterson.
  There, there.

  1. San Francisco Bay region—Description and
travel—Tours.   I. Title.
F868.S156D62   917.94'6'045   78-7894
ISBN 0-89141-055-4

Photos: Mare Island photo, p. 289, by Cathy Fox.
Treasure Island photo, p. 161, by U.S. Navy.

Cover art by Muriel Schmalberg Ullman

Book design by Hal Lockwood

Printed in the United States of America

This book is dedicated to Charlotte McGregor for *auld lang syne*.

CONTENTS

INTRODUCTION

Learning to Walk,
Really Walk

"Where did you learn to walk, Mrs. Doss?" The first time this question hit me was in June 1961, about the time the "walking column" I had originated began. It was asked by a young newspaperman on the *Chronicle*. I looked at him incredulously. Where does anyone learn to walk? Groucho's answer is as good as any: At my mother's knee. . . .

In the wake of the thousand or so weekly walks I have written since, the question has come my way many times. Recently a little inactivity enforced by an injury has given me the time to speculate on what people really mean by it. Some of them undoubtedly mean "Where did you learn to enjoy walking?" The answer is the same.

Parents and grandparents often took me for walks when I was a child. I remember these fondly. Each walk had a different character. As Trevelyan says, "There is no orthodoxy in walking. It is a land of many paths and no paths, where every one goes his own way and is right."

1

High adventure might await one on any of Grandmother's walks. She gathered cleavers, kinnikinnick, and wintergreen berries, discovered the first arbutus to peep through the snow, taught me how the Chippewas gather sweetgrass for weaving baskets, and which herbs were best for dyeplants. Once, coming upon a plague of big grasshoppers in a meadow, she inspired us to collect a bagful on the promise of a feast of roast grasshopper legs. As I recall, they tasted rather like bacon.

Another time, coming upon a swamp abloom with wild blue flags, she showed me how to lay two planks, over and over again, to reach the wet center of the marsh where the flags were most plentiful. A pioneer in the North Woods, she was also a dead shot with a Colt .45 and could put her initials or mine into the broad side of an abandoned barn at 40 paces, something a child who has seen it once is not apt to forget. Yet this was the same grandmother who tucked an extra pair of white gloves in her reticule once a week and paid formal 20-minute calls.

Grandfather had a more philosophic turn of mind. To him, the rest after exertion was half the pleasure. With a pipe in his mouth, often unlit, his stride measured to accommodate short legs and his big collie Jack a few paces ahead, Grandfather would give his thoughts free run. One day he might ask, "Do you think there is a God, lass?" or "Have you ever considered the inequalities of men?" Children were still to be seen and not heard when I was six, so I knew I was only expected to listen while he tried his speculations on me for size.

Mother was an artist and her walks made a game of beauty. "Let's stop here for a longer look," she might say, and make me peer through the crotch of a tree or under the arch of a bridge at the landscape visible beyond, then bid me step aside and view it unframed. We laid our ears against telephone poles to hear the buzzing, as if a thousand bees were trapped inside each pole.

Or again she might command suddenly, "Stop, stock still. Now close your eyes and tell me what you smell." The scent of daffodils, ripening pears, new-mown hay, wild onions, a vixen, wet fallen leaves, all rush upon me in memory of her walks. Bird song, the chitter of squirrels, flickering sunlight on a still pond, the wind in ripe wheat, tinkling springtime rivulets, silence of early morning snow sharpened by the crunch of footsteps are the wild sounds memory lets loose. If you stop to smell, you also see and hear.

Father's walks were more athletic, for he was an exuberant man. "Let's run 50 paces, then walk 50, then run 50 for the next mile," he might say. We children would try to keep up with him until we came to a huffing, puffing stop and threw ourselves panting under a tree to rest. He liked to play follow-the-leader with us. We learned to walk a single railroad track, leapfrog over stumps, turn cartwheels, skip, hop on one leg, walk blindfold, and sing marching songs tagging after him.

We walked to school, to the store, and elsewhere and loved it in the safe cities of my childhood (indeed those cities were made safer by the many walkers in them).

It was not that we didn't have vehicles to spare. There was an electric car, a horse named Babe, and a carriage and a cutter, which is a kind of sleigh, in the carriage house behind my grandfather's home.

Father had a succession of cars that would grace any concours d'elegance—a Mercer, a Buick touring car, a seven-passenger Stutz with jumpseats, nicknamed Lord Greystoke, which was Tarzan's real name, a Reo, an Auburn, a Cord. We children were taken "touring" in them. It was fun. But there was never the magic in an auto ride that there was in a walk.

For one thing, isolated in the back seat, you were always past the thing you wanted to see before you had a chance to really look at it. For another, the big parental hand was on the steering wheel, instead of folded fondly around the trusting child's.

"Where did you learn to walk, Mrs. Doss?"

In some other world.

PART ONE

IN AND AROUND OAKLAND

1

A New Look
at the Mudflats

"How do we get down to the East Bay mudflats for a better look at the sculpture?"

This question pops up in my mail almost as regularly as the tide ebbs at Emeryville. And Emeryville, that once totally industrial minitown sandwiched between Oakland and Berkeley, is the clue to remember. There is excellent mudflat access in Emeryville under the Eastshore Freeway at Powell Street. It has, alas, very little parking.

Don't despair. With a little ingenuity, one can do a pleasant mudflat walk despite the obstacles. First and easiest choice is to approach that significant corner on any of four AC Transit buses—F, G, H, or L. They all stop at Powell Street.

If you prefer your own wheels, once across the Bay Bridge, head for the Marketplace, 5800 Shellmound Street, a nearby factory building recycled into an infinitely better mousetrap of a shopping center. It can easily accommodate 1,000 cars.

Enciting as the Marketplace is, plan to leave your exploration of it for the end of this walk (you are sure to emerge heavily laden with shopping bags). First, put on your oldest sneakers and walk resolutely away from the big seductive building toward the curve of street that fronts the parking lot.

If you had come along here around the turn of the century, there would have been a festive scene at Shellmound Park surrounding the tremendous kitchen midden that gave the park its

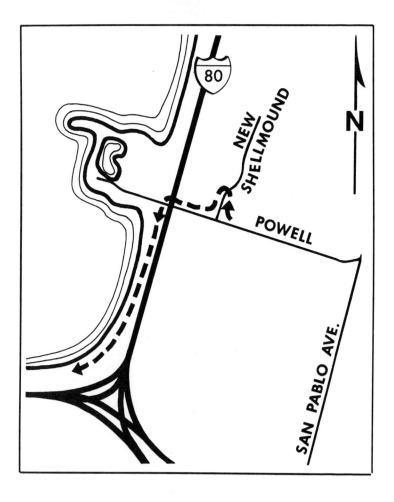

name. It held two of the largest dancing pavilions on the Pacific Coast, a racetrack accommodating 2,000 people, bowling alleys, shooting ranges with 200- and 400-yard targets, swings, rides, games, ice cream and fruit stands, restaurants, and in the center, the 1,000-foot-long, 300-foot-wide, and 22-foot-high shell mound. The Indian artifacts are now at the University of California, retrieved when the mound was leveled for factories in 1924.

Bear right, or west, to Christy Avenue, then south one block to Powell. Follow Powell under the freeway. Because the intersection is complicated by freeway ramps along a frontage road, the going gets hectic for a moment. Nevertheless, it is possible to cross with the stoplights. Be careful.

When you are safely on the southwest corner (away from Scoma's restaurant, whose found-object sculptured airplanes in the water may tempt you in that direction), you will discover 400 feet of paved sidewalk parallel to the freeway. Take it through the landscaping to its end.

From this point onward, the route is via a simple and sometimes muddy footpath. Come at low tide and if you are spry enough to jump Temescal Creek, and the occasional rivulet from a storm drain, you can make it almost to the curve onto the bridge approach. You may find student artists from the College of Arts and Crafts at work creating ever more monumental pieces of found-object sculpture as you walk.

Tremendous dragons, huge camels, heffalumps, knights in fantastic armor, a grandfather's chair for a giant Edith Ann,

plyboard castles, cacti, missiles, thistles, madonnas, and prima ballerinas have all burgeoned here at one time or another. Sometimes they stay for months. Other times they may be transmuted by the next whim of tide. For a long while there was a wonderful scene of a windmill approached by an unlikely Don Quixote and his faithful Sancho Panza. Another season, an entire parade of wooden people advanced along the mudflats on square-wheeled tricycles, octagonal-wheeled bicycles, turtles made of packing boxes, serpents of cables, and an un-wheeled wheelbarrow, all like some misshapen merry-go-round gone awry.

The San Francisco skyline looms off to the west as you walk, Camelot above the waterline.

2

New Life for an Old City

Consider a horserace of fashionable notions pounding pell-mell toward the year 2000 . . . and here comes Recycling, neck and neck with the pacer Gourmandise, as Rediscovery-of-the-City edges up from behind. . . .

Prodded by youth, we are taking second looks at yesterday's artifacts, often cheaper, better crafted, and more interesting than contemporary counterparts; at unprepared foods; at gracious spaces in the hearts of old cities.

All three idea-surges can be seen dramatically in the compact Old City area of downtown Oakland. In a few short blocks the walker will find a honeycomb of thrift shops, many of them housed in what well may be the most distinguished composition of late Victorian architecture west of the Mississippi. Nearby is a collection of markets that offers an international cornucopia. Some of the foods for sale here are available nowhere else on this continent, as more than one grateful gourmet or restaurant owner has discovered with delight.

The ideal way to begin this walk would be via BART, for the main subway station is located two blocks away at Broadway and 12th Street, but check the schedules on the weekend. For San Franciscans, cross the Bay Bridge and take the Nimitz Freeway, Highway 17, south to Oakland. Take the Jackson Street offramp, make a sharp left on Harrison, left again on Eighth, then look for parking around Washington and Clay streets.

Once parked, seek out first 821 Washington Street, for eighty years home of Ratto's International Grocery, where Martin Durante, grandson of the original owner, serves his clientele with Victorian courtliness as rare as some of his manioca flour or African red palm oil. Brazilians come here for the makings for feijoada, Britons for whistling copper teakettles, Indians for the snacks native to Punjab and Bombay, gourmets for the Gick soupfat separator. Mustard and mayonnaise stand on a barrelhead for businessmen who come for noontime sandwiches, mingling with shoppers who like to pick up their vinegar from another nearby barrel.

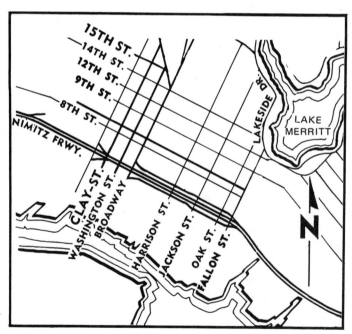

When you can tear yourself away walk north to Ninth and Washington. Pause first for reconnaissance. The eye is immediately torn between the contemporary street furniture and trees of Washington Mall on the one hand and Victorian Row, as the unbroken succession of handsome old buildings that line both sides of the 900 block of Ninth has come to be known.

Walk east on Ninth to tap a treasure trove of thrift shops surrounding Ninth Street Meat Market, which does both wholesale and retail business. *The Oakland News,* the city's first journal, once had its offices in this block. As you walk east, look across the street to get perspective on the sophisticated architectural details. Notice the lion heads on the overdoor at the Portland Hotel.

At Broadway, fishermen might want to bear left half a block to locate upstairs at 927, McClintic's Sporting Goods, a mecca for executives who bring expensive tackle here for repair. Otherwise, cross Ninth Street at Broadway. At the corner of Washington and Ninth, a barrow of melons near the curbstone may signal the goodies within. Don Abraham has sold as much as 21 tons of melons on July Fourth weekends. Look closely, for every conceivable melon turns up here, including white chayote and orange watermelon. On Washington Mall, bear right to discover at 926 the Peerless Coffee Company, whose delicious smells perfume the street from its open counter. Oakland City Council member George Vukasin, one of the owners, sometimes helps in the blending and roasting.

Cross the street to Swan's Food Center. Like the great old municipal markets of New Orleans, Baltimore, and many European cities, this is a collection of stalls, a great bourse all under one roof. The locksmith may loom behind a collection of embroidery patterns, a dressing-room front on a birdseed counter, dried fruits neighbor with fabrics, or hardware dwell nigh optometrists in this friendly place where the market basket is commoner than the plastic bag.

At Clay Street look north to spot the gracious old building whose sky-high sign says Synanon. This was the old Athens Club, to come down in the redevelopment. Then walk west, where the ornate red and white Chinese architecture, which for many years housed herbalist Fong Won, gives a hint of the Chinatown nearby. The next corner reaches Lafayette Square where one can rest on a bench in the shade.

Start back by walking one block south to Ninth Street to discover another block-square market under one roof. This one is the Housewives' Market, every bit as wonderful as Swan's, whose stalls lure the shopper who may want a whole hog's head, a tripe, or dried bananas. Plan to return with shopping bag in hand, but walk east along the south side of Ninth Street to see the handsome Della Robbia medals of Pascal lambs, fowl, fish, and fruit that adorn this old white building. For the explorer, nearby are many more secret shops to discover, among them Mexican, Polynesian, Filipino, Chinese, Korean, Hawaiian, Spanish, Japanese, Greek, Middle Eastern, Indian, Italian, and Brazilian.

Then if you'd rather have food for the eyes than for the stomach, continue east on Ninth to Laney College, bear left, and there you are at Oakland's celebrated museum.

3

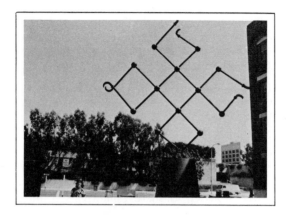

The Unusual
Oakland Museum

"The most brilliant concept of an urban museum in America" is located, of all unlikely places, in Oakland. This accolade was laid on the Oakland Museum by Arthur Drexler of the New York Museum of Modern Art, an institution that has held such laurels for many years itself.

What gives the Oakland Museum such cachet is twofold: unusual architecture by Kevin Roche—an associate of the late Eero Saarinen—designed to blend unobtrusively into the cityscape; and equally unusual exhibits within, particularly one that will appeal to readers of *Bay Area at Your Feet*—an ecological "Walk Across California" that former director Jim Holliday once told me took its inspiration from my newspaper column.

To make this walk, go to Oakland via the Nimitz Freeway, take the Jackson Street exit to Tenth Street between Oak and Fallon. (There is parking under the building.) You can also take BART.

On first glance the building will seem like an almost impenetrable block-square concrete fortress. Actually it is more like a Mayan temple in its interior levels. In another way it is not unlike the hanging gardens of Babylon, for the building surrounds many levels of outdoor gardens in its open center.

If you enter on Tenth near Fallon, off to the right will be a long carp pond surrounding a square island whose central cedar sometimes boasts a resident live blue heron. Walk into the museum foyer to find a tremendous redwood burl sculpture by J. B. Blunk entitled *The Planet*, which has come to be the spot museum buffs choose for rendezvous, with "Meet me by *The Planet*" as a casual line to drop.

Just beyond is an elegant open bookstore. On one wall is a dedication plaque dated September 20, 1969, which says the museum was "designed to share California's continuing heritage of life, art and history." There is also a docent desk where the coordinator pleaded, "We have so many classes coming we can't accommodate them. Please ask teachers to call us ahead at 273-3514 to make appointments for tours."

From *The Planet* bear left. Immediately you are flanked by a series of tremendous side panels and above your head are

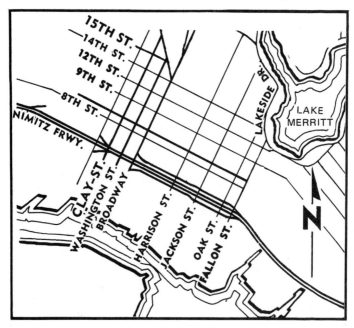

such quotations as "Nature speaks in symbols and signs" or "Nothing happens in living nature that is not in relation to the whole." Within a few steps you have reached an orientation room of the Hall of Natural Sciences. Absorb the orientation, then bear right and you have begun the "Walk Across California" at its coastline and are headed for the High Sierra. In quick succession you will pass through dioramas, transections, photomurals, displays, models, and specimens that represent the coastal mountains, the great valley, chaparral, foothill pine woodlands, the Sonoran zone, savannah, and the Sierran slope.

Since education in ecology seemed the only relevant goal in a threatened world, designer Gordon Ashby and former curator Don Graeme Kelley have explained in the arrangement of cases the interrelationships of the biosphere so well that even the littlest walkers can understand them even without the well-worded captions. At one point, for example, there is a series of cases that show terrain with its plant and animal population before, immediately after, and during recovery from a fire. Another beautifully done section is a redwood grove. Many displays show prey and predator. All show the sweet land that was California before it was befouled at the hands of the engineers, developers, and exploiters.

When you have completed this floor, climb up to the second level to find, equally well done, an exposition of California's history. This is also a California walk, but through time, beginning with Indians, through the conquistadores, the whalers, the Gold Rush and Silver Bonanza years, and the coming of the railroads. As Lewis Clark—a former president of the Sierra Club and a docent in the museum's excellent guide organization— showed me the railroad exhibit, he said: "The other morning I heard a train whistle and I knew from the high thin sound of it that the weather that day was going to be cold and clear." Remembering that lonesome indicative sound out of childhood, I found a lump of sadness gathering in my throat for the world foregone.

There is yet a third floor, this devoted to California art from earliest times to the present, but wisdom says save this for another day lest museum fatigue dull one's appreciation.

4

Where the *There* Is

Anyone who thinks there's no *there* there in Oakland, hasn't been to Lake Merritt.

This natural saltwater lake covers 155 downtown acres. Once a tidal lagoon, it became the first state game refuge in the United States, in 1870. Now it affords a handsome setting for Oakland's Civic Center and offers some of the most pleasurable strolling in the Bay Area.

Best of all, it is easily accessible by public transportation.

For starters, the southwest end, surrounded by Civic Center, has a few surprises motorists may not suspect. There are two tunnels under the highways so cleverly placed they are visible only to the walker. To discover them, and explore this area, take AC Transit's transbay Line A to 12th and Fallon and head for the Auditorium, or any of Lines 14, 15, 18, 40, 41, 43, 80, 81, 82, or 83 to the Oakland Auditorium stop. BART is handy to Lake Merritt, too, but remember to check schedules for the weekend.

Once at the Auditorium, walk to the side facing the lake. Look up over the four tremendous arches over the doors (one of them has the word "Intellectual" carved above it). Do an about face in front of this door and walk straight ahead. Within 50 paces you will be on a ramp that leads down to the lake through a gleaming white tunnel. In it sunlight streams down between the roadways overhead.

When you emerge, look to the right to discern Oakland's very own watergate at the Twelfth Street Bridge. Built by Dr. Samuel Merritt who dammed the lagoon adjoining San Antonio Creek in 1907, its hydraulic gate controls the water level of the lake. Pioneer Horace Carpentier once charged a toll to passersby here.

Look straight ahead next. You will discover that you are on an unexpected little sandy beach with a small fishing pier nearby. Up until 11:00 A.M. on weekends, the waterfront trail is reserved for bicyclists. Thereafter it is for walkers. Look past the beach and on the broad stretch of water, pintails, baldpates, coots, grebes, canvasbacks, scaup, and other diving ducks may be swimming at this season.

The little Lake Merritt excursion boats, the *Cabrillo* and the *Portola,* may go chugging past. One of the best buys for your

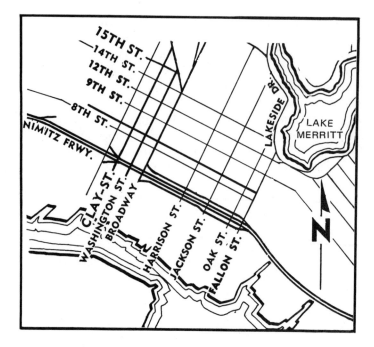

money left today, either boat may be rented for a pittance to take a birthday party of small fry out on the lake for half an hour. The water often rings with their merry-making. A scull manned by a crew from the University of California may scoot by like a waterbug.

Turn left and walk about 50 more paces to locate the second tunnel, but save it for your return trip. Climb the steps to the right of it and you soon have another whole perspective on the lake.

Oakland's remarkable museum is the fortress parallel to the Auditorium. The taller building across the street is Alameda County Courthouse. The smaller building adjacent houses sirens. Beyond is the Oakland main public library, worth a visit on weekdays to see the remarkable Knowland collection of historical pictures that line second-floor hallways.

Walk along the balustrade and "the Lady of the Lake," an

elegant Victorian house, last of many that once ringed Lake Merritt, comes into view. This was Oakland's museum for sixty years. Now a special project of the Camron Stanford House Preservation Association, it has been given a new coat of paint and carpenters are at work, restoring a veranda.

As rehabilitation of the fine old house progresses, the two front parlors will be period exhibition rooms, the others will be leased to civic organizations. One of the old house's distinctions is that President Rutherford B. Hayes and his spouse, "Lemonade Lucy," were entertained here. (Lucy won the name because she permitted no alcohol in the White House.)

Continue past the Camron Stanford House and take the first asphalt walkway that angles toward the lake. It reaches the water at the main boathouse. To make a loop of this walk, bear right at the shoreline and return toward the bridge.

Give your attention to the more distant hills from this sweeping vista and you can pick out areas where trees frostbitten a few years ago in a cold snap have been cleared to leave the hills as bare as they were "before the gringo came."

5

Oakland in Bloom

The most spectacular annual display of chrysanthemums in the world falls into place like a kaleidoscope every October in Oakland: chrysanthemums reign at Lakeside Park, alongside Lake Merritt.

From September until the winter rains scatter the petals, Oakland's noble cascaded chrysanthemums, each one a waterfall of blossoms, outline a great semicircle enclosing the chrysanthemum garden south of Lakeside Garden Center.

Within this living backdrop are 4,000 plants of 300 varieties, each with masses of blooms. Many are new introductions. Some are sports developed from name varieties in the garden. Others are displayed with ball and bat to make a great "A" in tribute to the Oakland Athletics.

To see this floral spectacular, transport yourself to Oakland. (AC Transit buses 12, 18, and "B" stop half a block away at the corner of Grand Avenue and Park View Terrace.) Walk past Children's Fairyland and continue past the bandstand, past the bowling greens, past the Lakeside Park Garden Center until you reach a boulder by the roadside whose bronze plaque calls attention to the torii, gateway to heaven, presented to Oakland from Fukuoka, her sister city in Japan. Walk through the torii on your left.

Immediately you will be in the dahlia garden, which remains a spectacular sight well into October, after almost two months of continual bloom. Annuals that border the dahlias are removed to ready the beds for new plantings.

At the first crosspath, pause to locate the nursery and lathhouse visible beyond, the site of a Polynesian garden which draws crowds in queues. There will be four Italian stone pines in a circle on your left and behind them the garden center building. Bear right, away from the building toward the archway of flowers.

Go through it, pause and look to the left and right to enjoy the wall of living color. Cascaded chrysanthemums, all grown in gallon cans in an oriental technique that is as challenging as bonsai cultivation, have been arranged in masses of bronze, ochre, purple, lavender, pink, gold, canary, and white to make a splendid setting for the central beds.

Bob Castro is the gardener who tends these remarkable

cascades. His partner, Bill Witmer, nurtures the spoons, quills, cushions, and mounds of the central beds. Both men are members of "Compost," the organization of professional gardeners for Oakland parks, a club that spurs the men to competitive pride in their efforts.

If you thought chrysanthemums had to be head-sized flopsies, typical of football game corsages, prepare to be amazed by the varieties here. The big football "mum," created by disbudding, is not challenging enough for these pros.

When you have oohed and ahhed to your heart's content, walk to the septagon of cascades in the center, then bear left

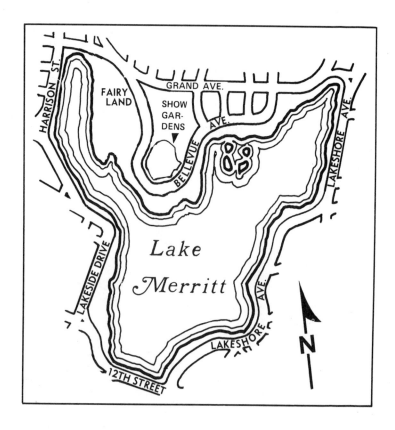

toward the main floral display and left again, past the boat toward the building beyond. Soon you will be abreast of a stunning cactus and succulent garden, created not long ago by Ann and Charles Genasci of San Francisco, who tend it regularly as volunteers. Walk alongside it to spot the "Old Mission" opuntia, the beaver-tailed cactus on the left. The fruiting one is *Opuntia arenacia,* while the spiny cabbage is *Agave huachuchensus.* The one that looks like a hand of bananas, reputed to be poisonous, is *Aloe plicatilis.*

At the fountain, go into the lathhouse, past the hanging baskets of ivy geraniums and campanulas, to reach the Polynesian garden, an inspiration of gardener Earl Kuklo. A total expenditure of $500, plus the labor on their own time of many of the dedicated gardeners of Lakeside Park, brought it about.

When you have enjoyed its tropical ambience, retrace your steps to the succulent garden, then cross the grass toward the lake to find a charming little waterside restaurant near the geodesic dome which is the center of bird activity. Thousands of migrating birds have made the islands offshore of it their fall and winter resort since before 1870, when Lake Merritt became the first wildlife refuge in the nation.

If you'd like a closer look at the birds, walk south along the shore from the restaurant to the dock, where, for a nominal fee, a little launch leaves every half hour for excursions on the water.

6

A Magical Walk

"It is the mark of an upward looking civilization that men make beautiful gardens, that the joy . . . be shared with others." Richardson Wright, the famous contemplative gardener, wrote in 1922. If he had lived to see today's gardening craze, when every other bar, boutique, and bay window has blossomed, he might well give an appreciative nod and chalk up a few points in favor of the progress of the human race.

The supreme irony, of course, is that right at the height of this gardening fever, along came the California drought to—one could scarcely say dampen—well then, to stunt the gardener's enthusiasm. Ahh, but wait. . . . Hope lurks in Oakland.

The Lakeside Park Garden Center opens its annual spring garden show on May 1 every year. A walk around the show and its environs, in the Mediterranean sunshine for which Oakland is famous, always gives hints on how to deal successfully with any water crises in your own backyard.

To enjoy this walk, go to Lake Merritt at the corner of Harrison and Grand. Best public transportation to this point from San

Francisco is the AC Transit B bus. The nearest BART exit is near Capwell's five blocks away at the Oakland 19th Street Station. Walk from Harrison and Grand into Lakeside Park following the trail along the water's edge. It will take you past Children's Fairyland, the charming pergola bandstand, and the big free-form play sculpture in its sandpit near the putting greens.

As you walk, the children's train may toot by. Joggers, strollers, cyclists may all pass, for this downtown park is surely as urbane as any in the Bay Area. At times a group of women rowers in a big whaleboat may pass. Music from the municipal band will echo across the water as you walk if you come this way in the afternoon on Sundays.

When the park road, Bellevue Avenue, seems to swing close to the lake, you are at the tip of the Lakeside Park peninsula. Walk away from the water, cross Bellevue Avenue, and head toward the colorful scene visible through trees and fencing to reach one of the two admission gates that lead through the outdoor show gardens toward the Garden Center building. Admission is $2, a pittance by today's inflationary standards. Children over 12 are half price; under, they are free.

No oriental carpet was ever half so vivid as the beds of indigo and gold pansies, those coy faces bordered here by drifts of snowy white or purple alyssum. When you have absorbed all you can, especially if you are a cook with gourmet intentions, seek out the southwest border of the garden, a year-round trial garden for the National Herb Study Society, which has planted such rarities as burnet and hyssop.

Linger awhile here to let the modest herbs restore your senses before continuing into the display of firemen-red petunias or Day-Glo orange nasturtiums. During the drought, horticultural sleight-of-hand began near a series of waterfalls and pools where the Business Men's Garden Club of Oakland and the East Bay Municipal Utility District installed an exhibit called "Plants for a Thirsty State"—drought resistant greenery. If not teetotallers, at least these plants were guaranteed not to drink you out of bath and laundry.

Designer Gordon Courtwright, who put together 1977's

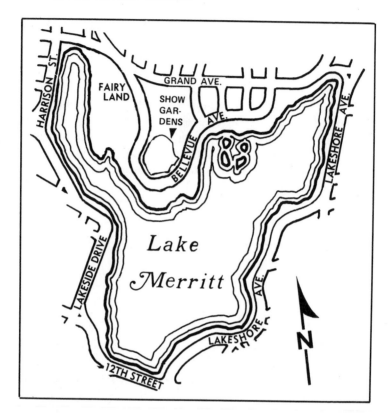

six-acre show, says the recycling pools used water salvaged
from the California Department of Weights and Measures. Before it came here, it was used to check capacities of trucks and
other vehicles, and in the past had been going down the drain.
Funds for the ponds came from the Lakeside Club and will be a
permanent part of the park in an area formerly filled with
chrysanthemum racks.

Walk toward the octagonal pink building, which houses a
tropical nursery, to see en route the strong sculptural forms of
desert plants maintained year round by the Cactus and Succulent Society. Never heavy drinkers, all cacti and succulents
here will thrive on neglect. Go through the bamboo gate across

from the citrus grove to experience an instant change in the intimate tea garden. If you sit awhile in this shady nook, you may even discover where Mamma Mallard raises her broods of ducklings. Clue: Her nest is in plain sight in the most obvious safe location.

Go into the building to see the roses or the irises. Educational exhibits and demonstrations on propagation and cultivation are also located indoors, with a covey of experts to answer questions. Cut flowers, plants, flower arrangements, bonsai trees, and orchids all go on sale when the show closes. Then, within the next two hours, Lakeside Garden Center sees as much as $10,000 turn over in sales in one of the most frantic bargain basements in the world.

The rest of the time, this serene scene is, like any garden, a lovesome spot, God wot. Wander as you will in it, before following Bellevue Avenue back past the lawn bowling gardens to Grand Avenue to complete this loop walk.

7

The Oakland Squares

February in the Bay Area is a month for celebrating both national patriots and Chinese New Year; it is a time to consider a walk from Oakland's Madison Square to Lincoln Square to Washington Square, which combines facets of both. The squares were among Oakland's original seven public plazas that fan out from Broadway on an axis somewhat in the pattern of hopscotch. All have seen their share of changes.

The two-acre park now called Lincoln bore the name of Oakland Square from around 1853, according to Kellersberger's map, until the 1898 anniversary of the birth of Abraham Lincoln. According to the Works Progress Administration's park history:

> On February 12 of that year, it was renamed Lincoln Square in honor of the Great Emancipator, in a formal ceremony at which Mayor John L. Davis presided.
>
> The occasion was the planting of a young sequoia tree around whose roots was deposited soil from each of the nation's 46 states and two territories; soil also

from the Washington, Lincoln, and Grant tombs, from the Bunker Hill Monument and the famed Sloat's Monument in Monterey. And here (circa 1933) the Lincoln Sequoia stands today. Nurtured by such cosmopolitan soil, it has attained a height of some 50 feet and is 12 or more inches in diameter.

Three fourths of the children of Lincoln school (adjacent to the square) are Orientals. . . .

In contrast, Madison Square, originally named Caroline, was not only renamed but bounced across Madison Street from one square of land to another. Its relocation came in the wake of BART. Dedicated anew in 1973, its trees and lawns have had time to mellow a little.

Old-timers who grew up in the area miss the abacus fence, moon-gate, and other play equipment of oriental motif, now removed to Knowland Park. Since the Corbusier-inspired BART administration building at Lake Merritt Station standing on the

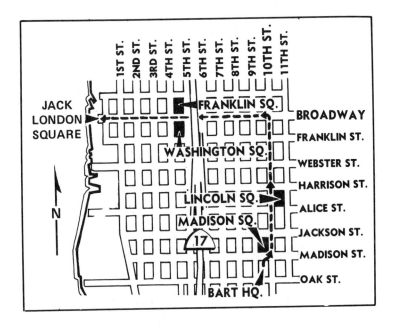

old park site has nice ground-level landscaping, the change is really more like doubling Madison Square acreage, however.

To see for yourself, begin the walk in the block bounded by Eighth, Ninth, Oak, and Madison streets, the original square. Ideally you should be able to come by BART. At least you should walk through the station's street level and look down the Circle. Inside, a fantasy of tropical plantings and water gives pleasure not only at street level and to passengers below but to all the offices in the building overlooking it, a fine multiple use of space.

Then walk past the flagpole to peer into the glass box that is the BART lobby, decorated with hanging banners and a big planter. The circular staircase leads to a mezzanine boardroom right out of "2001."

Cross Madison Street, once named Julia for the wife of pioneer Moses Chase. On the west side, you are in the new Madison Square. Stroll toward the left, past berms to find a playground whose sandpit is totally surrounded by a low "undulating" wall that turns out on second glance to be a dragon. The swings are supported by a torii gate. Architect John Sue was the designer.

Meander through the lawns toward the pergola in the direction of the big Buddhist Church of Oakland, which annually holds its Obon Festival in Madison Square. Both Hanayagi Japanese dancers and Chinese Lion dancers participated in opening ceremonies for the park.

From the Buddhist church at Jackson at Ninth, walk past the Goodwill north one block, bear left on Tenth alongside Lincoln School and in one more block you will be at Alice Street, now closed to automobile traffic. It is the eastern border of Lincoln Square. Although the square is defined by a redwood lane, it is nevertheless the tremendous magnolia trees and huge Chinese junk jungle gym that predominate.

Come along this way around 2 P.M. on a Saturday near the first new moon on the Chinese lunar calendar, and you may discover the Children's Chinese New Year Parade, a charming festival which has grown from modest beginnings ten years ago to rival in length its adult counterpart across the bay.

When you have observed the old tile-roofed recreation center in a back corner, and the new one under construction at the Harrison Street corner, make your way three blocks west on Tenth to Broadway. Bear left on Broadway four blocks, go under the freeway and there on the east side will be Washington Square, and for good measure on the west side is yet another of the seven originals, Franklin Square. (What do you mean they don't look much like parks, all filled up with civic buildings?)

Oakland became the Alameda County seat by offering the land on either hand for a courthouse in 1874 when the stench of tanneries and slaughterhouses drove legislators out of a nearby town. The new courthouse near Lake Merritt dates from 1934.

For something more recreational than welfare buildings and a hall of records, if you are a real walker, continue dead ahead on Broadway to the waterfront. That's what both Bret Harte and Jack London used to do.

Oakland, which has always loved and honored its writers, has named a nearby place for Bret Harte and the relatively new square at the foot of Broadway for Jack London.

8

Something's Afoot
in Oakland

Oakland's wonderful waterfront grows ever better. Four recent blooms on what was once a "rotten row," two the contribution of private enterprise, the others of government, are so pleasant and stimulating that any walker will enjoy them, no matter of what age or interests.

To end the suspense quickly, this paragon of places is the new Estuary Walk which links Jack London Village with parts of Estuary Park by way of the Portobello development. The ease with which it can be walked is part of the charm.

To discover this romantic promenade, transport yourself to Oakland. By public transportation, take AC Transit bus 11, 31, 33, 34, 59, or 76 to Broadway at the Embarcadero. Walk south on Embarcadero to Harrison Street. (Using your own wheels, park in Jack London Village at Embarcadero and Alice Street.)

For starters, enter the handsome two-level quadrangle of wooden arcades that is Jack London Village, easily identified by its gray rustic watertank. This is a marketplace so beguiling that many a walker could be diverted into browsing the day away in the shops here.

For the moment however, look for the Jack L, a derelict fishing boat beached in its own tidewater pond alongside Spider Healy's restaurant. According to Village manager Dick Cober, the boat cost only $50, but helicopter delivery to the site was $1,400.

Walk to the Estuary railing nearby for a little leaning. The maritime activity below makes it lively all day. Lights outlining the restaurants on the Alameda shore make it romantic by night.

When you have filled yourself with the lively scene, look for the Captain's Locker, on the upper level immediately north of you. Climb the stairs to look at the old pictures of this area in the antiquarian chandlery.

Back on the lower level, go through the gate abloom with Burmese honeysuckle, bear right and you are at the Alice Street minipark, a quarter-acre provided by the Port of Oakland, complete with benches, grassy borders, landscaping, and a great view of Alameda's houseboat community. Lounge awhile and enjoy it.

Then go through the hiker's stile to follow a dirt fire road

skirting the water. As you walk, look across Santa Fe railroad's vacant lot to locate the Alameda County Courthouse, the Oakland Tribune tower, and the Clorox building. On clear days the Mormon Temple looks like a Mediterranean villa on the East Bay hills.

The Rusty Scupper, which does not look rusty, is the contemporary gray building with the fine stained glass you soon reach. Owners tie up their boats alongside to dine here for Sunday brunch, or late suppers. Standing in front of it, look away from the water to discern the double lane of sycamore trees that outlines Oak Street from here to Embarcadero West.

Continue along the waterfront, noting the yachts berthed on your right and the mirrored windows of the building, which give the illusion of two estuaries.

When you reach the foot of Fallon Street, you are at the 7½-acre Estuary Park, which stretches along the water to Fifth Avenue at the Lake Merritt channel. For the fisherman, picnicker, baseball player, sunbather, canoeist, boatman, or windsurfer, this is a bountiful place. It has a double fishing pier, the only public boat ramp on the Oakland Estuary, two finger piers, any number of tie-up cleats, and five broad stairs to the water. Under those nine diamonds in the sky that comprise the pergola is a row of the sturdiest picnic tables in the Bay Area.

And as a testimony that things industrial need not look funky, consider the colorful blue, white, and yellow wheels and reels in the nearby Ford Tractor Company parts yard. It looks like the playbox for a giant and very neat child.

Follow the shoreline around under sycamore trees to the bridge to find both telephone and comfort stations at the Embarcadero across from Lyons Storage. Across the street the unusual tower is used for training firemen, while across the water, the brightly painted dock is launching point for local high-school crews.

At the bridge, reverse your direction and follow the sidewalks and tracks back to Oak Street.

As you stroll, the Southern Pacific may present what Wendy Silvani, who conducted me on this walk, described as a "rolling geography lesson of freight cars," in fine counterpoint to the movement of boats on the estuary.

In front of the Portobello apartment complex, walk down Oak Street's double line of trees to return to the water and make a loop that brings you back to Jack London Village, food, transportation, or the delights of the marketplace.

9

Bay Area Refuge

"Want to catch a fish . . . watch the sun set into Bay waves . . . scuff your feet on a sandy beach . . . launch a pleasure boat . . . gather driftwood . . . barbecue a hamburger in the salt air . . . stretch out on green grass a few hundred feet from the bow of an oceangoing freighter . . . or spot a rare shorebird in its natural habitat?"

This enticing list of invitations is extended in a new little yellow-covered booklet called *The Port of Oakland Pleasure Guide,* which offers "Six public parks and a variety of access paths and walkways" along the 19-mile shoreline Oakland's port has on San Francisco Bay, Oakland Estuary and San Leandro Bay.

Since there is very little parkland that touches the water along the Port of San Francisco shoreline, it is interesting to see what the metropolitan rival across the Bay has done. Its new parks and walks are impressive. Like Avis, Oakland evidently tries harder.

To see for yourself, consider a walk along that stretch of

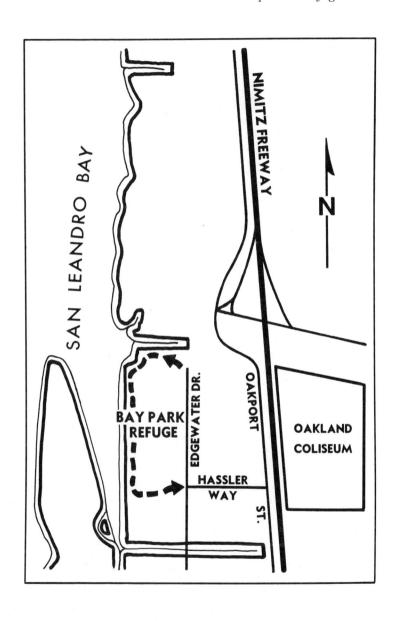

shoreline nearest the Oakland-Alameda County Coliseum Complex. It's the one you see from 66th Street as you approach the moat of parking lots that surrounds this pair of handsome contemporary sports palaces. The formal name is Bay Park Refuge.

To reach it, coming from San Francisco take Highway 17, the Nimitz Freeway, south when you come off the San Francisco-Oakland Bay Bridge. Go off on the west side at the first Coliseum Airport offramp and stay on Oakport, the frontage road, to Hassler Way. Turn right on Hassler to Edgewater Drive and right again on Edgewater. Drive this aptly named road to its end at Damon Channel. There is plenty of free parking.

An odd structure, rather like the crow's nest of a beached derelict ship, seems to invite the eye as you approach the shoreline of San Leandro Bay through the nearby industrial flatland. Use it as a landmark if you will. It stands in the middle of a sandy tot plaza within Bay Refuge Park, and you will be within 50 feet of the crow's nest when you shed your wheels.

At the outset, walk over to examine this witty wooden tower, designed to be a children's lookout surmounting a deck that is equally good as a stage for executing a tap dance or shouting "Avast you landlubbers." Deck and tower stand within a sandpit whose rocks and pilings are so well placed they must surely have been inspired by a Zen garden. When you have examined it, walk away from the Oakland Arena, which looms, from this vantage, like a giant bandbox stranded by an extremely high tide. Follow the walkway as it curves along the bayshore. In a trice you will be abreast of a marsh often throbbing with dabbling ducks. Dedicated birdwatchers have spotted the semi-palmated plover, the marbled godwit, the long-billed curlew, the black-necked stilt, the dunlin, the dowitcher, and the killdeer here. No one has reported a broadbreasted pushover nor a branded cutpurse, although sanderlings, egrets, herons, sandpipers, terns, and seven kinds of gulls are common. Come along at the right time and a ranger from the East Bay Regional Park District may be conducting a birdwalk.

Indeed, the area is so popular for birdwatching that in addition to the shoreline birdwalk in Bay Park Refuge, the park district leases eighty acres of diked shoreline around the huge tidal basin. Look across the water to vast open land this side of the airport to discern another part of the San Leandro Bay Regional Shoreline, Arrowhead Marsh. Hiking and biking trails outline much of it.

As you curve with the walk past the parking lot, several picnic tables snuggle into the sheltered shrubbery. Then an eight-sided fishing pier appears on the route. Digress out onto it for a closer look up and down the length of this arm of San Leandro Bay. Homes visible across the water on your right across Airport Channel are located on Alameda island. The bridge leads across the channel via Route 61, Doolittle Drive. Look past it if the day is clear for a fine view of the San Francisco skyline.

Grindelia, Scotch broom, star thistle, California poppies and the marsh plant called Fat Hen, bloomed here when this was part of Rancho San Leandro and owned by the heirs of José Joaquin Estudillo. At that time hide droghers went up the creek. The native plants bloom still along the shore, but the passing craft are more apt to be yachts. Cyclists, dogwalkers and joggers also frequent this length of trail between the water and the tall fence which hides the City of Oakland Service Center, a euphemism for corporation yard. It teems with activity during the week. Weekends the big vehicles look like tremendous insects at rest.

At one point along the trail a jackrabbit, big as a cocker spaniel pup, started from the brush. If you can take your eyes from the water, look back at the East Bay hills. When Charley Parkhurst, the stage driver who was revealed at death to be a woman, drove her team and coach along the county road (which ran between the trail and the Coliseum) this was farmland. Later, after the Southern Pacific Livermore line came, there was a stop along here called Elmhurst. The conductor would also call out, "Fitchburg, Melrose, and Fruitvale," before the trains reached Oakland.

The Bay Park Refuge trail takes an abrupt right angle turn at a line of camphor trees. Bear left on it and you will emerge in about the length of a city block at Edgewater Drive and Hassler Road alongside an AC Transit bus stop for the 57 Heggenberger Road, BART Coliseum line. The message on it says, "Commute Hours only. Phone 653-3535 for further information."

Since no sidewalks front the lawns of warehouses and such that front on Edgewater Drive, return the way you came. There is always more to see and enjoy along a waterfront.

10

Mosswood Park

Beautiful Mosswood Park, an oasis in sprawly old Oakland, stands sanely calm and green at one of the world's busiest intersections, trying to hear itself think over the combined roars of West MacArthur and Broadway boulevards and the MacArthur Freeway.

A walk through it is one of the unexpected pleasures of the mysterious East Bay. Here in a gracious tree-dotted area roughly three blocks square there are often more people enjoying themselves in less space and more ways than the average man could list—put to the spot question.

To see for yourself, begin this walk some pleasant day at the corner of Webster Street and MacArthur Boulevard. One sidewalk borders the park. Another goes diagonally, catapulting the walker instantly into the thick of horseshoe, basketball, volleyball, tetherball, and other gamecourts, hard by two playgrounds and a clubhouse.

If the games and crowds of kibitzers seem to be jumping, it is the better part of wisdom to walk along Webster Street first, skirting the playing fields. This route leads under shade trees,

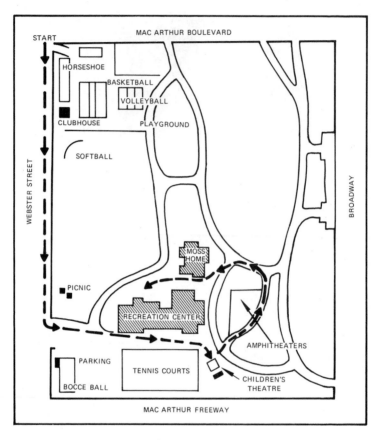

past a hot dog stand, bleachers, a softball diamond, picnic and barbecue areas to an entrance parallel with 38th Street.

The unusual Victorian house visible in the center of the park, usually described as a Gothic villa, was the home of Joseph Moravia Moss, better known as J. Mora Moss, a pioneer associated with San Francisco's first telegraph and gas companies and an early member of the University of California's Board of Regents. He built the house in 1864, naming the surrounding 32-acre estate Mosswood, a combination of his name and that of his bride, Julia Wood. The city purchased the land from heirs in 1905, formally opening the city park, now reduced to 11 acres, in 1912.

"When I was a child growing up nearby," novelist Floyd Salas, author of the prizewinning *Tattoo the Wicked Cross*, recalls, "a creek ran through Mosswood Park, a mysterious creek that little girls shunned and boys thought it high adventure to explore."

Glen Echo Creek was piped underground in 1945, but part of its contours are still apparent in a children's outdoor theatre, one of two such amphitheaters in the park. To see it, turn into the park near the few remaining redwoods. A bocce ball court and clubhouse are sheltered by them.

Walk between the tennis courts and the contemporary building. The building contains a recreation center in one half and an arts and sciences complex in the other. The children's theater is just beyond the tennis courts. Cross the walk to see its larger mate, which has its stage built around a tree.

For 30 years, outdoor theatre was a unique feature of Mosswood. A report of the Recreation Department says, however: "Use of the theatre was abandoned in 1960 as a result of adjacent freeway construction." Once in a while someone tries to read or sunbathe on the benches, but not for long.

Attrition or no, drama for other parts of Oakland still gets a boost in Mosswood. Walk back toward the Moss house (which becomes magically haunted near Halloween) to see a stage workshop building that is also a "teen drop-in" center.

Once within the building area, the walker will be dumbfounded at the evidences of activity. Signs announce programs for tiny tots, adults, old-timers, and families, tennis tournaments, hikes, campercrafts, skits, games, cookouts, nature lore, competitive sports, scuba and skin diver classes, orchestra tryouts, exercises, archery, and dog training, to name a few. This is the Junior Center. Oakland's recreation philosophy is that people need diversity.

A sleek, imperturbable Benny Bufano seal watches the kaleidoscope of comings and goings sparked by a staff of 14 lively recreation and park people. In a sense all of them, old-

timers say, barely replace George W. "Curly" Freeman, a leg-
less World War I hero who made Mosswood Park his headquarters between 1919 and 1944. Curly umpired, counseled, baby
sat, and greeted all comers.

You won't see Curly today, but it is his indomitable spirit
that carries on in the park that, like him, has been maimed by
civilization.

11

Pocket of the Past

Every city has its unsung charms. Oakland has a rural pocket, once known as Oak Tree Farm, where yesterday clings tenaciously, surrounded by today.

Within it, one can find a natural watercourse, Sausal Creek, and a footbridge crossing it; a public recreation area, Sanborn Park, which began as a private horticultural garden; and an elegant 93-year-old Victorian mansion still in the hands of the family that built it.

If you'd like to explore it, transport yourself to the corner of East 14th Street and 29th Avenue, an area of east Oakland known for the last hundred years as Fruitvale, so named for Henderson Lewelling's orchard, a little further up Sausal Creek, where the first Bartlett pear trees were established in California.

From the corner, look about. It doesn't seem very promising, with strip-shopping, (which is not to be confused with strip poker) all rather unprepossessing and with little pretension to chic. But turn up 29th, catercorner across from the big mail-order department store and walk a hundred feet until you are abreast of the house numbered 1440. Stop for a searching look. M. W.

Wood's *History of Alameda County,* published in 1883, records that "On January 20, 1859, W. A. Bray established himself on the Oak Tree Farm and commenced agriculture."

Emilita Cohen, for whose mother, Emily Bray, the mansion at 1440 was built, says, "This area originally was the vegetable garden for the farm. Grandfather Bray built this house for mother's wedding, in 1884." Notice the fine old trees, the stained-glass windows, the beautiful vestibule, the tower.

Fittings inside the house are as old as the exterior, and include a tank in the attic which supplied water, carpets woven to size for the rooms, and a tremendous mirror that came from Fernside, the legendary Italian villa of A. A. Cohen, attorney to the Big Four railroad magnates. Because of him, Fruitvale Station was established nearby. Fifty-two descendants of the Bray and Cohen families traditionally gather here for Christmas when the redwood panelled "alcove" is decorated with a grove of conifers.

Walk east, picking out other Victorians interspersed with smaller, more recent houses, until you reach Hawthorn School. Then bear right. In a few steps the street dead-ends in a clump of greenery. Go up close to the trees and lo! a hidden footbridge. Leaning on it, watching the untrammeled creek, one could imagine Antonio Maria Peralta, whose land this once was, fishing for the salmon and steelhead that came up here to spawn in his time.

Cross the bridge and there is yet another surprise; the neatly clipped grounds, informal walks, benches, and clubhouse of Sanborn Park. From 1879 until 1889, John Sanborn tended the horticultural treasure trove, many of whose plantings were the first, and often only ones of their species in the United States. His widow, Elizabeth, treasured the pioneer horticultural introductions and tended them carefully until 1925, when she sold the land to the City of Oakland for a scant $36,000.

Sit awhile and enjoy the sheltered sunlight. Notice the fine old ivy, the palms and other plants. Then walk out, away from Sausal Creek to reach Fruitvale Avenue. Bear right to return to East 14th and right again to find 29th Avenue, completing a loop that takes you back to your starting place.

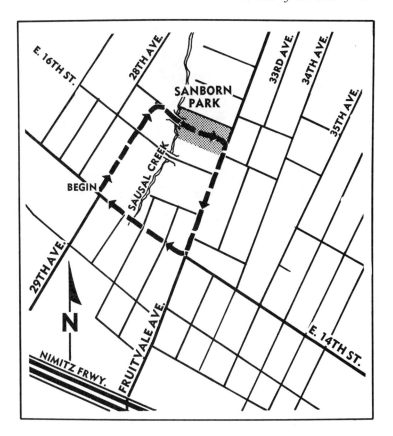

En route, you will find a street that commemorates pioneer Bray's friend, E. H. Derby, who took up residence here in the spring of 1860. Walk to the end of it, for an interesting digression, then look at the creek from the nursing home parking lot. Sharp-eyed amateurs of archeology should be able to discern the gate across the creek that once opened on a footbridge that led from Oak Tree Farm to Derby's.

12

Street-Wise Piedmont

"Mountain View cemetery is about two miles from Oakland and its approach is the finest drive in Alameda County," wrote historian J. P. Munro-Fraser in his *History of Alameda County, California*. The cemetery, lovingly designed by Frederick Law Olmstead, was twenty years old in 1883 when the history was published.

Today Oakland has totally surrounded Mountain View, but odd vestiges of past glory remain on the land. The once beautiful drive to the cemetery, formerly called Webster Avenue, is now Piedmont Avenue. It is short, straight, and most of its trees have been replaced long since by the business establishments of stonecutters, florists, and headstone merchants. More than one observer, noting the hospital at one end and the cemetery at the other, has described Piedmont Avenue as the short distance between birth and death.

Meandering down from the cemetery's parklike 200 acres there is, however, an unexpected urban treasure, Glen Echo Creek. Miraculously spared, possibly through more than a hundred years of benign bureaucratic oversight, it still tinkles musically through the arroyo to which it gave its name. Many a house in the neighborhood shares the pleasures of birdlife, frog conversation, tadpoles, and even an occasional fish that the creek brings to the urban setting.

To discover Glen Echo, transport yourself to the corner of Piedmont and Echo avenues. Begin walking south on Echo across from the Piedmont Avenue School. In the 1940s, Works Progress Administration buildings replaced the old wooden school built in the 1890s, around the time Glen Echo tract was developed.

As you walk, look for 63 Echo, a little complex on the right that is like a small town. Notice the Piedmont Avenue Children's Center and the vegetable garden made by children of working parents.

Bear right at Rose Avenue. The point at which you reach lush street trees is the discernible city line for Piedmont, whose street tree program is one of the best in the Bay Area.

At Linda and Kingston, bear left on Linda into the garden-like "hill town of Piedmont" which permits no highrise. Just past Lake Street, across from the Piedmont School, go on the footwalk on the uphill side of the barrier. In about 100 paces, you will find benches surrounded by pleasant plantings and a fine overview of tennis and basketball courts. Bear right at the footpath's end onto Oakland Avenue. Go one block to Oakland and Olive to reach the uphill corner of the Oakland Rose Garden.

At Bayo Vista, bear right, crossing this cruel commute corridor as well as you can on the intersection that totally ignores the needs of pedestrians. Bear right again on Harrison to seek out 3911, listed in Gebhardt, Montgomery et al *Architecture in San Francisco and Northern California.* Number 3912 is a lovely Queen Anne, while 3932 has gorgeous old palms.

At Monte Vista, bear left away from the Town House, a center of community activity. Park Sequoia Apartments at 323 Monte Vista have nicely preserved old redwoods in their back central garden. Downhill in the 250 block of Monte Vista is a fine old garden court that once faced the creek. Its own interior sidewalk fronts a series of brown-shingled homes dating

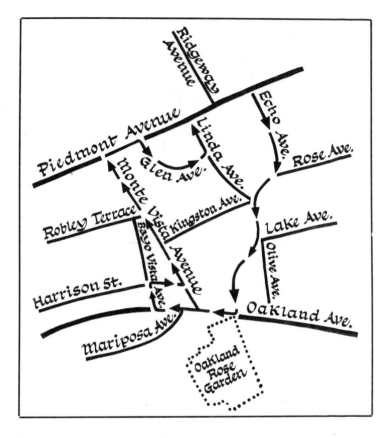

from 1908. Green Gates, the home just beyond it, has the same architectural style with a stuccoed Mediterranean overlay. Look for Robley Terrace, a charming lane.

Then, to spot Glen Echo Creek, look on your right across from 169 Monte Vista. There is the precious open water, scintillating under trees.

Continue on and surprisingly soon you are back on Piedmont Avenue. Bear right on it to find Pierson's country-style hardware store, which still sells cowbells and washboards.

Turn right on Glen, passing a unique dressmaking establishment owned by three black sisters who are talented triplets.

Steven Pride's tiny shop at 17 Glen creates handkerchiefs for the Pointer Sisters. The miniature house at 65 Glen stands right on the creek, visible beyond its yard.

Bear left on Linda and return to Piedmont to discover something unusual in a neighborhood theater, the Piedmont Cinema, a first-run house. The charming church at Ridgeway is St. Leo's. The Woolery is not a shop, but a school for weavers.

For a smash ending to this outing, stop at Fenton's Creamery, if only to see the wooded landscape mural on the back wall whose sign announces "Our good dairy cows are in the meadow behind the trees." There isn't a cow to be seen, but the milk shakes are thick as mud pies.

13

Elegant Claremont

"Would you like to take a walk? Ah-ah-ah. Just to. . . ."

If you recognize the tune, dial your mind back to innocence—the wholesome prewar nights of 1939, say. Radio was still a novelty. Big bands could draw 2,000 dancers any night of the week. Music was unashamedly romantic and half the nation tuned in to hear the music of Tommy Dorsey (or Lawrence Welk, Hal Girvan, Jack Fina, Paul Neighbors, or Russ Morgan) coming from Hotel Claremont "high atop the Oakland-Berkeley hills overlooking San Francisco Bay."

In these days when the sterile stacked boxes that pass for hotels are indistinguishable one from another, whether in Cairo, Chicago, or Calcutta (and sometimes indistinguishable from welfare housing) the big white Resort Hotel Claremont is one of the Bay Area's more unlikely and more charming anachronisms.

The deep purple still falls nightly over its 22 acres of sleepy gardens, walls, tennis courts, swimming pools, trees, and trout pond. Quite possibly nothing closer than the Empress Hotel in Victoria, B. C., can compare with it.

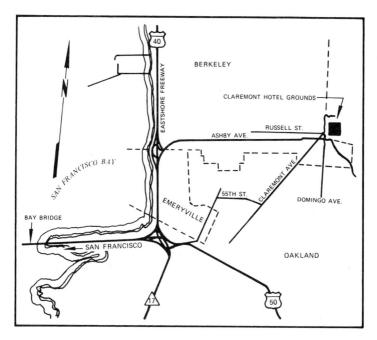

For thousands of Berkeley High graduates on balmy June nights, like their parents who danced the Chesterfield, and their grandparents who danced the Charleston, the Claremont is that romantic spot, forever frozen in time, the scene of the First Prom, the Big Prom, the Best Prom, the Prom of Proms. The walking around its spacious gracious grounds is pleasant indeed.

To make this walk, go (humming "Handsome Harry Gray," "Tea for Two," or "Help" depending on your own vintage) to the corner of Russell Street and Domingo Avenue, Berkeley. Until a few years ago this was the end of the line for Key System E trains. The cars stood in that narrow alley now lined with planter boxes between courts of the Berkeley Tennis Club, scene of many of Helen Wills Moody's triumphs. Walk uphill on the tree-bordered lane at the north end of the courts toward the castle-like building.

No one today remembers who designed the hotel, the second "castle" to stand on this site since the Gold Rush. The first was built by a Kansas farmer named Bill Thornburg whose wife had dreams of glory. To please her, Thornburg created an English country estate, complete with stables, pedigreed hunters, Cockney grooms, and fox hunts, on 1,300 acres purchased from heirs of Don Luis Peralta, who was granted old El Rancho de San Antonio in 1820. An English lord took Thornburg's daughter off to become his bride.

Of many subsequent owners, one of the most interesting chapters in the Claremont's long history was its exchange as the stakes in a checker game played at Oakland's Athenian Club by the famous miner "Borax" Smith, a Berkeley capitalist, John Spring, and realtor Frank Havens (best known today as poet George Sterling's uncle). Havens won, but it was another miner, Erick Lindblom, the Klondike millionaire, who built the hotel in approximately its present state, completing it in 1914 for the Panama-Pacific International Exposition.

To see the Olympic-size pool where Gail Peters, winner of eight national championships, works out, bear ever left, past the front of the carriage entrance and the old wing, which now houses, among other businesses, the BART computer. The pool is beyond the gate, but normally the pool and courts of the Pool and Racquet Club are open only to hotel guests and members.

To get the real resort "flavor" of this Bemmelman's-like establishment, retrace your steps through the gardens to the north wing and enter under the marquee. Here the grand hallway is an up-to-date "Peacock Alley" of shops, ice-cream parlors, and 38 party and convention rooms. If you're over the legal age limit, be sure to visit the Terrace Lounge (reputed to have been located here exactly one mile from the University of California campus) for a look at the San Francisco skyline. Then end this walk in the famous Garden Court, scene today of great plumes, a Hawaiian luau, and a fountain that dispenses more California wine than any other restaurant in the Bay Area.

The late Frank Lloyd Wright, one of the world's great architects, said the Claremont was "one of the few hotels in the world with warmth, character and charm."

14

A Hike
through the Canyon

Interested in communication? Consider a walk through the East Bay canyon where the first transcontinental telegraph cable was strung in 1858, an historic event that linked the West Coast with the eastern states.

Telegraph Canyon, as it was then known, begat Telegraph Road. From Telegraph Avenue and Claremont, Telegraph Road rambled over the hills toward Mount Diablo and then northerly to the Sacramento River at Martinez, following the wire overhead.

Known today as Claremont Canyon, the road through it is also Claremont Avenue, though the telegraph still goes through this gorge.

To make this walk, transport yourself to the vicinity of the Claremont Hotel and the adjoining Berkeley Tennis Club. From San Francisco take the E bus to the Domingo Avenue stop. From the East Bay, AC Transit buses 65 and 37 stop at Claremont and Ashby.

Walk around on Claremont Avenue northeasterly until you are behind the hotel. At the back gates you will be walking over

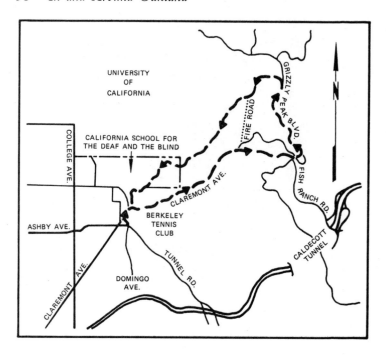

Harwood Creek, the north fork of the Temescal, with an old cobble wall on your left.

Follow the road as it follows Claremont Creek. As soon as you pass the fenced telephone company equipment and its junipers you will be abreast of Garber Park, a gift of the family of John Garber.

If you take the walk in May, look for patches of blue on your right. This will be jimbrush, the *Ceonothus sorediatus,* an inland version of the coast blue-blossom. Once past an oak forest and a country mailbox, you will have reached the northernmost extent of the "East Bay Burn" of 1971 in which 37 houses were destroyed. Now a "fire climax" landscape, few traces of the destruction are visible.

The walker now has two choices. The shorter is to cross Claremont Avenue at the fire road on the left, follow it up the hill past the quarry to reach a single footpath that goes off left again down the ridge.

The longer and more spectacular is to follow the footpath through the meadow. This is well worth the extra climb for the superb view east at the junction of Fish Ranch Road, Claremont Avenue, and Grizzly Peak Boulevard, once the site of Summit House, where stagecoaches paused for water or food.

On the longer route, bear left across Claremont and take the dirt road uphill. Take a sharp left back along Grizzly Peak Boulevard and within a hundred yards one sees the Bay Bridge. Rockhounds may be scraping for blue agates along here.

Another 500 feet and one seems to be on the rim of the world, looking at Tamalpais and the Golden Gate Bridge. When a fire road is visible on the downhill side, strike off into the logged area on your left. Follow the fire road, which soon becomes a single path.

At the next fork, take the left trail along the ridge. This is property belonging to the California School for the Deaf and Blind, whose roofs are soon visible as you walk downhill. Falcons are often seen hovering around here.

Bear right at the next fork, left at the following one, and soon you will have made a horseshoe loop that brings you out on Stonewall Road, which ends downhill on Claremont Avenue to complete the canyon walk.

15

Where a Poet
Left His Mark

"Rose-land, sun-land, leaf-land, wide crescented in walls of stone," wrote poet Joaquin Miller as he looked down on the Bay Area from "The Hights," his 80-acre home in the Oakland hills. Now part of Joaquin Miller Park, "The Hights" is also the place where pathfinder John C. Fremont camped, looked across the water at sunset and named, with an idle phrase, the Golden Gate.

Before Attila the Developer ran rampant on the land, San Franciscans could look across to the Contra Costa hills and pick out "The Hights" easily. It was marked by a tremendous cross on the land created of living Monterey cypress trees planted in the shape of a classic cathedral and equally as grand.

Sharp-eyed cognoscenti aboard helicopters or landing jets sometimes discern the cruciform even now, although part of it has been sacrificed to a road-widening.

Historians and walkers who seek out oddities on the land will find this nave of trees, and other surprises, in a special memorial walk to Joaquin Miller taped by Ranger (Digger) O'Dell of the Oakland park system.

To reserve a tape and player, call the ranger station (number 531-2205) any weekday between 10 A.M. and 4 P.M. If a robot narration isn't available, one can easily make the pleasant hour-long walk without it. In either case, go to Oakland and thence via Warren Boulevard (freeway no. 13) to Joaquin Miller Road at Robinson Drive.

For the first half, the trail is downhill, following Sanborn Drive and leaving it only occasionally. The first digression is about 100 yards along. Take the path to the right of the trail until you reach a funky little round tower, complete with miniature merlons and crenels. It was built of fieldstone by Joaquin Miller about 1894 to honor his friends and fellow poets, Robert and Elizabeth Barrett Browning.

Backtrack to the road, go downhill a few hundred yards, cross both roads, then go past the picnic tables on Cheapskate Hill to get an overview of Woodminster Amphitheatre, dedicated to California writers, and the impressive Cascades that approach it. Then follow the road downhill until you reach a sign indicating the Moses Monument. This, too, is of fieldstone, built by Miller, but shaped like a pyramid.

From the plaque behind it, head through the meadow to a meeting of park roads. You will be on a slight rise, looking toward a parking area marked by a berm. Cross the road, go past

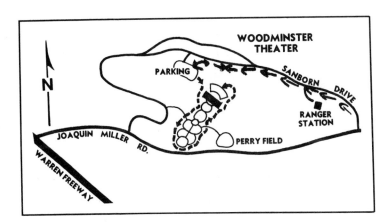

the berm, and you are suddenly in the stately lane of cypress trees that once formed the great cross. It leads one inexorably to monument three, a funeral pyre Joaquin Miller built for himself but could not use. City fathers didn't want him polluting the air. A ritual fire was burned here during Miller's cremation and later the ashes were thrown into it. While she lived, Juanita Miller, the poet's daughter, and a Chautauqua monologist, gave an annual recitation here of her father's best known work, wearing as she did so, a ring with relic fingernails and hair from his funeral pyre in it.

Walk downhill via the road to the lookout point for a good bay view, then cross the bridge, continuing downward until you reach the Abbey, an odd little white house Miller built for his own home in 1886. He lived here until 1913, and in it wrote, among other things, the poem "Columbus."

Go out of the park to the bordering parkway, Joaquin Miller Road, and head uphill past the statue of violent green; Joaquin Miller, once a Pony Express rider, is the horseman. Both he and his mount have lost their noses.

Continue on the walk to the Woodminster sign. Then go into the park again and begin climbing uphill beside the Cascades, a series of reflecting pools alternating with waterfalls and enhanced by stone steps and beautiful natural plantings.

Take the path that leads uphill, passed Craib Meadow, and skirts what was once park and is now a terraced series of seven parking lots. Where the walk meets the road, you will have completed the loop and can return the tape.

Or, since there are ten other good trails in the park, if you'd like a little wilder walking, pick up a map. Then you can go on and on and on.

16

Mills College

"To spell correctly, to read naturally, to write legibly, and to converse intelligently." This was the goal Dr. Cyrus Taggart Mills and his wife Susan set up for "the daughters of miners" at an advanced school for ladies they planned to name Alderwood College.

At first they rented the Benicia Female Seminary, a school launched in 1852, when sleepy little Benicia had hopes of developing into the state capital. Then with the small fortune scrupulously saved from their earlier efforts as missionaries, the dedicated Mills bought a foothill farm at the confluence of two mountain streams. They moved the seminary there in 1871.

As Mills College, the effort survives graciously in Oakland, where the "Vassar of the West" is now a 127-acre parklike oasis—the Mills College campus.

Thus, hidden in the heart of the city is a woodland ramble that has canyons, forest, streams, footbridges, old-fashioned double lanes of trees, a lake, sharp slopes, a pond where fish come to be fed when a bell is rung, and coincidentally, some of the finer architecture to be created in the last ten years in the Bay Area.

To make this walk, transport yourself to Richards Gate at the corner of MacArthur Boulevard and Richards Road. (The AC Transit's "N" bus from San Francisco's Transbay Terminal stops right there. Freeway 580 is also convenient, using the second, or southernmost, MacArthur offramp.)

Walk into the campus on Richards Road and follow its lovely long double lane of plane trees. Peaking over trees off on the left is Alderwood Hall, originally designed by Julia Morgan as the Ming Quong orphanage. On the right is Richards Lodge, known to alums as the Gate House, where many distinguished people have lived, among them author Jade Snow Wong and composer Darius Milhaud.

The first big new eyecatcher is a few hundred feet further, the 14-sided chapel designed by Callister and Payne (and reminiscent in its use of wood of the chapel at Fort Ross). Across the road, the Walter Haas Pavilion by Ernest Kump must certainly be the most inspired gymnasium this side of Delphi.

Snuggled into the giant rhododendrons in another few hundred feet is the music building designed in 1927 by Walter Ratcliff. The building, by the way, contains an electronic music studio and had one of the first Moog synthesizers. Immediately past it is the pond whose carp know for whom the bell tolls.

At Kapiolani Road, marked by double lanes of eucalyptus planted by founder Cyrus Mills, bear right to pass in quick succession three more remarkable new buildings, the Cowell Health Center, Lisser Hall, and Lucie Stern Hall. The latter has an octagonal building completely surrounded by, but not touching, a square one.

Once past it, cross Kapiolani Road and walk uphill into the forest via the steps. Bear right after the first street light and continue climbing until you emerge at the Prospect Hill parking lot behind Mary Morse Hall.

A marker here indicates that captain Don Pedro Fages, Father Juan Crespi, 14 soldiers and an unidentified Christian convert Indian camped here on March 27, 1772, taking a

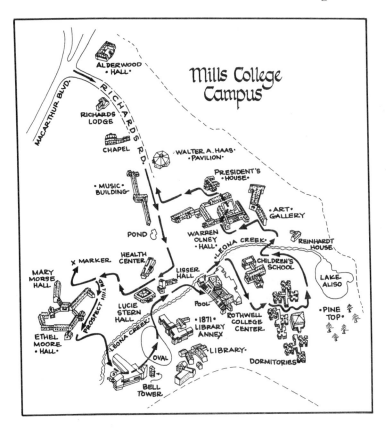

latitude sighting on the Golden Gate. Tall trees today would obscure their sights.

Retrace your steps to the Prospect Hill road and come down it until you reach two red bollards parallel to Ethel Morse Hall. Go down the steps, take the first right and then go down another set of steps, cross the road and take the red footbridge that leads over Leona Creek. No matter how enticing the banana trees may seem, bear right, go up the brick steps toward the gnomen, which of course tells sun rather than daylight savings time.

Beside it take a sharp left under the passthrough to emerge

by El Campanil, the old belltower designed in 1904 by Julia Morgan. One of the earliest reinforced concrete structures in California, it survived the quake of '06 intact. Inside are ten bells cast originally for the Chicago-Columbian Exposition of 1893. Pause beside it for a look across the Oval, once a croquet court, toward the mansard-roofed Mills Hall, now a national treasure.

When it was completed in 1871, students and faculty came from the original seminary in Benicia by horse and buggy. The flowering peach trees and banksia roses that festoon the facade were brought from China by the missionary Mills family. The Julia Morgan Library to the southeast and its annex, house the famous Albert Bender rare book collection.

From the front of Mills Hall, bear left across Leona Creek, again on a footbridge lined with benches, peek in at the interior gardens of Lucie Stern Hall, then with the creek at your right, follow it past waterfalls and through redwood trees until you reach the Rothwell College Center, a student union building surrounding an outdoor swimming pool, and well worth a stop for the Prieto Pottery Gallery.

From the nearby outdoor patio (where tables are sheltered for picnicking) walk with the creek on your left following the redwood rounds around the building and bear right on Post Road past the post office until you reach a road that reminds you of the wiggly block of Lombard Street. It meanders through a complex of handsome dormitories designed by Skidmore, Owings, and Merrill, bringing the walker out at a superb view-spot below Pinetop. Cross Pinetop Road for an overview of Lake Aliso, which waters all these lush grounds, then bear left downhill.

By the Children's School, bear right across the brown bridge, take a sharp left in front of the Reinhardt Alumnae House and begin looking for the marble Fu dogs that mark the Bender Art Gallery, open Sundays from noon until 4 P.M. When you leave the gallery, start along Kapiolani Road until you reach Warren Olney Hall, then cut through its underpass diagonally across the court and through a second underpass.

Suddenly you will be facing a country farmhouse which antedates all the surrounding buildings. Preserved and renovated as the president's house, it has served generations of Mills girls as a model for historic thriftiness. From its formal front door, walk along the tree-bordered lane for a quick return to Richards Road, to complete this remarkable ramble.

17

An Island City's
Victorian Legacy

Alameda, the six-by-two-mile East Bay island port known today for its underwater tunnels, its drawbridges, beaches, fine old trees, classic Beaux Arts high school, naval air base, and flea market, is one of the Bay Area's oldest settlements. Costanoan Indians were in residence among its oak trees when it became part of the vast Peralta land grant in 1820. Shell mounds reveal tribes had been there for 4,000 years.

The Peraltas called Alameda, then a peninsula, Encinal de San Antonio, the "oak grove of St. Anthony" for trees near a creek that then drained what is now Oakland's Lake Merritt. A few of the oaks still stand, though most went down before charcoal burner's axes.

Development began in 1850, "after the gringo came." To tout the island they had bought from Antonia Peralta for $14,000, pioneers Gideon Aughinbaugh and W. W. Chipman offered "watermelon picnics" and excursions via a small steamer, the *Bonita*. By 1853 there were 100 homes near High Street.

Copra and cod brought Alameda to her heyday as a port. They also brought her a fine legacy of elegant Victorian homes. Many, built by sea captains of the Alaska Packers along what came to be known as the "Gold Coast" for its fine waterfront views of San Francisco, still stand, now landlocked by fill that converted their open bay into a lagoon. Though the views are no longer patrician, Alameda still has its charms for the walker.

Recognizing this, city planners have included several walking tours in a booklet entitled *Scenic Highways Element, City of Alameda*. Among them, my first choice is based on Map 10, in the southern part of the Gold Coast, partly because it includes the famous Captains' Row.

To enjoy this viable Victorian lode, transport yourself to Alameda via the Nimitz Freeway, taking the Webster Street tube and Scenic Route 61 by way of Webster, Central, and Encinal to the corner of Encinal and Morton streets. Two tall palms make a good landmark. Park where you can and bear right on Morton Street, away from the long white trellis fence, to Franklin Park, noting the nice shiplap siding on the house at 1023 and spindlework on 1015.

Alameda was one of the first cities to have street lights and the driveway at the dead end of Morton boasts an old short-style lamp pole.

At San Jose Avenue, bear left, skirting the park past the ball diamonds. Behind the barbed wire, oddly enough, is a private pool in a public park. Families must have kids under school age to belong to its club.

At the next corner, the beautiful oak trees predate the city. The turret at 1615 San Jose has been lopped off, but observe the nice paint job on 1616.

At Grand and San Jose, the yellow Victorian with lions guarding its steps has a lovely fanlight. Cross Grand, whose street trees are among the finest in the Bay Area, and take a look at the three Victorians numbered 1001, 1007, and 1011, which you have just passed. Old trees and generous lawns help keep the small town ambience which makes Alameda so livable.

As enticing as it is, for the moment overshoot Grand and continue on to Union Street, passing a home whose carriage

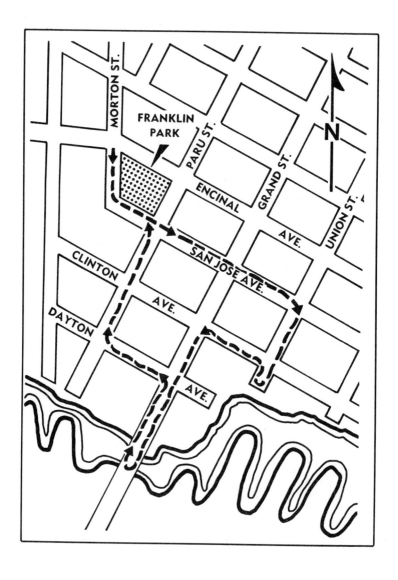

canopy has been glassed in to make a library. At 1711 the wisteria twining over an arch almost hides a cottage.

At Union bear right to Clinton, then cross both streets for a look at Captains' Row, the 800 block of Union. The three handsome Queen Anne Victorians, brown shingle, green shiplap, and white side by side, are reminiscent of New England seaports. Houses across the street are no longer single-family homes but could be just as elegant if they were as well maintained.

Go to the end of the street, once the seawall overlooking the open bay, to see the lagoon, courtesy of the unloved Utah Construction Company. Longtime residents nicknamed the lagoon "a drainage system" at the time it was dredged.

Retrace your steps to Clinton Avenue and bear left, passing a stunning Italianate home. The house at 911 Grand, more than 100 years old, now Frenchified, began as a mansard-roofed Gothic country cottage.

Bear left at Grand, one of the few streets on which a pedestrian can cross the lagoon, and walk to the far side of the bridge for an over-the-water view of number 650, a former beach house on pilings. Cross Grand and retrace across the bridge to see another, beyond its brick seawall, in the Craftsman style of architecture. From the bridge, note the slide into the water from one tract home landing, and the distinguished line of "featherduster" palms on Eighth Street at the far end of the lagoon.

At Dayton, bear left to Paru to see at 800 Paru a classical Federal Greek revival home. (Plane trees along Paru give a hint of the size San Francisco's Market Street trees can attain.) As you reach Clinton, look to the right for a surprise. Inez Kapella, who conducted me on this walk, calls the rhapsody in blue that you see here "the paint job of people who dare to be different."

One block more lets you end this loop walk at Franklin Park. Alameda planner Tom Lee says it, too, was once the site of Victorian homes until philanthropic citizens dedicated their land to create a much-needed park.

18

A School
Everyone Recalls

"It is probably safe to say that no town in California takes more pride in its schools, and sustains them better, than Alameda," wrote Capt. Thomas Hinkley Thompson and Mr. Albert Augustus West in the illustrated *Historical Atlas of Alameda County* in 1878. Down through the years, the island city just offshore of Oakland's Lake Merritt still has a handsome claim to that early reputation. It is the imposing neoclassic Alameda High School, now listed in the National Historic Register, and happily for the walker, included in a *Downtown Alameda Walking Tour Guide* available free from the Alameda Historical Advisory Commission office, 1361 Park Street.

The walker who goes to explore Alameda on foot will find it has many other pleasures to discover, among them a genuine village heart, old Victorian homes, a drawbridge, and the long Robert W. Crown Memorial State Beach.

To make this walk, transport yourself to Alameda via the Bay Bridge and the Nimitz Freeway south to the 23rd Avenue offramp, which merges into 29th Avenue. It will take you across

Alameda's fine old drawbridge over the channel, cut through in 1902 to join San Leandro Bay with the Oakland Estuary and make an island of what was once a peninsula.

Once across the bridge, 29th Avenue becomes Park Street. Bear right at Santa Clara Avenue, one block to Oak Street to shed your wheels where you can park near City Hall, the first of 67 buildings on the downtown walking tour. The Alameda City Hall is guaranteed to bring out the nostalgia in any small towner, and if it seems familiar to you, it could be because you have seen copies of the fine old-style red brick municipal building with its three graceful arches. One is in Disneyland. Until its 120-foot tall clock tower, damaged in the 1906 earthquake, finally had to be removed in 1937, the City Hall often appeared in movies.

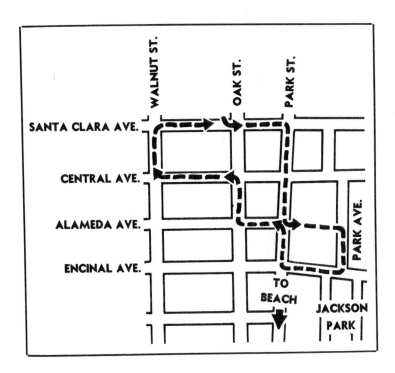

The building across the street, the Alameda Public Library, built in 1902 with a grant from the Carnegie Foundation, is equally classic with its Corinthian columns and broad stairway.

Walk south on Santa Clara Avenue, once served by the old "loop line," Alameda and Oakland Horse Railroad. By 1880, there were five stops on Alameda. Now AC Transit comes in here. As you stroll past a dozen old storefronts, try to imagine the blacksmith shop where the fruit stall is today. Many of the old buildings, like Nos. 2309 to 2311, reveal their Victorian origins in the 1880s with false gable and stick-style window details and brackets. Ionic pilasters and double-hung windows on the hardware store place it in the Edwardian period, while the corner building, originally built in 1878, was given a Moorish flavor by renovation circa 1937.

Bear right, or westerly, on Park Street, whose wooden sidewalks were replaced with macadam in 1872.

Proud of its village-like ambience, Alameda residents recently have passed an ordinance regulating design standards that does not permit new buildings taller than two stories nor larger than a duplex within city limits.

Redwood Square is not a square but a lane. When you reach it, bear left one block, past the trendy shops and restaurant, to reach Park Avenue, easily confused with Park Street one block away. It leads to Jackson Park, the green oasis visible to the right. Given by property owners whose homes front on Jackson Park, it would revert to them if any other than park use were made of the land.

At Encinal Avenue, bear right again, past the dairy, which now seems to deal more in beer than in milk. Turn right again on Park Street. When this block got its electric lights in 1903, Alameda became known as "the best lighted city in the Bay Area." Bear left on Alameda Avenue to see at midblock, a fine view of the East Bay hills beyond the fabulous Art Deco Alameda Theatre, designed by architect Timothy Pflueger in 1931.

Bear right on Oak Street, then left on Central to reach the *pièce de resistance* of this walk, the stately colonnaded Alameda High School.

It, too, has had its movie career and looks, according to Inez Kapella who graduated from it, "like a high school should look." Critic Allan Temko has called it "The greatest 1,000-foot facade in the state." City planner Tom Lee says, more formally, it is "a statement of the importance of education to the community . . . of a time when a high school diploma was no inconsiderable thing."

Architectural buffs may well want to visit and study in detail every building on the loop tour, which ends again at City Hall.

If Junior is tugging at your coattails by the time you come this far, head back to Park Street to locate Oly's Coffee Shop, famous for its waffles, the fast food of the fifties.

Then follow Park Street to the shoreline and bear right to find a mile and a half of shoreline beach reserved for public use, which widens out at Westline Drive to become the vaster Robert Crown Regional Park, a great place to conclude any exploration of Alameda.

19

A Beach
Against Time

A hundred years ago, the most romantic date a San Franciscan could offer his best girl was a day at Neptune Gardens, across the bay in Alameda. Early on, it began gaily, with a ferryboat ride on the little steamer *Bonita*.

The "Coney Island of the West" as it came to be known, flaunted its pleasures to those who approached by water. Before the passengers came streaming down the gangway, there would be the merry music of a carousel lilting across the water.

You could swim and sun and promenade. In the heyday of Neptune Gardens, you could take rides, dance the bunny hug, gorge on the new invention, the popsicle, chew Blackjack gum, and if you were too young for Wetmore's Cresta Blanca wines, drink that elixir of the sand gods, Green River.

At sundown, clambake fires would dot the beach. There'd be banjo and ukelele music on the warm bay wind. Finally, happy, sandy, and tired, one arm around the girl, darkness adding piquancy to the boat ride back, the San Franciscan sailed off into the west toward the welcoming lights of home. What, today, could match it?

The romantic Alameda ferry is long gone. The Alaska Packer's big square riggers that berthed in Alameda are ships in memory only. The Rotten Row of forsaken craft that loomed hard by has mouldered away. Croll's Gardens, Strehlows, and the U.S. Martime Training School that superseded them during World War II, are half forgotten.

But there is new life for the famous shallow two-mile Neptune Beach. As Alameda Memorial State Beach, it sparkles again with ten thousand or more swimmers, sunners, splashers, toddlers, canoeists, kayakers, and frisbee flingers on any fair Sunday. In the East Bay, the warm weekends are frequent.

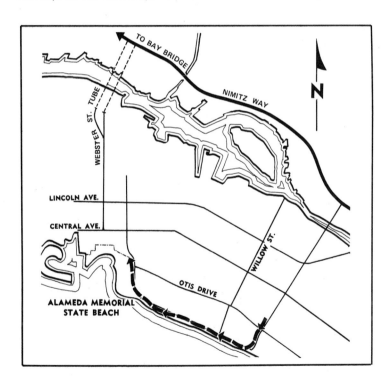

To sample the blandishments of this precious stretch of bay shore, pack your swim gear and transport yourself to Alameda, via the Bay Bridge, Nimitz Freeway, the Webster Street Tube, and Central Avenue, if you drive yourself. Shoreline Drive skirts the length of the beach.

By bus, the excursion begins at the Transbay Terminal. Get off at Lincoln and Webster, cross the street and board the 64 bus to the beach (63 on weekdays).

When you leave the bus, walk toward the water. If things urban and maritime interest you, head north to see how wall-like San Francisco begins to look from the East Bay, or to enjoy the loom of aircraft carriers at the U.S. Naval Air Station. If birdlife and marshland are your choice, walk south toward Bay Farm Island.

Either way, at high tide, the beach is a narrow strip of sand, 20 to 30 yards in width. Low tide leaves warm pools in the sand where toddlers can puddle safely. The beach is shallow 40 to 50 yards out, so parents relax with their beer and transistors while the puppies and babies swarm as they will.

As one walks, a marvelous metropolitan melange of people surges along the sand. Against a backdrop of development where suburbanite living seems to focus on the barbecue and balcony, bicyclists scorch along Shoreline Drive. From some aspects, the walker can look up the streets of San Francisco's Twin Peaks area. Joggers huff by. Oakland's metropolitan airport sends up a jet, leaving a brown feather of exhaust, every few minutes. Underfoot, castles in the sand emerge in fantastic shape. One Sunday recently, the best one on the beach was made in the replica of an Indianapolis stock racing car.

The north end of the beach has a free shower, a not-so-free snack bar, picnic tables, and some half-submerged log booms that are great for balancing acts. 10 P.M. is the beach curfew.

PART TWO

A LITTLE
FURTHER
SOUTH

20

A Second Chance
in Eden

"Eden is that old-fashioned house we dwell in every day/ Without suspecting our abode until we drive away," wrote poet Emily Dickinson at just about the time San Leandro was first surveyed. Its early inhabitants knew San Leandro for the fertile garden it was. They named the township in which it is located Eden.

Cherry orchards were once so widespread in this Eden that San Leandro held an annual Cherry Jubilee. Later when floriculture became a big business, the town called itself, "The Home of Sunshine and Flowers."

It was an open secret in the Bay Area that San Leandro supplied flowers for the Pasadena Tournament of Roses, the Portland Rose Festival, and the New Orleans Mardi Gras. Visitors made pilgrimages to see the flower fields. One local man had the nickname of "The Dahlia King."

One can still see a wide variety of flowers and trees and an interesting intermixture of old-fashioned houses and contemporary buildings near the village heart. First famous as a stage stop on the road between Oakland and San Jose, San Leandro had a notorious stagecoach driver, Charley Parkhurst, an eyepatch-wearin', gun-totin', tobacco-chawin' hell roarer, who was revealed after death to have been a woman. Charley voted regularly 50 years before women's suffrage.

One can reach San Leandro by AC Transit. From San Francisco, take Lines R and H from Transbay Terminal; from Oakland southbound buses 80, 81, or 82. Get off as close as possible to Cherrywood and 14th Street. BART also has a stop at San Leandro.

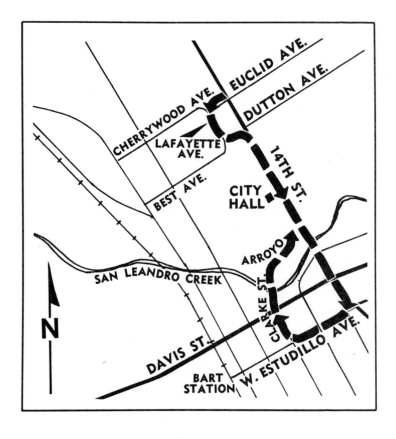

Walk southwesterly to 561 Lafayette to reach a tremendous magnolia tree shading the pink Alta Mira Clubhouse, once the home of Ignacio Peralta, whose father held the original Rancho San Antonio land grant. Constructed of brick in 1860 by W. P. Toler, who raised the first American flag over Monterey, it has seen the evolution of Alameda County from cattle range, through orchard paradise to the present residential-cum-industrial stage.

Take Best Avenue back to 14th Street and bear right. The Civic Center is discernible ahead down the handsome double row of street trees.

At Lorraine Boulevard, one reaches City Hall. Most recent in the municipal complex is the Public Safety building by Wong & Brochini, completed in 1967. The Pacific Telephone Directory Assistance building, 550 East 14th, was designed by Howard Johnson and appears to owe a design debt to Corbusier. The antiquated house across from City Hall sheltered Federico's blacksmithy within the memory of Bat (Battling) Larsen, a life-long resident of San Leandro. Pioneer Dr. Benjamin F. Mason, who delivered Bat, lived on the site of City Hall.

Continue south past the dahlia test plot to Root Park on the bank of San Leandro Creek. In Charley Parkhurst's time and until 1901, a covered bridge sheltered this crossing. Now an historical marker shows the boundary between Rancho San Antonio of the Peraltas and Rancho San Leandro of the Estudillos.

A modern statue salutes San Leandro's Portuguese community, largest in the state. Headquarters of the United Portuguese organization is in the next block across the street.

At Davis Street one reaches the triangular plaza, replanted for San Leandro's centennial in 1972. Don José once had a stage-stop hotel, Estudillo House, facing this half-square. Daniel Best, whose name lives on in the Best Bank building at the south end of the triangle, and who built San Leandro's first horseless carriage, later merged his company with Caterpillar Tractor.

Turn right at Penney's, originally the site of Hersher's Cheap Cash store, to reach at 384 West Estudillo, San Leandro's best-known building, Casa Peralta, remodeled to its present Mediterranean magnificence by Herminia Peralta Dargie, whose husband was the founder of the *Oakland Tribune*. The building is now owned by the city and has a museum upstairs. Go into the court to see adobe bricks from the original Estudillo home and ceramic tiles depicting the epic of Don Quixote. The redwood and deodars on the right are known as The Three Graces and were planted by John McLaren. Come along this way about noon and a carillon concert issues from the tower.

The charming old Victorian catercorner across the street is the Best house. Brent Galloway, president of San Leandro's Living History Society, says his Grandmother Best keeps the furnishings inside unchanged. To him, this is Eden indeed.

Bear right on Clar, pass St. Leander's School, then cross Davis, and ignoring the Not a Through Street sign, continue to the footbridge. Galloway also tells a tale of a schoolmaster in his mother's time who daily crossed a wooden bridge here until students removed a plank, sending him into the water below. The concrete replacement is safe from this.

Linger awhile to watch the streamside life, then cross, bear right, and make your way back to 14th Street to complete this walk through an Eden not quite forgone.

21

Central Park West

If every site in the Bay Area were unbuilt on and available to you, where would you locate your base of operations? Fray Fermin Francisco Lasuen, founder of Mission San Jose de Guadalupe, 14th in the long chain of California missions, let prayer and the law of gravity solve that stickler for him in 1797. A tremendous stone was blessed, then rolled down one of the steep flanks of what we now call Mission Peak. Where the stone rested, the mission sits today.

Mission Peak is also the landmark for all that rapidly growing South Bay agglomeration of neighboring communities that calls itself Fremont, after John Charles, the pathfinder. It is one of the more enlightened and visionary of the "sudden suburbs."

Largely because it has planned trails, lakes, creeks, canals, open space, nature areas, and recreational places, Fremont's amenities make for more interesting living than most new towns. The walking around Lake Elizabeth in its 412-acre Central Park on the plain below Mission Peak is a great foretaste of even better things to come.

Thanks to an advanced city government, backpackers can

now get off the trains at a nearby BART station, go through landscaped areas to Central Park, then via linking trails, up into the hills capped by Mission Peak.

Lake Elizabeth Trail is more urbane. To sample it, transport yourself from San Francisco across the Bay Bridge, pick up the Nimitz Freeway, Highway 17, south toward San Jose. At the Stevenson Boulevard intersection, go east toward the hills to Civic Center Drive. Here, bear right toward the remarkable new Civic Center building and park in its large lot.

Walk through the brick plaza. As you do, notice on your right the nicely articulated staircase that wraps around the octagonal part of the building. Architect Robert J. Mittelstadt's design was chosen in an international competition, partly because

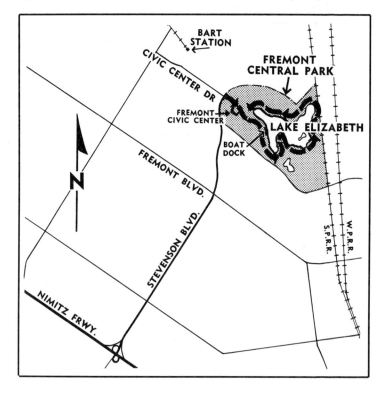

its deliberately unpainted cast concrete surface requires no maintenance.

Go under the ramp section that links the two parts of the U-shaped building and bear left on the macadam path that leads toward a low-lying temporary library building and Lake Elizabeth, visible on the left. The lake surrounds the Civic Center building like a moat, reflecting pillars and plantings.

Take the meandering path left past a children's play area and head toward the boat launching ramps. On weekends, the shoreline blossoms with trout fishermen, duck feeders, and the surface with El Toros, Lidos, and Sunfish. Go through the boating area and follow the path that parallels the shore. Soon one reaches a beautiful bridge that crosses a babbling brook, created to drain the adjacent five-acre swimming lagoon in a natural way. Bathhouses visible on the right have won several prizes for design.

Follow the shore of Lake Elizabeth and soon, abreast of a wooded island, one reaches a sluiceway between the lake and a nearby flood-control channel. Tule rushes on the right will be maintained as a natural wild area with a little elevated wooden sidewalk bridging a nature study area. As you skirt the shore, look uphill to spot Mission Peak.

Near at hand are the Western and Southern Pacific railroad tracks. Former mayor Bill Van Dorn and park director Ted Harpainter were the moving figures behind this park, as great an undertaking today as Golden Gate Park was 100 years ago. Pedestrian underpasses leading to the hills are located at the northeast end of another lake extension to go into this open turf area.

There are already 412 acres of land in the park and 63 in the lake.

As you swing around the lake, use the Civic Center building, in all its changing aspects, as a landmark. Wildflowers bloom along the trail side. Horsemen pass; bicyclists, dog walkers, and strolling lovers all swing by.

The imaginative can already envision a time when this emerging park will jump like its New York namesake.

22

History–Conscious Fremont

Sixty-five years ago if you had come out of church at Mission San Jose de Guadalupe between Good Friday and Easter Sunday, you would have been startled by an explosion in one of the trees.

Judas being blown to bits!

"The figure of Judas, hanging in some conspicuous place, consisted of a bundle of straw in which were encased some explosives," according to an account in the *History of Washington Township.*

"As the people came out of church, a fuse was lighted which set fire to the figure and exploded its contents, amidst a great din. This curious old custom continued from the founding of the Mission in 1779 until 1902." It is common in Mexico even today.

Even without fireworks, the walking in this modest old village at the south end of San Francisco Bay, one of the five small communities absorbed into the 96-square-mile city of Fremont, is very pleasant.

Fremont, far more advanced in its planning and zoning ordinances than most suburban areas, had the vision to make a place for walkers. Five pathways emerged. Two of these are bucolic walking trails within the Cabrillo Park and Mission Valley private housing developments. These are not merely sidewalks bordering the tract streets, but thoughtfully placed, elongated, landscaped parks that connect homes and schools, with the least possible exposure of the pedestrian to the automobile.

A pedestrian mall has been built into the Downtown Park

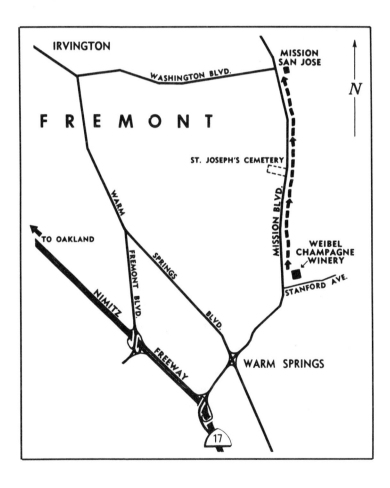

Plaza. A nature trail and arboretum has been established bordering Mission Creek south of the Mission San Jose High School between Palm Avenue and the Hetch-Hetchy right-of-way. The right-of-way is also a trail.

Out at Weibel Winery tasting room at Stanford Avenue, one of the most charming of historic sites, there is a country walk through vineyards to a little park. In it a pair of handsome gazebos have been built for band concerts and picnicking.

To get perspective on Mission San Jose, the walker should begin his explorations in an area known as the historic zone, the two blocks of Mission Boulevard divided by Washington Boulevard in which all construction must be compatible with the mission and its surrounding gardens.

Begin at the northern approach on Mission just across Mission Creek, beyond the great iron gates of Palmdale, once a winery of Don Juan Gallegos and now a Holy Family novitiate and junior college. A noble line of palms planted by pioneer E. L. Beard around 1850 marks the approach.

The parking lot at Mary Gibson's House of Antiques will accommodate 25 cars (and the shopping center on the next block west will take many more). Bottle collectors will find a bonanza of cobalt bottles here that have washed up in the mud-flats nearby. After picking out your favorites, walk south.

On one side of the road is a country orchard with olive trees, almost concealing a school. Next to it is the mission cemetery, where many a progenitor of San Francisco's first families rests eternally.

Beyond it is the mission church, reconstructed after a fire, and the adobe, once a monastery for Franciscan padres, now a museum. Behind are the gardens and orchards that entranced journalist Bayard Taylor so greatly in 1849 that he returned for a second visit with his wife in 1853.

On the other side of the road, half hidden in pepper trees and chinaberries, are old houses and shops interspersed in the quaint way of country villages. Walk slowly, and try to envision Don Jose de Jesus Vallejo, whose home was once here across from the mission, assembling his daughters in their mantillas for a fiesta.

Or imagine Father Duran boarding his *calesa,* the crude, two-wheeled cart drawn by six rare white mules, for which Mission San Jose was once renowned.

The cigar store Indian at DuBurg's Antique Trading Spot stands where many an Ohlone Indian stood when this was a center of the hide trade. Notice the chinaberry trees in front of the Olive Hyde Community Center, where Chileno, an Indian community leader, may have strung up the Judas Day effigy. If Washington Boulevard, the intervening street, seems enticing, there is still an Ohlone cemetery about a mile west of the mission.

Continue along Mission to find an architect's office, situated in a handsomely restored building, a real-estate office that has been everything from a stage stop and pub to a blacksmithy, and another treasure trove of old artifacts at the antique shop.

Then end this walk with a visit to the museum before making a visit to Weibel to enjoy a respite overlooking the vineyards from the new gazebos as seen through the mellow light of champagne.

23

The Movies'
One-Horse Town

History lurks in the least likely of places. Try, for sighs, envisioning the prototype of western towns, from the days "when men were men and women were double-breasted." The railroad threads its umbilical tracks along the base of the golden hills. Civilization, represented by Main Street, is a series of one- and two-storied false-fronted wooden or brick buildings, facing the depot. There is a hotel, of course, across from the station. On the corner there's a batwing-door saloon.

The streets of Laredo? Dodge City? Panamint? Jackson Hole? Not at all. That mainstay cliché of western movies, established in the days of the black and white nickelodeon, when flickers really flickered is—would you believe?—Niles.

Yes, Niles was the authentic one-hoss town of Broncho Billy (Gilbert) Anderson, first cowboy star of motion pictures. Made famous by his role in "The Great Train Robbery," Broncho Billy starred in 150 flickers, most of them filmed between 1910 and 1915 "on location" in Niles.

According to film historian Geoffrey Bell, producer of the

documentaries "The Movies Go West" and "The First Motion Picture Show," it was Anderson who took filming out of the studio and into the real world. The place he brought his cameras and railway car laboratory was Niles. Already sold on the climate, the open country, and the look of the place, but to make sure of community reception, Broncho Billy tested Niles storekeepers by asking each one to donate $10. "Thereafter only those who had made a gift received Essanay studio business."

All told, Essanay produced 450 pictures in and around Niles, using Broncho Billy, Ben Turpin, Wallace Beery, Jimmy Gleason, Zasu Pitts, Ethel Clayton, Marie Dressler, and nearly 50 lesser-known talents. It was also down one of the tree-lined country lanes around Niles Canyon that a winsome little comedian named Charlie Chaplin waddled his way into the sunset and the hearts of filmgoers as "The Tramp." That final fadeout, in which the rejected tramp with the expressive cane walks off down the lane toward a brighter tomorrow, became the signature as well as signoff of later Chaplin films.

Although Niles has been swallowed into the 98-square-mile megalopolis called Fremont, Broncho Billy's picturesque western town is still there, hidden in plain sight. Essanay studio and stables are gone, but old barns, hotels, storefronts, cottages, and even Broncho Billy's office-cum-dressing room still exist.

To discover its charm for yourself, set out from San Francisco via the Bay Bridge and the Nimitz Freeway, Route 17, for Niles. Follow the Alvarado-Niles offramp east. It becomes Niles Boulevard as it swings in close to the railroad tracks. Niles Boulevard is Main Street by another name.

Park by the boarded-up depot, ideal for a community center or railroad museum, and take a look at that train station and its palm trees. The bow at the ticket wicket and the columns topped by Victorian window pilasters are such perfect architectural details, the station should be nominated for the National Historic Register, an idea that has appealed to many townsfolk here.

Walk toward the flagpole, one of the tallest in the Bay Area,

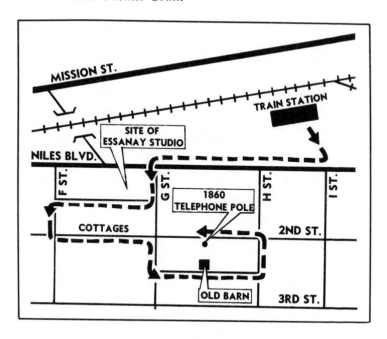

and cross Niles Boulevard at I Street and bear right one block to the hotel at the corner of H Street. The handsome overdoor gives an unexpected bit of photogenic swank.

Continue on to the corner to the Iron Horse Saloon, where many a villain has come flying out the door. If it is open, go in to see the original bar stools, which look like sawn logs. The dance floor and platform at the end of the barroom have been the scene of many a staged brawl. Old pictures on the wall show Niles in its Essanay heyday. One includes Chaplin and Turpin. Another locates the Essanay studio properties.

Walk another block along Niles Boulevard, noting Don's Antique Autoparts and the cigar store Indian in front of Devil's Workshop Mercantile, as you pass. At Niles and G, Holland Gas, a suitably simple service station, stands on the site of the old Essanay building. Bear left on G half a block to number 153–155, which was Broncho Billy's office and cottage.

Continue down the alley, past hollyhocks and vegetable

gardens for the film cliché of homey middle-America. At F Street, bear left, past the vacant lot and the cherry tree, a legacy from another significant chapter in Niles history, fruit-growing.

At Second Street, bear left along the lane of California sycamore trees. In 1912, this row of cottages was built to house performers on location. Many of the homes in this block are modifications and alterations of those early "dressing rooms."

At G Street bear right, crossing Second. Sidewalks, installed in 1930, have yet to be extended here. At the alley, cross G Street and bear left. The ramshackle shake-roofed barn is where Broncho Billy stabled his horse. Walnut trees, other barns and buildings along the Tom Sawyer-like lane were all much photographed in the pioneer film days.

Bear left on H Street for the fun of finding a telephone pole midblock that dates from 1860 and another view of the Essanay barn down a garage driveway. There is also a big pyracantha bush so lush it shades the sidewalk.

Wander as you will, or return to the depot at I Street to find your wheels.

Which was the tree-lined lane of the Little Tramp? Today, only the Lord and Chaplin know.

24

The Patterns of Serendipity

Coyote Hills is an unlikely line of grassy knolls rising in the vast marshy Alameda Creek floodplain. Once, like Angel and Alcatraz, the hills were islands in San Francisco Bay. Now, thanks to the silt carried down through Niles Canyon for thousands of years by Alameda Creek, they are *graben,* islands slowly sinking in the marshes, meadows, and salt-evaporating ponds near Fremont.

Commuters meandering through the salt ponds at the eastern approach to the Dumbarton Bridge pass Coyote Hills daily without realizing there is another 600 feet of the rock mass below ground. If they think about the hills at all, it is perhaps to wonder idly why quarries should be chewing away the only elevation along an otherwise monotonous shoreline, an area in all-too-visible proximity to the surrounding 23,000-acre San Francisco Bay National Wildlife Refuge.

Approach Coyote Hills from the San Mateo Bridge to the north, however, and the illusion is far pleasanter. As one comes closer to the softly rounded chain of low golden hills, they seem like an oasis of rural serenity in the burgeoning South Bay tracts. And so they are, for 907 acres of *Potrero de los Cerritos* (Pasture of the Little Hills), as it was known in Spanish days, now comprise Coyote Hills Regional Park, where the walking is very fine indeed.

There is a choice of willow run, marsh, meadow, canalside, and Indian mound trails to entice the walker to this predominantly flat but richly varied land. For the first-time visitor, however, the best introduction is Red Hill Trail, a mile-and-a-half ramble over the highest eminence in the park—not only for its spectacular 360-degree views but also for the opportunity to reconnoitre all the trails below.

To make this walk, transport yourself southeasterly from San Francisco via 101. Once across the San Mateo Bridge, bear right on Hesperian Boulevard. (Union City Boulevard-Newark Boulevard.) A single sign announces Coyote Hills Regional Park entrance via Patterson Ranch Road, a west, or right-hand turn. Follow Patterson to the Coyote Hills visitors' center, an attractive low sprawling building nestled against the hills. Free trail maps are usually tucked in the racks near the main entrance.

Your map in hand, your dog leashed, your lug-soled boots on, make for the south end of the building. Just across the utility road look for a monumental stone trail marker whose legend, oddly enough, has yet to be installed, although the park was opened in 1968.

Walk past the marker and go right uphill on the path at the end of the chainlink fence. Double back toward the corporate yard along the shelf of land above the fence. The visitors' center will be on your right as you go through a browning acacia woodland. At the fork bear right again. Red Hill, elevation 291 feet, will be visible ahead.

At the broad road, cross and go up the hillside, angling to your right through the old stand of trees that once led to a duck hunting lodge. At the picnic grove, go to the far side and take the trail that leads uphill toward your left from the two highest picnic tables. The big holes in the trail were made by ground squirrels, only half-tame here. Stick to the best beaten path and

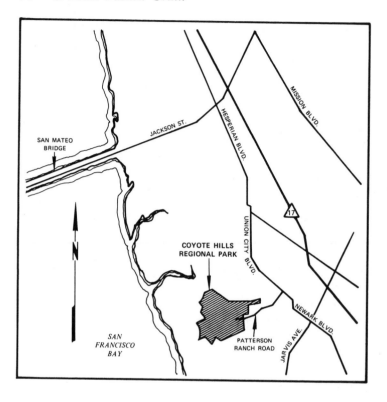

in within a hundred feet of steep climbing you will be in a saddle between hills. Digress toward the bay for the first of many fine views, this one toward Redwood City, the Dumbarton Bridge, and on a clear day, San Francisco.

Hang gliders used to take off from the hill on your left. Return to the path and bear left along the fire road. Mission Peak is the highest point in the Hayward Hills, as Wolpert Ridge, the range to the northeast is commonly known. Niles Canyon is the gap, with Tolman Peak to the left of it from this point. Water of Alameda Creek carved the canyon, depositing the alluvial soil that makes up the Niles Cone, en route to the sea.

Another 50-foot climb brings you to outcroppings of radiolarian chert. From this point you look down on the marsh, pond, canal, and Indian mound trails across from the visitors' center. Continue to the second outcropping to find a U.S. Geological Service reference mark on one of the Red Hilltop rocks.

Naturalist Norman Kidder, who introduced me to this walk, says, "The fantastic view all around gives you the feeling of sitting in the middle of a bowl." On a clear day, Mounts Tamalpais, Diablo, and Hamilton are discernible. So is the 11-mile route of the Alameda Creek Trail, following the flood-control canal from Niles to the bay. The most striking element in the landscape is the long line of housing, business, industry, and commercial development that with cavalier disregard for possible consequences follows the Hayward fault line along Mission Boulevard below the distant hills.

Take the fire road down to the next saddle, turn right at the cross trails and swing down along the edge of the marsh to return to your wheels.

As you walk, the lonely call of a freight train may echo across the marsh. Zebra-striped yellow swallowtail butterflies may dance along the path with you. Red-tailed hawks and white-tailed kites may soar overhead.

And once the storms of autumn begin in Canada, hundreds of thousands of migrating birds may fly, light, skim the water, or float nearby, for this bird resort is the Woodstock of the Pacific flyway.

25

No Ordinary Boardwalk

In the fall, thousands of migrating land and water birds populate that great highway in the sky between Alaska and Central America. As many as 25,000 sandpipers have been counted in the marshes of the South Bay in a single day, and some 250,000 move through them in a year. Great flocks of dowitchers, avocets, cormorants, mallards, coots, scaups, pelicans, pintails, shovelers, teals, grebes, and baldpates are just a few of the birds that move through the marshes like poetry in flight.

A great place to observe them is the boardwalk at Coyote Hills Regional Park, the 1,000-acre miniature mountain range that rises in the salt flats east of San Francisco Bay between the San Mateo and Dumbarton bridges. If boardwalk to you means Atlantic City, Coney Island, or honky-tonk commercialism, walk this one some day and be prepared to change your mind.

To make this walk, drive south from San Francisco via Highway 280, east on Highway 92 across the San Mateo Bridge, then south on Hesperian Boulevard. En route, Hesperian (you will note from the previous walk) will change names twice, first to Union City Boulevard, then to Newark Boulevard. As soon as you cross the Alameda Creek flood-control canal, begin looking for a small sign that announces the Coyote Hills Park entrance. Immediately past the sign, take a right on Patterson Ranch Road, drive to its end (past two park parking lots), and find a place for your wheels near the park visitors' center.

Once parked, go to the south end of the lot, look for a crosswalk marked on the approach road, and cross the road. Bear right about ten yards to find the trailhead for the boardwalk. At first glance it seems to be a modest wooden bridge. Once you are on it, however, it is like a Japanese garden walk, bending seductively into the cattails and duckweed. Within a few feet of the first bend, there is an octagonal platform out over the water, the first of three. These are designed for sitting and waiting for the shy creatures of the marsh to emerge. Pause awhile on this observation pad, and listen.

Once seated, you will be aware how cleverly the architect has sited the platform, for nothing man-made intrudes. One could be 400 years back in time and a thousand miles away from civilization, with hills on one side, marsh on another, and open water of a slough meandering between. Soon the charm of the freshwater marsh will manifest itself as polywogs, water striders, and wrigglers skitter past below, damselflies and dragonflies zoom lazily above, and the conversation of birds emerges.

When you have absorbed some of the marsh's tranquility, wander on to the next raftlike octagonal pad. En route if you walk quietly, you may spot the shy clapper rail, or a pair of ruddy ducks cruising near a clump of the marsh plant known as Fat Hen. The third pad overlooks the main marsh on your left.

After you return to the trail, the adjoining Muskrat Trail comes in on your right. Continue left and in a short while you will reach the unmarked Chochenyo Trail, which also accommodates cyclists. If it is a weekend, bear right on it to reach one of the four excavated Indian kitchen middens, or shell mounds, within the Coyote Hills Regional Park. The next right leads to the fenced mound area, locked unless a ranger is present.

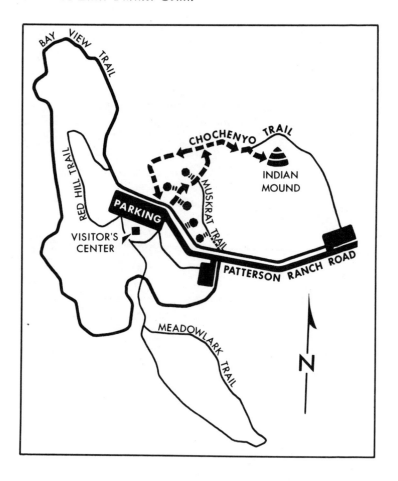

On other days (or if you would like more birdwatching over open water) bear left on the Chochenyo Trail which overlooks the big north marsh. During a recent walk here, a white-tailed kite landed on a telephone pole in the distance, a young golden eagle soared, a flight of mallards rose from the water, and woolly bear caterpillars rippled along unaware of them all. Bear left with the trail at the foot of the northernmost of Coyote Hills to loop back to the visitors' center.

If you think you saw everything, walk it again, for a marsh is a subtle place, changing almost imperceptibly moment by moment. Next time around you may see a muskrat swimming, a sparrow hawk feeding, or surprise a twinkle of sandpipers that will scatter before your approach like a handful of confetti blown on the wind.

26

Down by the
Old Salt Flat

"Old as the hills" is the common cliché to describe something whose age staggers the imagination. What could be older?

Well, for one thing, Alameda Creek, which flows through Niles Canyon to San Francisco Bay, draining (and in the past frequently flooding) 623 square miles of South Bay shore land.

Known to geologists as an "antecedent" watercourse, Alameda Creek is older than the hills that surround it. Through prehistory, it cut downward as fast as earthquakes and block-faulting made the hills rise.

Many San Franciscans think of this area around Newark, Union City, and Fremont as "the salt flats." For at least 4,000 years, salt from solar evaporation has been available in the wide basins through which Alameda Creek flowed. The Costanoan Indians gathered sea, or more accurately, bay salt here. So did early pioneers, and salt is produced by the same method even today. Oddly enough, Alameda Creek basin is underlaid by the greatest fresh-water well field in the Bay Area.

Thanks to the U. S. Army Corps of Engineers, it is now pos-

sible to take a good walk through the salt flats. Two trails sur-
mount the levees of the Alameda Flood-Control Channel. Both
are for pedestrians, but the southside trail may also be used for
bicyclists and the northside one for equestrians. Both trails are
surfaced appropriately, and thanks to landscape architect Ted
Osmundson, planted with trees, though with few of the poplars
that gave la Alameda its Spanish name.

The trails begin at Niles Canyon and make their way for 12
miles beside the water to Coyote Hills Regional Park at the bay
shore.

The walking along this linear park is level, easy enough for
oldsters in street shoes, and well enough surfaced that Captain
Phil Lamme and I could walk it in a pouring rain without stepping in a puddle. Devotees of the natural or wild riverbanks
might find the banks tame, but no one will deny that the walking along Alameda channel is unique.

To sample a few miles of it, drive south from San Francisco
via the Bay Bridge and Highway 17 to the Beard Road offramp
in Fremont. Follow Beard Road (not Beard Court) about seven-
tenths of a mile to find a parking area planted with native
California sycamores and Monterey pines adjacent to the channel. Park, note the portable privies, read the special East Bay
Regional Park trail rules posted for the Alameda Creek Trail (alcohol, motor vehicles, and shooting are no-nos), then climb the
ramp at this trailhead.

If flatness of the terrain makes directions seem confusing as
the channel swings along in its great wide arcs, pause a moment to look at the water, then follow the current left toward
the bay. (At some points along this trail Mission Peak makes a
good eastern landmark, San Francisco's Transamerica pyramid
a good northern one, but the movement of the water is in-
fallible. It goes to the bay.)

Shortly you reach a ramp that leads safely under the Nimitz
Freeway. Other ramps along the trail between Beard Road and
Coyote Hills go under the Alvarado-Fremont Boulevard (which
changes from one name to the other exactly at the channel), the
Southern Pacific tracks, and Newark Boulevard. Occasionally

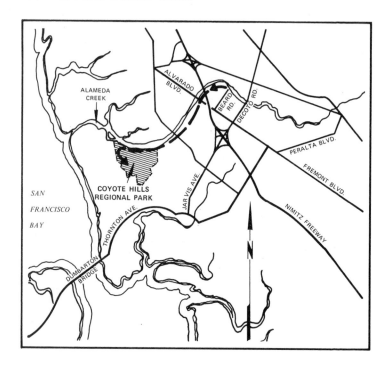

one looks down on a housing tract, or worse, trailer court, which, alas, has been allowed too close to the trail.

More often the trail overlooks flat open farmland or salt flat. Here and there are rest areas for walkers. One oversight seems to be the lack of canoe launching places.

After you have passed under Newark Boulevard, start looking on your left for two fenced plots of ground parallel to the high-tension towers. These are Indian digs that have been excavated for more than 20 years by Bay Area universities, most notably by the late Dr. Adan Treganza of San Francisco State.

When you are abreast of the two hills divided by the channel, look for a trail sign. The Coyote Hills Park path leads uphill on the left. If you want to go to the park, take this trail, bearing ever left; but if salt flats and shorebird watching are for you, continue instead on the road.

To return, retrace your steps. Once you have discovered the route, plan to return and try the eastern half of it, which goes past Decoto Road and Jameson Road to wind up near Vallejo Mills Historic Park at the junction of Mission Boulevard and Niles Canyon Road.

27

A Park of Springs

"Fifty years ago California was famous for its mineral springs," writes a Berkeley reader who recently stumbled on Dr. F. C. S. Sanders' book published in 1916, *California as a Health Resort.* "What happened to them? Are there any springs left one could walk around? Maybe even drink a glass of mineral water as it comes from the ground?"

For him, and for any other Bay Area walker who would like to sip soda water fresh from a rock crevasse, there is still in the Bay Area an enchanting public spa. It is "Little Yosemite," San Jose's municipal playground, Alum Rock Park, which in 1972 celebrated its hundredth anniversary.

Within the park there are 27 springs with mineral water of seven varieties including soda, sulphur, magnesia, and iron. The terrain, fed by the springs along Penitencia Creek, is interesting indeed.

To make the walk, transport yourself south via Highway 101 (from Berkeley take 17 and 680) to San Jose. Alum Rock Avenue takes off from 101 as State 130 and goes six miles east directly to the park.

Follow the lower road within the park past the cluster of quaint old buildings that includes a natatorium (now condemned, alas), a bandstand, carousel, junior museum, and outdoor dance floor. Although this land was designated as a "City Reservation" by Spanish land grant in 1779, like much of California, it had its squatters. Among them were pioneers J. O. Stratton, for many years operator of a hotel here, and his predecessor, Woolsy Shaw, who built the hotel on the 700 acres then called Alum Rock Ranch. The park was created by the state legislature in 1872.

Drive as far as you can and park, prepared to pay a modest fee on weekends and holidays. Cross the nearest stone footbridge and bear left. Soon you will discern the charming niches and grottoes of stone built long ago to enclose the springs.

Parks crew leader Sam La Rocca assures me the waters are potable. Taste freely as you wish. The sulphur water, which has a heavy eggy smell, is supposed to be a great tonic. My own favorite is the zippy soda springs whose water has a refreshing carbonation. (It's the one with the white and green train.)

Let the bridges lead you back and forth following the trail. (If you find the trail ends beyond one bridge, it is only 50 feet back to retrace to the last one.) Go through the picnic areas that line the creek side, including one whose long table could seat 50 people, until you reach the first wooden, aquamarine-colored footbridge. Then bear left on the north side of the creek and cross a second aquamarine footbridge. This will keep you on the trail to the main falls when the creek forks. (South fork also has a much longer trail to a smaller falls, but for this first exploration, continue along the more exciting Main Falls Trail.)

Cross each aqua bridge in turn, zigging and zagging with the creek. The last footbridge you cross is painted maroon and has no sides to it. From there on, the trail is single-file, mounting through ever-steeper canyon walls. Skirt up the cliff and round the canyon horseshoe to follow the creek through alder and sycamore trees until it reaches a steep cul-de-sac.

Here, like Yosemite's Bridal Veil, the water courses down in a lacy frill. Dan Holley, who guided me the first time I made this walk, said he likes it best of all in a rainstorm when the cliff face is glorious with lacy blown spume from the 60-foot-high falls.

When you have enjoyed both the upper and lower falls observation points, retrace your steps along this half-hour walk to return to the main floor of Penitencia Canyon. From it, 26 more miles of trail for hikers and horsemen take off to Eagle Rock, long an aerie for eagles; Alum Rock, the potassium alum pinnacle that gave the park its name; and Inspiration Point, a high overlook.

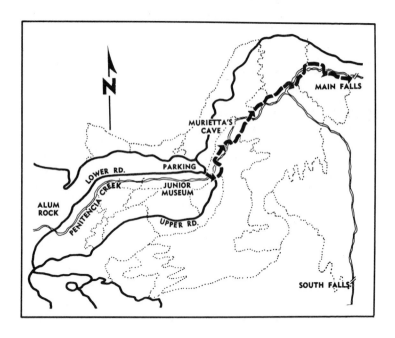

28

Knowing the Way

For great cross-country walking in the middle of a city, it's hard to top the city heart of old San Jose. Most of the "there" that was there for nigh onto 200 years isn't there any more. On the site of the first pueblo, and later the first capital of California, today there are mostly good intentions, temporarily open spaces, vacant parks-to-be, and financial plazas-to-come.

What's left of the old is so good, one yearns to have seen what is gone. The central district also has an uncanny mirage-like quality. Sometimes when one looks back on the terrain he's passed from a remove of two or three blocks, there are upper stories and roof lines revealed so handsomely one almost feels he's been somewhere.

Braided through town are the Guadalupe River, Coyote Creek, and Los Gatos Creek, their banks unspoiled. Meandering streams that have escaped the straitjackets of the U.S. Army Corps of Engineers are scarce these days. This alone would make San Jose worth seeking out, but there are also sweeping views of the Santa Cruz Mountains to the west and of Mount Hamilton to the east.

To make this walk, take the train from Fourth and Townsend streets in San Francisco. The San Francisco and San Jose Railroad, built in 1864, long since has been absorbed into the upstart Southern Pacific, but its tracks run the pioneer route through five tunnels and along 45 miles studded with as varied a collection of attractive train stations as one could find.

Get off at the end-of-the-line station, walk to its south end and head east on West San Fernando Street. Inside of a block, one becomes aware of modest "workingmen's Victorians."

When you reach a wrought-iron bridge pause to look down at Los Gatos Creek, its banks rich with willows and wildflowers. The second bridge you reach crosses the Guadalupe River, where fishermen sometimes still catch striped bass. Frogs call, red-winged blackbirds trill, and the distant "Big Ben" chiming "Lest we forget" seems anachronistic in this little wilderness under the bridge.

City fathers plan a riverfront park here like the one that has made San Antonio famous. The berm of earth across the street is that familiar disrupter of community continuity, the beginning of a freeway.

Abreast of the new construction, look right to discern the attractive civic theater San Jose would like to forget. Its round moveable roof tumbled in May 1972, shortly after completion. A new ceiling is now completed.

At Almaden Avenue, brace yourself to walk a block and find the next street called Almaden, too. One new plaza and the old adobe have been completed here. After you've explored, continue to Market Street where St. Joseph's Catholic Church, established 1803 and rebuilt in 1877, is worth a visit. Even television could learn from the red backlighting on the crucifixion tableau. Stations of the cross are individual oil paintings on canvas.

Cross the street to find the Civic Art Gallery, born a post office in 1892 and later used as the public library. Then head for the oval park across from it. This was San Jose's historic plaza, once lined with adobe houses, some of which had their own spouting artesian wells. Pause here in the plaza to try to imagine the lazy village of 1777 before continuing on to First

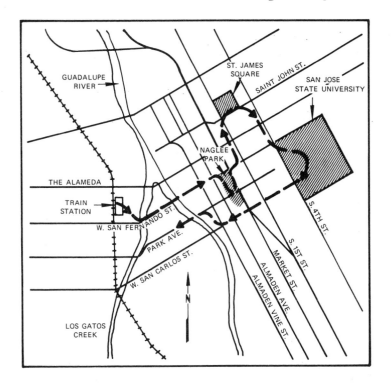

Street to find St. James Square, site of a lynching of two kidnapers in 1933. Newspaper accounts of the time say the men who beat and strung up murderers of a wealthy merchant's son wore pillowcases over their heads. Like buildings that carried much of San Jose's history, the trees from which the kidnapers hung nude have been cut down.

A rotunda honoring Kennedy and a statue honoring McKinley stand in the park, however.

If there's still time before your return train leaves, seek out San Jose State University, the campus that was the state's first "normal" school. Near it is a colorful student quarter, with old bookstores and "head" shops, and beyond is Naglee Park, whose fine old houses, large trees, spacious lawns, and old plantings are a reminder of all that was best in San Jose.

29

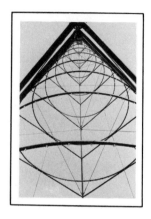

A New Walk

San Jose has always been a robust town, lusty innovative, sprawling and perennially vital. For example, as early as 1881 it installed electric arc lighting on four 237-foot towers intended to illuminate the entire business area. It was an outgrowth of the U. S. Centennial of 1876. (History-conscious grads of St. Ignatius College will recall that one of their professors, Fr. Joseph Neri, inventor of the arc light, brought fame to the college when he strung the lights across San Francisco's Market Street as part of the 1876 celebration.)

A hundred and more years later, visitors to San Jose will find the city still robust and innovative. For its own bicentennial celebration, a replica of one of those tall light towers was constructed in the new 16-acre San Jose Historical Museum within Kelley Park. Around the tower is an entire full scale village — houses, shops, offices, hotel, a reconstruction of native son A. P. Gianinni's first branch bank, a post office, firehouse and stables. Most of its buildings are originals moved into the park from earlier sites. Some few are reproductions built from original plans. To San Franciscans the museum will seem like a land-based version of the completely outfitted museum ships of the Hyde Street Pier. To Los Angelenos, it may seem more like a Hollywood film lot for Dreiser's "Valiant is the Word for Carrie", or Sinclair Lewis' "Babbitt." To anyone who sees how charming, parklike, and spacious this San Jose of the 1800's was, it may well seem like Eden. In this setting, less certainly seems to be more.

To make this walk, transport yourself south from San Francisco via Highway 280 to the Tenth Street offramp in San Jose. It leads to Keyes Street. From Keyes turn south on Senter Road to find the appropriate Kelley park entrance (beyond the Japanese

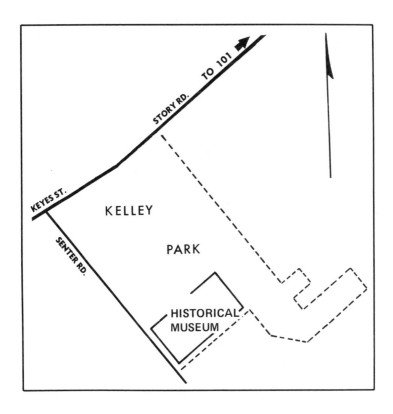

Friendship Garden) with a left turn on Phelan Street to No. 635. The San Jose Historical Museum is open weekdays from 10 A.M. to 4:30 P.M. and Saturdays and Sundays from noon to 4:30 P.M. Park, pay the modest fee, and walk into Grandfather's San Jose.

At the outset, stop in the print shop to see a Liberty hand press on which early newspapers were printed and a display of Museum Association publications. A placard credits Theron Fox with the whole idea of the museum. Then cross San Fernando Street to the doctor's offices for a look at the home and equipment of Santa Clara county pioneer H. H. Warburton. Then, as now, birds of a feather flocked together so it is not surprising to find a dentist's office around the corner. Among the final total of fifty buildings projected for this museum, one of the most elaborate, a brick Chinese temple will one day go between the clinic and the smithy beyond. Drop in at the Dashaway Stables visible in the lawns beyond the clinic at the right time and you may find the blacksmith at work here forging tools or shoes. When you have examined the vehicles here, look across the vacant lots, one of the greatest pleasures of childhood in the 1800s (and fosterer of our national pastime, baseball), to spot the electric tower. At 117 feet it is substantially shorter than the four originals that stood a few blocks away in 1881. It is still high enough, however, to dwarf all the other buildings. Head for the tower. En route you will pass a parked parade of harrow, wagons, democrat, drays and peddlar's cart that might well have stood on a market square any Saturday in town.

Look them over, then sashay, as they used to say here, across to the Pacific Hotel. Its neighbor, O'Brien's candy store, like the original, could easily become an institution with children of all ages who like sodas and ice cream. Most elaborate building thus far in the park is the Bank of Italy, first outpost of the empire that is now called the Bank of America. Fronting it, a placard for the tower reveals that after a storm blew down the original, the lighting system was discontinued. Director Don DeMers says land for the park was the gift in 1953 of Frank J. Kelley and that the adjoining Grilli orchard was part of the Kelley estate. Fruit trees, typical of San Jose, are being replanted near the tower.

Stroll back toward the bandstand. Like the streetlights, this was the gift of the E. Clampus Vitis organization, a group of pioneer businessmen interested in history, who take a lighthearted view of it. Continue down San Fernando Street to visit the lovely little Umbarger house, a workingman's Victorian, sometimes described as carpenter's Gothic in its architectural style. The Chiechi house nearby, a farmhouse, has not yet been renovated, but will be equally correct both inside and out when it is done. Work on the buildings, as one feels while passing the Empire Firehouse, now under reconstruction, lends another authentic note to the museum. When wasn't there work in progress in any city or town or village?

Meander as you will for there is something here to entrance every walker. Wolf (number one) may have claimed, to the tune of several hundred thousand words that *You Can't Go Home Again*, but if home were like this today, it would be a pleasure.

30

San Jose Bicentennial

San Jose celebrated its bicentennial in 1977 as California's oldest town. A commemorative 13-cent stamp issued featured a sketch of its oldest building, the Peralta Adobe, and the label "First Civil Settlement Alta California 1777." About ten years earlier in anticipation of its 200th year, local history buffs started looking around seriously for vestiges of their past. It is pleasant to report that their findings, unlikely as it seems in an area known for its burgeoning growth, have been significant. "Most of our history," Hilles Podesta, Santa Clara County director of the California Heritage Council, says "was buried under progress."

The Peralta Adobe itself, the only known one remaining in San Jose, had been buried under plumbing supplies in a tin-roofed warehouse at Almaden and St. John street until recently. The stampbuyer who seeks it out to satisfy his curiosity, as I did, will also discover San Jose's newest park has been created surrounding it. Nearby a colorful restaurant row calling itself Farmer's Union Plaza and San Pedro Square is emerging in Victorian era buildings that were called "a ghetto" by local press and planning commissioners not very long ago. And on Sundays in harvest time a midblock parking lot is the scene of an impromptu farmer's market of locally grown produce.

To walk through this exciting revitalization of an old urban heart, transport yourself south from San Francisco via Highway 280 (or via Southern Pacific) to downtown San Jose. If you are burdened with your own wheels, park where you can near Almaden Avenue and St. John Street. The Peralta Adobe stands at 184 West St. John. Believed to have been built by Manuel Gonzales, an Apache Indian, prior to 1804, for nearly 50 years it was the home of Don Luis Peralta who came to California with the Anza expedition of 1775. Seventeen children were born to Peralta in those two rooms of the adobe's modest interior. Although he was awarded the 48,000-acre Rancho San Antonio in 1820, while he lived, this was his home. When Don Luis died in 1851, the great rancho, which today makes up most of the East Bay, was valued at $1,383,500. It was divided equally among his four surviving sons. Members of the San Jose Junior League can take credit for the restoration, a bicentennial gift to school children of the Santa Clara Valley.

After you have looked at the displays and heard the recorded stories, notice across the street the former home of Capt. Thomas Fallon, mayor of San Jose in 1859, now in the process of renovation and recycling. Walk along St. John and bear right on North San Pedro Street alongside the great old tubs that now contain geraniums at The Laundry Works, once Soon Lee's Chinese Laundry and now a garden restaurant whose decor wittily incorporates the artifacts of its former use. A municipal parking garage presents a blind face behind street trees on one side of the street. Walk on the lively side. The first restaurant to thrive in a reclaimed building here is The Old Spaghetti Factory, located appropriately enough in the old Ravenna Macaroni Factory. Walkers will be delighted with the long walkway that cuts midblock through to Almaden Avenue.

Continue along San Pedro, enticing as the byway seems, to find beneath a billboard-size copy of the San Jose commemorative stamp, the weekend farmer's market. The prunes one buys here, and much of the other fruit, was first introduced to California two blocks away at Louis Pellier's nursery "City Gardens," now St. James Park. The prune cuttings he introduced from France ultimately made Santa Clara County's prune industry a 43-million-dollar business. Park plans for replanting the nursery to the original La Petite Prune D'Agen variety and other introductions are in the works.

The Old Mill Building was a mill and feed warehouse around 1882, but the one that has given its name to the plaza is the Farmer's Union, on the corner, part of a cooperative that grew into a bank under the guidance of the pioneer McEnery family. Like his father, Banker John McEnery, young Thomas McEnery, a moving force behind this "Experiment in Humanism," as the injection of new life is known, serves on the planning commission. "San Pedro Square is San Jose businessmen financing their own downtown improvements," he told me. "All without government money."

Bear right at West Santa Clara Street to discover the Hotel Vendome, where winemaker Paul Masson once lived. His cellars, which stretch under much of this block, will once again be a tasting room if Tom McEnerny's plan continues in its present pattern. The Chinese Lantern has been at the same location for 30 years, but its neighbor, Arley Brewster's restaurant and pub occupies the old Lyndon Building, once home of the *Times Herald,* and indeed, of the *San Jose Mercury.*

Go into the Tower Saloon for a look at the great old photos of this area in its earlier heyday ranged around the walls. The Tower, which gives the Tower Saloon its name, is long gone, however. It was a 237-foot-tall electric lighting scheme that "frightened the chickens as far away as Los Gatos" until it blew over in a storm in 1881.

PART THREE

BEYOND THE
COAST RANGE

31

Skyline National
Recreation Trail

Project Skyline is a dramatic new 27-mile-long National Recreation trail which skims the crest of the East Bay hills from Richmond to Castro Valley. The first 14-mile segment was dedicated in 1970. When completed, the total trail will run on East Bay Regional Park District lands from Wildcat Canyon on the north, through Tilden, Sibley Round Top, Huckleberry Regional Preserve, and Redwood and Anthony Chabot regional parks. Ultimately the trail will become a link in a regional backpacking loop with six overnight camping areas.

The trail is already on the land. When there were still a couple of four-mile pieces that were a little rough, walkers were invited by the co-sponsors of the trail, the East Bay Trails Council and the parks district, to an old-fashioned two-day pioneer-style work party on a Thanksgiving weekend. A little like the community barn raisings or quilting bees of our forebears, the work party had food and fun to go along with the labor.

Members of organized hiking groups who got the word through club bulletins started the party with a day's work that wound up with dinner, campfire entertainment, and an overnight encampment at Gillespie Youth Camp in Sibley Regional Park.

To hike a completed section of Project Skyline and enjoy the fun, put on your most comfortable hiking duds, boots, and gloves. Then transport yourself to Skyline Gate at the north end of Redwood Regional Park, Oakland. On the border of Alameda and Contra Costa counties, this gate has a big parking circle where Pine Hills Drive meets Skyline Boulevard. Highway 13, the Warren Boulevard Freeway, is the way to go. From either direction, exit from Highway 13 east on Joaquin Miller Road, stay on it to Skyline Boulevard, then take a left. In three miles, at 8500 Skyline Drive, you are at the gate.

This major trailhead was the rendezvous point for the work party. Park your wheels here. To orient yourself to the land, observe that West Ridge and Stream Trails come up on the right, East Ridge Trail on the left. True to their names, the ridge trails run the ridges and have fine distant views, while Stream Trail goes down the canyon following the stream. Until the great work weekend, West Ridge Trail was the northern end of the Skyline National Trail.

Look for the stone chateau on your left. This is the residence for the parks district fire chief. Walk toward the public privies downhill from it. Go through the stile on the asphalt road and follow East Ridge Trail.

Trails Coordinator Jana Olson, who took me on this walk recently, says, "We hope making the trail completely by hand will preserve the naturalness of the terrain the way pioneers did." About 1,000 feet along, the path leaves the asphalt uphill on the left. Climb 30 feet and bear left through cutover red gums. Bear right in another 20 feet and if the day is clear, there will be a sensational view on the right of Mount Diablo with Gudde Ridge in the middle distance.

From the next high point along the trail, the knoll ahead is the volcanic cone known as Round Top in Sibley Regional Park. Looking at the tennis courts visible to the right of Round Top, one can discern that from 50 feet below it, everything is park.

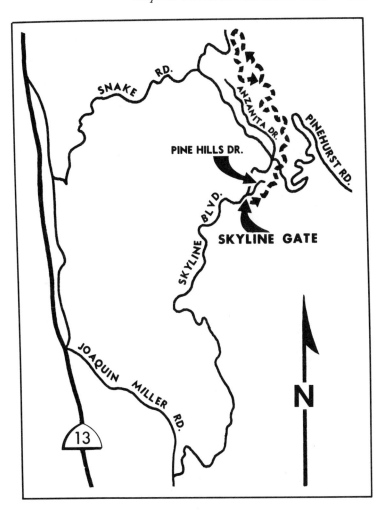

As you bear along the trail, Pinehurst Road is visible looping its way toward the little town of Canyon.

At the bootleg auto road bear right, and right again at the fork. At the junction of Pinehurst Road, Skyline Boulevard, Shepherd Canyon, and Manzanita Road, you are at the first of the only two major road crossings in the 27 miles of trail. (The other is Fish Ranch Road.) Cross Pinehurst. The trail goes on parallel to Manzanita, the uphill way. This is also an entrance to the trail through Huckleberry Botanic Preserve. Go in, climb over the eucalyptus log and after 30 feet of scrambled cutover brush, bear left along the east slope of the Oakland hills. Work on this length of trail has largely been done by the Contra Costa Hills Club, a group of hikers who are all about 65 years old.

Huckleberry Trail goes uphill on the left at the fork. Instead, take the right fork downhill to stay with Project Skyline.

Old ranch maps show much of the land through which the Skyline National Recreation Trail passes as public domain. Early on, much of it served as watershed for private reservoirs that ultimately came into the hands of the East Bay Municipal Utility District. The utility district transferred it around 1934 from watershed to the park district. Below the Huckleberry Preserve, stagecoaches once came from Moraga to Oakland on the Old Thorn Road. A good place to view the stage road is from the parking area to the right of 7090 Skyline Boulevard, slightly north of Snake Road.

Gung-ho hikers with the stamina of John Muir can continue to Tilden Park via the Skyline Trail. Since 27 miles is a goodly distance for most Sunday walkers, this parking area is a good place for those of lesser prowess to loop back via the Huckleberry Trail.

32

A Mile-Long Treasure

"Up, up, my friend and quit your books," wrote William Wordsworth to his fellows one spring more than a hundred years ago. "One impulse from a vernal wood may teach you more of man/ Of moral evil and of good than all the sages can."

If Wordsworth had lived in Oakland then, or now, his Pan-piping might have led his friends to Winding Way, better known to botanists by the equally descriptive name of Huckleberry Trail.

For Huckleberry Trail is unique, a rare island of native vegetation that meanders across the northeast-facing slopes of the Oakland-Berkeley hills between Roundtop and Redwood peaks. In the spring it is glorious with pink, gold, and lacy, white chaparral in bloom.

To explore this mile-long treasure, a well-kept secret of botanists for many years, go to Oakland via the Bay Bridge and Highway 580.

Take the Oakland Avenue-Harrison offramp. Go left on Oakland to Highland, left again on Highland to Moraga.

Turn right again on Moraga to Snake. And go uphill on

Shepherd Canyon-Park Boulevard to a tricky intersection with
Skyline and Manzanita. Right on Skyline brings you to an unexpected parking lot across from 2365 Manzanita.

Pull in and park here. Put on your heavy boots. Short as it
is, this is a challenging natural trail.

Walk north along the road about 50 feet. As soon as you
pass under the high-tension wires, take the gravel road that
leads downhill on your right.

In a few steps you are in that vernal wood, en route to a
graveled knoll.

Go out on it for a superb overview of surrounding ridges
and valleys, with Mt. Diablo in the distance.

When you have seen the splendor of the site, backtrack to

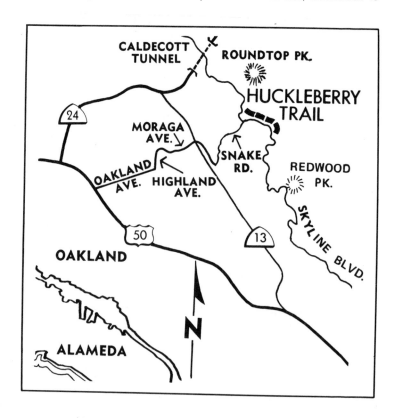

the first path that goes off to the right from the gravel road. It passes a stand of the rare western leatherwood, or *Dirca occidentalis,* a "living fossil" like the oso berry, *Osmaronia cerasiformis,* which is also found along this trail.

On this trail, experts have found golden chinquapin, the silk tassel bush, wax myrtle, ocean spray, red flowering currant, coffeeberry, several manzanitas, blue elderberry, California hazelnut, and the huckleberries that give the trail its name, as well as the equally native, though not rare, poison oak. Stay on the trail to avoid it.

After passing under a tremendous bay tree with at least 20 rooted trunks, you will come upon another of the gravelly approaches to a second knoll.

Once more digress from the main trail to pause for the broad view of the ridge of Robert Sibley Regional Park off to the northeast. The trail takes up as you return from it about 30 feet east of the place it came onto the approach.

Plunge into the woods again and shortly you will come out above the Old Thorn Road, once the stagecoach route to Moraga. In the future it may become a horse trail as part of the Skyline National Recreational Trail.

Huckleberry Trail passes a deep gorge, created by slides through many years (and recently littered unfortunately with boxes of gaudy household trash). Then the trail turns a curve. You are back on Skyline Boulevard at a little meadow blocked off from cars only by a low split-rail style fence.

Since it is three times as long to return from this junction (shown as Winding Way on many maps) via paving, retrace your steps instead and discover how many things you see on the return trip that you missed the first time along the trail.

33

Las Trampas—Space on The Fault Lines

Las Trampas means The Trap. When Joaquin Moraga, José Martinez, and their friends hunted in the Contra Costa hills, they found an odd land pattern that made a natural trap for elk and gave it the nickname. Sixty years later in 1894, geologist Andrew Lawson, surveying through it, discerned and named Franklin, Las Trampas, and Bolinger faults, which defined the strange geological conformation.

Today it is a park, the newest in the East Bay Regional Park system. For the thousands of recent residents who have poured in nearby, attracted by the aerospace industry, it is a welcome breathing space.

For anyone who has wondered why the Alameda-Contra Costa county line zigs and zags so much near San Ramon, it is a chance to understand the map. Given one of those scintillating blue and gold days of October when the smog count drops and the air is like wine, it can be a wonderful country walk.

To make this walk, transport yourself toward Castro Valley via Highway 580 south from Berkeley and Oakland. Leave the freeway at the Center Street-Crow Canyon Road exit and follow Crow Canyon Road seven miles toward San Ramon. Half a mile beyond the Alameda-Contra Costa county line sign, take a left turn on Bolinger Canyon Road. Drive four miles and park near the picnic tables and charcoal braziers.

Look for a small footbridge on the Bolinger Road side of the parking lot that leads to a grove of California buckeye trees shading a pleasant group of tables. In the late summer and early fall, Bolinger Creek is a scant trickle.

Notice the narrow macadam road that leads out and uphill

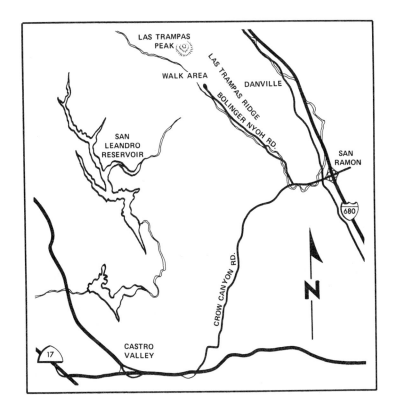

toward the communications antennae visible on the ridge. Follow it uphill one mile to the boundary gate of the East Bay Municipal Water District watershed for San Leandro Reservoir and a military reservation.

From this point, look off to the left to find two cow trails. Let your eye follow further uphill toward the ridge top to locate an elderberry bush. Take the upper of the two trails toward the elderberry.

As you go up, the steep walls of Las Trampas Ridge will come into relief behind you, behind exposing folds of a thrust fault. Thrust faults along here meet one another like the blades of shears. There are also transverse faults in evidence, so Lawson believed, of a gigantic overturned syncline.

As you walk, Mount Diablo is to the rear. The climb up to the cow trail is sharp but short. Soon you are on the crest of Rocky Ridge and up against a fence with a park boundary sign. Follow the old cow path, now widened by human use, continuing along the ridge to a large California bay tree. From this vantage, if the day is clear, Mount Hamilton will be visible to the south, St. Helena to the north, and to the west, San Francisco's Bank of America building makes a landmark as distinctive as Marin's Mount Tamalpais.

When Andy Lawson's surveying party came through this way they found the region almost devoid of trees, except for the digger pine, *Pinus sabiniana*, on the east slopes of the San Ramon Valley.

Earlier lay botanists among the Spaniards who first came through here with Pedro Fages stumbled on an oddity that they took to be an oak with a willow grafted on it, giving San Ramon Creek its first name of Arroyo del Ingerto. Ramon, by the way, was never a saint, but the sheepherder or majordomo of Mission San Jose, whose flocks came through all these high valleys. He may have found the strong breezes on Rocky Ridge as compelling as they are today.

When you have surveyed the East Bay from this high lookout, picking out your own neighborhood or even house if the day is clear, retrace your steps to the parking area.

34

A Walk That Began as a Gamble

"Don Guillermo Castro was a high stakes gambling man who fancied Three Card Monte," according to Leonard Verbarg in his informative little East Bay pamphlet, *Celebrities at Your Doorstep.* "That accounts for his opulent Rancho San Lorenzo Alto or Upper San Lorenzo Rancho being 'fairly struck off . . . for $400,000 at a forced sale' with the sheriff presiding over the proceedings" 112 years ago on the San Leandro Courthouse steps.

The 25,722-acre Rancho San Lorenzo Alto once encompassed 41 square miles on land that has since become San Lorenzo, Hayward, and Castro Valley. Three large unspoiled areas of it have also become part of the East Bay Regional Park District. One of these is Cull Canyon, named for pioneer stock farmer S. W. Cull. The walking and horseback riding in this segment of Don Guillermo's former domain is choice indeed.

To explore Cull Canyon, transport yourself to Castro Valley from San Francisco via the Bay Bridge and Route 580. Take Castro Valley Boulevard to Crow Canyon Road, swing left on

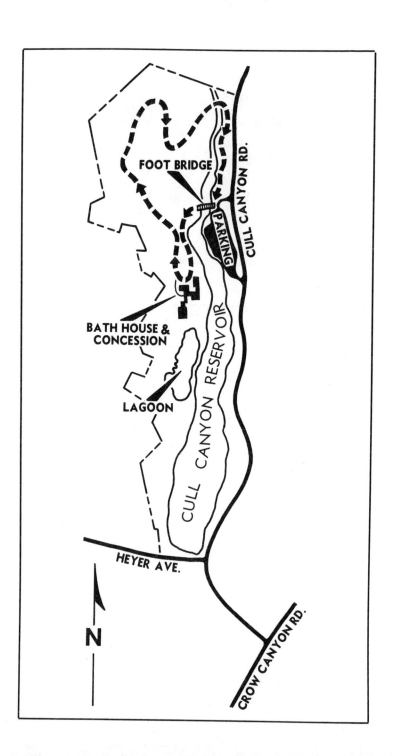

FOOT BRIDGE

CULL CANYON RD.

PARKING

BATH HOUSE &
CONCESSION

LAGOON

CULL CANYON RESERVOIR

HEYER AVE.

CROW CANYON RD.

N

Cull Canyon Road and look for the parking area on your left about the distance of a city block past Heyer Avenue. The cacophony of duck and goose conversation on the reservoir may alert you to the location of Cull Canyon Park before you see the water, a standby supply for the Alameda Flood Control and Water Conservation District.

From the parking area, walk north and cross the footbridge over Cull Creek. Linger awhile for a look at the water below in this romantic setting.

During the summer, thousands of children, clutching dimes in their hot little hands, stream across here to reach the most intensely used swimming facility in northern California. They swim, not in the reservoir below, whose steep sides and deep soft muddy banks make it unsafe, but in a specially constructed mile-and-a-half-long lagoon.

From the bridge, bear left to discover the prize-winning pavilion with its bathhouse, lockers, snack bar, well-groomed lawns, and vine-covered pergola. Then take the trail that veers uphill.

In a few minutes you will reach a small corral, left over from the time when this was a farm. Bear right and shortly this north end of the park reveals itself as a little wilderness.

Bear consistently to the right and you soon reach a meadow decked with the big feathery plumes of pampas grass. Handsome as it is, ecologists believe pampas grass is a threat to native vegetation.

At the creek, if the water is low enough to ford, cross and return on the trail following the far shore. Otherwise stay on the west bank to return to the footbridge.

When you reach the parking area again, go south along the east side trail to reach the spillway for the dam and enjoy the great display of waterfowl that gathers here, attracted by the resident geese and ducks.

Don Guillermo Castro might not appreciate what happened to this land he lost to pay gambling debts, but his seven children would have had a great time here. As gardener Jim Scroggins, who tends this land, says, "Its hundred acres is not large enough to get lost in, nor small enough to get bored with."

35

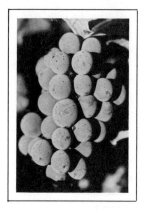

A Loop From Town to Vine

Livermore Valley memorializes the first English-speaking settler in these parts. It has ever been a place of changes. Since 1835 when Robert Livermore, a sailor who had jumped ship from the merchant ship *Colonel Young* in Monterey harbor in 1822, settled on Rancho Las Positas, it has been cow country, sheep country, mining country, orchard country, and wine country.

In our time it has been famous for the University of California's Lawrence Rad-Lab and infamous for proliferating suburbs and Santa Rita correction facilities.

In the town of Livermore, changes have emerged. Not the least of interest to the walker is a civic center park on the old rodeo grounds and a seven-block-long promenade called Quetzaltenango Parkway. For an interesting half-day walk, one can make a triangular looploop, partly through vineyards, that includes a visit to two venerable family wineries.

To make this walk, transport yourself east from San Francisco via the Bay Bridge and Highways 580 and 84 to the corner of Livermore and Pacific avenues. Go past both the Western

Pacific and Southern Pacific tracks, near what was once the town of Laddsville and now is absorbed into the town of Livermore.

Park where you can near the Livermore Library, a handsome new structure surrounded by a nicely contoured park. Start east on Pacific. Near Dolores, the building on your right is the community police building. City Hall is upstairs on the second story.

After passing a corrugated tin barn, a remnant of the rodeo days that now houses art shows, you will reach six recycling bins labeled clear, amber, and green glass, aluminum, tin, and steel. Just past them, follow the road beyond the sign that says "motor vehicles prohibited." Horses graze in the field on the left. Wild poppies and mustard festoon the path.

At the three-tined fork, go right on the dirt road to what is designated on some maps as Sunken Gardens Park. Sunken it is. Park it is not. At least not yet. Walk toward the fallen tree, go up the embankment, and at the dead tree with five bare limbs, take a sharp left along the fence across the road from it. You will then be skirting the sunken plot along a line of trees.

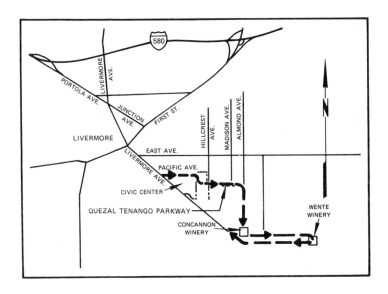

As you near the street at Hillcrest and Findlay streets, go between the house and farm fences to emerge at the western end of Quetzaltenango Parkway, completed in 1972 and named for Livermore's Guatemalan sister city. Cross Hillcrest and continue east on this well-planned and well-planted strip of parkway. It has paths for cyclists and walkers, benches, picnic tables, planter boxes, trees, and shrubs.

It passes a row of suburban homes equally well landscaped to end, alas, in a squeeze. Almond Park abuts the end of Quetzaltenango Parkway on the left, but for a narrow offset. The slender can make it between the fences. Portlier walkers may have to go half a block out of their way to continue the zigzag that cuts past the school and through the park to emerge on Almond Avenue.

Bear right on this country road to find at its end a hiker's stile that admits one to Concannon vineyards. Go through and bear right toward the pump house, then left toward the water tower. On the way one walks over the very gravelly loam that has been likened to the Graves district of France, between vines of Cabernet Sauvignon, Muscat de Frontignan, and Sauvignon Blanc grapes.

Bear left to reach the historic winery, dating from 1883, whose cool tasting room offers welcome respite for walkers. When you have revived, walk out the front lane, through Concannon's classic ranch gate, and bear left, walking on the vineyard road that parallels Tesla Road to reach the neighboring Wente winery, with its more contemporary double six-sided tasting rooms. It dates only from 1972, but the winery began in 1880. Go inside to see the lithographs of the Louis Mel ranch and the famous Bosqui lithographs of grapes.

To return, follow Tesla Road to Livermore Road westerly via the bordering vineyard lanes until you connect with Pacific again.

If you get the feeling a stagecoach might pass at any moment, your intuitions are in tune, for this was the route that gave Livermore Valley the name of "Corridor Country."

36

The Delights of the Wilderness

Sunol Valley Regional Park usually stuns first-time visitors, especially if they see the rare golden eagle circling overhead. Who would expect to find a mountain stream near Fremont?

Rugged terrain with ridge lines that include 1,688-foot Maguire Peak and 1,360-foot Flag Hill has kept these 3,213 acres of the old Rancho el Valle de San Jose little changed since 1839, when Spanish sailor Antonio Maria Sunol ran cattle here.

Bobcats, cougars, badgers, and black-tailed deer range the land as they have for thousands of years. The magpie's raucous calls echo through the canyon. Ground squirrels dart about. And the smoggy automotive world seems far away indeed from this walk-in park.

To discover Sunol Valley's special charms, cross the Bay Bridge from San Francisco and drive south on Highway 580. Follow the signs for Tracy to the junction with Highway 680.

Go south on 680 to Calaveras Road off-ramp just south of the minuscule village of Sunol. Continue south on Calaveras Road to Geary Road, which leads into the park. Leave your car

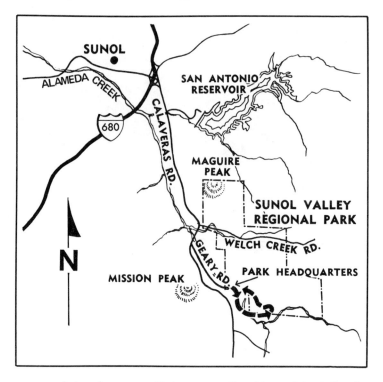

near park headquarters. Pick up a trail guide and look for the two pine trees that are the symbol for the 3.6-mile Canyon View Trail. This trail follows an old ranch road through a meadow filled with picnic tables, across a bridge with a gate locked to cars.

Then the trail follows Alameda Creek uphill past clumps of wildflowers to an aptly named overlook called Little Yosemite.

By the time you reach Little Yosemite, the cool mountain stream burbling happily will look inviting indeed. Cross the road and digress from the trail.

Park planners must have hiked this trail, rather than prepare it on the drawing board, for with unusual foresight, they have placed stone steps leading down into the canyon. The walker can descend to sit on the great boulders, wade in the cool water, or cross Alameda Creek on stepping stones to explore a block-fault cave on the far side.

When you have rested near this vignette of a Yosemite canyon and pondered the fault-line activity that created it, climb back to the trail, cross the road, and on the uphill side look for a trailmarker that says "To Headquarters."

Face the marker. On your left is a magnificent cliff, not unlike a miniature Half Dome. This is Lover's Leap, a name bestowed by local residents long before Sunol was brought into the East Bay Regional Park system in 1962.

Take the headquarters route and soon you will be standing on this eagle's aerie overlooking the lush valley from its best vantage. Thereafter the footpath winds easily back to headquarters.

37

Neither Walnuts
Nor a Creek

Larkey Park, near beautiful downtown Walnut Creek, may sound as though it were named by Christopher Robin but it was pioneer John Larkey, who owned it and the 750 surrounding acres in 1857, who left his name on the land. It is one of the most urbane small open spaces to be found in the Bay Area, and there is more to Larkey Park than first meets the eye, including some well-placed tennis courts, a swimming pool, a clubhouse for model-train buffs, a wildlife zoo, and a nature-study area.

Don't come expecting to see the native walnuts that first inspired Spanish settlers to call this part of Rancho San Ramon the Arroyo de las Nueces, or "Gully of the Nuts," however, because they are rarer than hen's teeth. What few walnut trees still stand in Walnut Creek are of an imported English strain that were grafted onto native rootstocks. They mark out old orchard lines in the yards of new houses whose developers had the good sense to keep existing trees.

"Surrounded by mountains and overlooked by the beetling cliffs of Diablo, the beautiful village of Walnut Creek is the most thriving of all the smaller towns in the county," historian J. P. Munro-Fraser wrote in Slocum's 1882 *History of Contra Costa County*. It owed its prosperity to the crossroads that had given Walnut Creek its early Yankee name of "The Corners."

It is still such a crossroads, although today the routes are freeways. To enjoy this oasis in the suburbs, from San Francisco, transport yourself east across the Bay Bridge, then via Highway 24 to Walnut Creek. Just before it merges with Route 680, take the Geary Road offramp west to Buena Vista Avenue. Turn left and look for the parking lot near First Street.

Walk toward the big warehouselike building fronted by

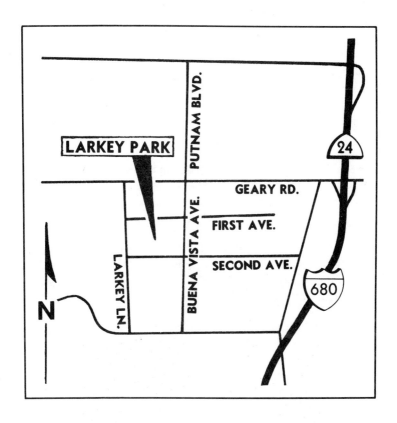

redwood trees. At the base of the broad steps, notice on the building's nearest corner a huge porthole that once accommodated a pipe. Formerly an East Bay Municipal Utility District pump house, it now houses the Alexander Lindsay Junior Museum, closed on Sundays to give the wild native fauna it houses a rest from the more than 112,000 visitors who go through this minizoo annually.

Bear right to find a weedy wild area in which botanist Jim Burtonshaw has reestablished indigenous native plants.

Leave the paved path to meander through the nature area, then return and follow its contours, dodging skateboarders and cyclists, toward the center of the grassy area. At about the middle of it you are standing on an East Bay MUD aqueduct.

Look to the northwest to discern the larger pumping station that replaced the one now recycled by the Lindsay Museum. Then look southeast toward Walnut Creek's open space area. This aqueduct right-of-way, about as broad as a fire lane, is part of a trail that will one day link several parks.

Given the energy crisis, vacationers may someday abandon their automobiles and again embark on the *Wanderjahren* or Grand Walking tours that wealthy young noblemen made on foot in Queen Victoria's time. When that happens, Larkey and Heather Farm parks, where cross-country hikers could pause for a swim, could make Walnut Creek famous as a rest stop.

Tempting as it is to head down the aqueduct path, for the time being swing along with the park again to locate near Buena Vista Avenue the clubhouse of Walnut Creek Model Railroaders, open from 8 to 10 P.M. on the last Friday of each month. Check the box office window for other special dates and plan to come back when the club sponsors its big public viewings of the layout, complete with villages and mountains, inside.

Check out the tennis courts across the street, still part of the park. Then if you are a swimmer, swing back toward the museum building to locate the 25-yard pool. It is open from 1 to 5 P.M. daily with a graduated schedule of modest fees. What could be a pleasanter way than a swim to end a warm day's walk?

38

A Long Walk in the Hills

"Geco," short for "gas-electric company ogre" is what conservationists have nicknamed the big high-voltage towers that stalk across rural landscapes like a chain-gang invasion of robots from Mars.

"It's only visual," a PG&E man said in a hearing not long ago, defending the company's proposal to march such a line through 3,100-acre Briones Regional Park, Contra Costa County's rare and beautifully unspoiled wilderness.

"For those who hike back into the wilderness to escape the sights and sounds of civilization, it can be very frustrating to come upon a line of gas company towers," a ranger told me recently, adding that "parks that have power lines are shunned by vacationers."

And that's the way the battle lines are drawn on one of the Bay Area's hottest ecological contests today.

In this, as in all such controversies, the best way to make up your mind which side is right is to go take a look, and preferably a walk around the area involved. Beautiful Briones Park offers some of the finest country walking in the East Bay. Unlike

Mount Diablo, a motorist's park, much marred by many communications structures, Briones, a natural study resource, has been preserved for hikers, bikers, horsemen, and especially students. Coincidentally, it is a refuge for the golden eagle and for the shy band-tailed pigeon, a bird that does not thrive in suburbs.

To make this walk, take the Eastshore Freeway (Interstate 80) north beyond Albany, then look for the San Pablo Dam Road-Orinda turnoff. Beyond the dam, when San Pablo intersects with Bear Creek Road, turn left and follow Bear Creek Road. Go two blocks beyond Happy Valley Road. Power lines and substations en route will give the casual observer a basis for comparison. A right turn on Briones Road leads directly into the park.

The easy five-mile loop of the park takes about two-and-a-half hours, none of it very strenuous. Shuck your wheels at the first parking lot on the left inside the park. At the opposite end from the map board, look for a service road at the foot of the small hill, a natural for kite flying. Facing the hill, take the road to the left into Pear Orchard Valley. Soon you will be abreast of Cascade Cre' k. Go over the hiker's stile at the barricade and leave civilization behind.

Don't let the white-faced cattle put you off. They are grazed to keep down fire hazard. Cattle have been grazed here since 1829 when Felipe Briones, a retired soldier of the Presidio of San Francisco, was granted the Rancho Boca de Canada del Pinole. In 1840 he was killed here in an ambush while chasing Indians who were running off his cattle. More recently the land has served as the watershed for Briones and San Pablo dams.

Look along the trailside for fruiting madrone and toyon trees, and for glimpses of the rare band-tailed pigeons. There are also fossil outcroppings and more than 50 kinds of wildflowers indigenous to the park.

By the big black oak and the water tank, bear left. Just beyond is a handsome youth camp center, erected by Girl Scout funds. In a pinch, 30 to 35 campers can sleep out of the rain around the covered fire pit.

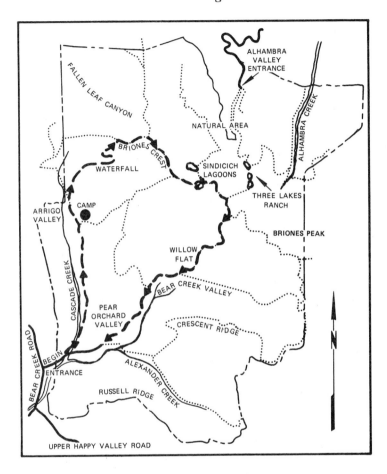

Return to the trail and at the next fork bear right up onto
the Briones crest. Within 400 yards, listen for the happy splash
of water. A charming waterfall hides in the grove of bay trees
on the right. Follow the road uphill or (if you feel adventure-
some) take the cow and deer path that strikes off uphill across
country. In either case, following the fence line on the ridge,
you will come out at the same place. En route are splendid
views of the mothball fleet, the Benicia Bridge, Mount Diablo,

Mount Tamalpais, the Farallones, and if the day is clear, snow on the Sierra crests. It is along this ridge that the power line may cross.

Notice the Sindicich Lagoon and its two neighboring ponds, which gave Three Lakes Ranch, now part of the park, its name. Take the stile and bear right beyond the second pond. If you're game for a climb, the next left fork goes to Briones Peak, 1,433.73 feet above sea level. Otherwise bear right through Willow Flat to Bear Creek Valley, a trout stream praised by W. E. Hutchison in 1915 for its "companionable nature."

If you come upon a mountain lion en route, don't panic. Leave the big kitty alone and she'll leave you alone.

The road will return you to the parking lot. If you feel the discovery of pristine Briones has been a windfall, make sure to come in the spring when the wildflowers carpet the hillsides.

39

A Hike in the
East Bay MUD

The enlightened East Bay Municipal Utility District, which owns 27,000 acres of reservoirs and watershed in the rolling East Bay hills, now has 55 miles of trail open to the public and is creating more.

The land through which this extensive trail system meanders is lovely, altered though it may be in some places by the clumsy thumb of man. Not really wild, as East Bay MUD's convenient new trail map explains, but land "on the edge between wilderness and civilization" where house cats, raccoons, opossums, squirrels, the familiar animals of suburbia, intermingle with foxes, coyotes, bobcats, weasels, badgers, deer, and even mountain lions.

Of the many routes available, one of the pleasantest, easy enough for the average Sunday walker, is a combination of the Hampton Trail and a length of the Oursan Trail along the north side of Briones Reservoir. Since it totals 6.2 miles, the ideal way to do it is via a two-car shuttle.

To make this walk, first obtain a Trail Use Permit from East Bay MUD, P. O. Box 24055, Oakland 94623. It costs $1 for a year and admits an entire family group. (On weekends, permits are also available at the San Pablo Reservoir recreation area located on San Pablo Dam Road between El Sobrante, reached from Highway 80, and Orinda Village, from Highway 24. Tell the attendant you have come for a trail permit and he will refund the $1 parking fee.)

Permit in hand, divide your party in two cars and head east from San Francisco via the Bay Bridge, take Highway 24 through the tunnel and go off at the Orinda-Moraga ramp taking Camino Pablo through Orinda Village. En route Camino Pablo becomes San Pablo Dam Road. Bear right on Bear Creek Road to the Briones staging area (it is on the left, after you pass the Briones Regional Park sign). Leave one car here, pile your daypack, lunch, canteen, and all the members of your party into the second car and continue along Bear Creek Road, to the junction with Alhambra Valley Road.

Bear left beside the weathered, graffiti-covered hut to the end of the road. Park here across from the little farm. This is the trailhead for Hampton Trail.

Ignore the two "No Trespassing" signs and go through the stile for walkers and horsemen at the right. For your own safety, sign in at the register just inside the stile. Then take off happily on the paved road to walk the 1.8 miles of the Hampton Trail.

At the privy, you have reached the junction with the Oursan Trail. For the young and spry who would like to reconnoitre, the knoll on the left makes a fine lookout. Pioneer Edward J. Hampton, 1878–1935, sleeps the long sleep on its crest. Otherwise go left under the large oak, taking the easy way through the stile. (The asphalt reaches a dead end at the water.) Now the trail follows an old dirt roadbed through an orchard and comes along the waterside, following the north shore of the Briones Reservoir.

East Bay MUD staffer Brian McCrea, who walked this trail with me, says credit for opening the watershed to hikers and horsemen goes to two persistent trail advocates, G. Howard Robinson and Clarence Wilson. Wilson, who beseeched East Bay MUD for 40 years, says when they finally opened the trails "they really went first-class."

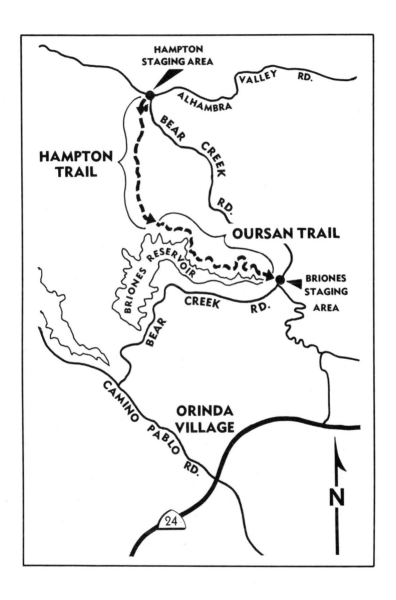

Trail markers are white posts with an arrow. Look for them whenever the trail veers away from the reservoir. You will find at the next down slope there is another view of the reservoir and that you have short-cut a small peninsula. Because land is leased, there may be cattle along here. (Farmers say "Huh! Huh! Bossy" loudly to scare the peaceable beasts from the trail.)

When the trail veers from the water a second time, pause on the uphill slope for a look around before you go through the next stile, downhill on your left. Self-closing gates are well designed to keep cows from straying. The only blight on the bucolic scene are the PG&E transmission towers. Signs at the water's edge that say 4/5 or 5/6 assist St. Mary's and Cal crews who practice sculling their shells on Briones.

On one point you will pass a beautifully exposed up-ended rock face of Oursan sandstone, one of many geological features identified in an educational land-use survey book prepared by Rodney Jackson that is available to teachers who use reservoir lands as living classrooms.

You will finally round a sunny curve and discover the ugly towers are concealed from sight, an ideal place to picnic. Please pack out all your trash to keep the watershed clean.

At the next junction bear right (the single path is a cattle trail) and at the inlet beyond, ignore the fire road and bear right again. At the next ridge on your left, the dead tree is a hangout for a great horned owl.

Follow the water consistently. Traffic noise may warn you that the highway is near before you see the sign "Swimming and Wading Prohibited by Law."

Beyond the Christmas tree farm, the trail ends at Briones staging area where you left car No. 1. Look for the register and sign out again before you call it a day.

40

There's Room
at the Top—Mt. Diablo

Concerned by the recent eruptions on Mount Etna, an East Bay resident asked me if Mount Diablo was ever a volcano. She also said, "My grandfather told me the Indians called it Koo Wah Koom, or 'Laughing Mountain.'"

Mount Diablo takes its name circuitously from the devil, by way of devil's woods (Monte del Diablo) for a thicket that contained an Indian rancheria near what became the village of Concord. Around 1811 it was called Cerro Alto de los Bolgones (High Hill of the Bolgones) for the Indians who lived at its foot. It has also been called "San Juan Bautista" but according to etymologist Erwin G. Gudde, author of *California Place Names,* the "Laughing Mountain" name was a hoax once swallowed hook, line, and guffaw by the state parks administration.

It was never a volcano either. Geologists call it a piercement structure and it is another indication of the great activity along the Calaveras, Hayward, and San Andreas faults. To get an understanding of how Diablo got its peaks, try to envision a giant bar of soap being held in an even more gigantic and slippery hand. The soap in Diablo's case is an oval of sedimentary rocks. The hand, tremendous serpentine dikes which "behave like a plastic and acted as a lubricant in facilitating relative movement between the wall rocks," according to geologist Earl H. Pampeyan in his definitive monograph on Mount Diablo. In simpler words, the slick serpentine greased an upward squeeze of the sedimentary rock that is now Diablo's peak.

If you wonder how a geologist knows what underlies certain areas, one indicator is natural vegetation. "Because scrub oak, manzanita and digger pine tend to be concentrated in areas of magnesian soils derived from serpentine, their distribution aided in locating small serpentine bodies," Pampeyan wrote.

The walker who would like to play geologist can try his hand at it at the Rock City Self-Guiding Nature Trail in Mount Diablo State Park. It has all the surface evidence a beginner could want.

To make this walk, enter the park from Highway 21 either

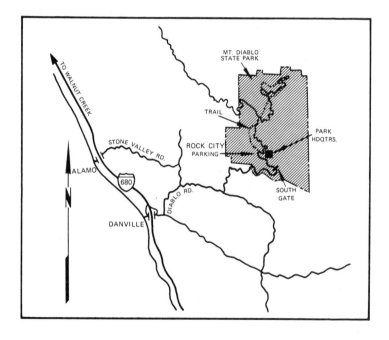

via Stone Valley Road from Alamo or Diablo Road from Danville. They join. Pick up directions for the self-guiding trail from the ranger-cashier at South Gate, continue along the road until you reach the Rock City camp area. Then park and look for the trailhead near a small ditch that drains a nearby spring, sometimes festooned with poison oak.

The trail heads out into grassland, then into oak woodlands. The blue oak here is deciduous and loses its leaves each winter, while nearby live oak hangs onto some of its leaves all year. The green cones, as well as seeds, of the digger pines, *Pinus sabiniana,* were valued as food by Indians.

Soon you walk from the oak woodland into chaparral, the collective name for brushlike vegetation. Here the chaparral includes chamiso (look for the needle-like leaves), pitcher sage, black sage, toyon, and manzanita. The woodrat can hide from his flying enemies here. Look below for rodent trails. Overhead, as you leave the fire-road portion of the trail and head across country, look for California vultures, red-tailed hawks, and possibly even an eagle.

Point 6 on the nature trail takes you near a species of manzanita indigenous to Mount Diablo and found in this area only. It has whorled leaves and earlike structures at the base of each leaf. Look also for the fine view of Sentinel Rock, a dominant geological feature of the park. There is also a good view on a clear day of the summit of the mountain.

Grotto Group Camp is one of four areas in the park reserved for large parties. One reaches it just before arriving at the Wind Caves, created by wind-driven sand particles eroding the boulders. If you haven't discovered by now what kind of rock those tremendous boulders are for which Rock City is named, you'll never make a geologist. They're sandstone.

41

Round a Reservoir

Wherever the pearly everlasting flower grows, the old gold teddy-bear hills of the Bay Area not only look, but smell like fall. It's a zesty, pungent smell, enticing to any walker. Usually the flower doesn't reach full maturity until September, but in a dry year, the season seems to be pushed ahead and reaches autumnal glory early.

Walkers who yearn to be out afoot and lighthearted in the East Bay can enjoy the pearly everlasting on Lafayette Reservoir's peripheral trail.

The first of East Bay Municipal Utility District lands to be opened to the public, Lafayette Reservoir Trail is more than ten years old. Its smashing success as a recreation area has led to opening of other East Bay MUD trails.

To make this three-mile walk, tuck a dollar bill for parking in your jeans, and go east from San Francisco via the Bay Bridge and Highway 24. Leave 24 on the first Lafayette offramp, labeled Acalanes Road-Mt. Diablo Boulevard. The ramp becomes Mt. Diablo Boulevard and crosses Acalanes almost immediately. Continue on Mt. Diablo east for a mile. The entrance to Lafayette Reservoir will be on your right. Turn in and feed your dollar bill into the toll barrier, then turn right to reach the parking lot above the boathouse.

During weekdays, when the park is less crowded, by the way, it is also possible to reach the town of Lafayette, three quarters of a mile east of the reservoir, by BART. One block south of the Lafayette Station on Happy Valley Road brings you to Mt. Diablo Boulevard. Take Mt. Diablo west. No fee or permit is required for walkers.

From the parking lot, drop down the steps toward the water to enjoy a staircase that goes right through the roof of the boathouse during your descent. Richard S. Kimatsu of El Cerrito was the architect who designed this attractive activity center.

Go inside to pick up a fine trail map leaflet and inspect the big fish tank containing black bass, rainbow trout, crappies, and three kinds of catfish, the varieties that can be caught in the reservoir. Rowboats are for rent.

When you have explored the little peninsula and discov-

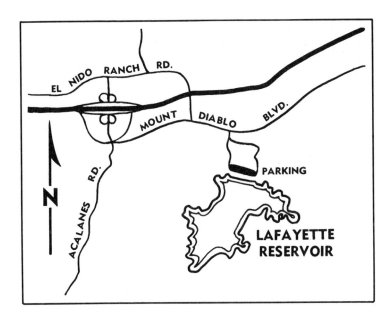

ered the resident Canada geese and mallards, return to the parking area above the center and continue past it on the well-paved road.

About a mile along, you reach a clearing often used by Campfire Girls and other groups for day camping. Digress from the main trail uphill on your right to the Rotary Outdoor Amphitheatre, recently enhanced with lawn and additional trees, to discover a fine view of Mount Diablo over the water.

Return to the paved road and continue along the waterside. Trails that go uphill reach the longer and more rugged Rim Trail that rings the reservoir at a higher elevation. Oddly enough, the upper route, a fire road, does not give nearly so much of a wilderness feeling as the easier peripheral trail, largely because the walker is often aware of the suburban surroundings from the upper trail.

Continue on the paved road and soon you reach the new Nature Trail, which loops back to the peripheral trail. As you walk on the paved road, big frogs may startle you from the reeds at the water's edge. Water levels seldom fluctuate here so the riparian life is rich.

After you pass the east lawn area, you will be walking on the reservoir dam itself. This is also the site of parking lot No. 1, and the toll gate. If you arrived by public transportation, peel away from the water here. If not, continue around the lake to return to your wheels and complete this loop.

PART FOUR

IN AND
AROUND
BERKELEY

42

Why They Call It
Treasure Island

Treasure Island—TI to thousands of sailors since 1940—is a 403-acre man-made island created on the Yerba Buena shoals with an airport in mind.

Partly to the greater glory of gasoline, partly to celebrate the completion of two great bridges, it was launched as a fair. For 372 magical days in 1939 and 1940, it may well have been the most entrancing spot in San Francisco Bay. Since then it has largely been "off limits" to the general public.

Harold Gilliam likened the Golden Gate International Exposition, as the Treasure Island fair was named, to "Tennyson's Palace of Art or the Pleasure Dome of Kubla Khan." Richard Reinhardt called it an earthly paradise and "a peaceable island crowned with towers and glittering with light, that seemed to float like a vision in a sea of gold." What conservationists would say if anyone tried a comparable bay fill project today probably isn't printable.

But there it stands, tied by a mile-long causeway to Yerba Buena, the rocky, tree-studded neighboring natural island.

Like other islands in the bay, Treasure Island has gathered its own mystique and history. Some of this was captured in a bicentennial project, the Navy/Marine Corps Museum, which filled the fair administration building, originally envisioned as an airport terminal. There are also enough other vestiges of the fair still standing to make a walk around the island a sentimental journey for those who remember it fondly.

To make this walk, since there is no longer ferry service, the way to go is via the San Francisco Bay Bridge. AC Transit makes frequent runs to the island from the Transbay Terminal at First and Mission streets. (Call 653-3535 for times.) Get off at the first

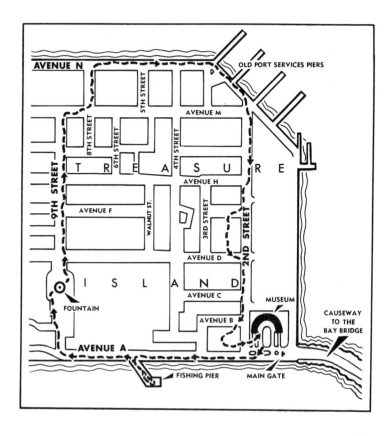

stop past the Main Gate sentry box on TI. By private car, take the Treasure Island offramp at the center of the bridge. (There is one from either level.) Once across the causeway, park by Building One, the museum. You do not need a pass, no matter what the signs say.

If the weather is fair, walk resolutely toward San Francisco, visible past the palms and water fronting the building, for a sensational view of the city, framed by its two bridges.

Once across Avenue A via the crosswalk near the sentry box, bear right on the walkway under the palms. This long line of trees, like others on the island, was planted for the fair. Walk away from the Bay Bridge, ducking under the ritual big guns, and follow the seawall.

Occasional patches of ice plant underfoot are the last remnants of 25 acres carpeted in mesembryanthemum by Julius Girod and Eric Walther of Golden Gate Park to create the fair's celebrated "Persian Prayer Rug" of plants.

When you reach the recreational fishing pier, go out and look around.

The walking gets rougher beyond the pier, but continue along the seawall, past two modern star-shaped barracks and the E. R. Taylor School, until the lane runs out of palms. This is at Ninth Street. Bear right on it, staying on the west side of the road until you reach four old palm trees, which reveal that prevailing winds are from the west.

Cross to the sidewalk on your right and approach the planting circle in the center of the roadway to see a fountain, now dry, which represented the Pacific during the fair. Statues surrounding it are in a "unique syncretistic style" called "Pacific Basin," no pun intended.

Cross to the right-hand side of the road to find a couple of picnic benches tucked under trees. Then follow Ninth Street across the island to the far side.

Once past the library, the Navy Exchange, and Basilone Theater, named for a Marine hero, bear right on Avenue M around the playing fields and tennis courts to Eighth Street. Then go left past another picnic area and restrooms to reach the east boundary of the island, also sheltered by palms. Although there is no formal walk, skirt under the trees on the road and turn the corner with the land to go alongside old port services piers.

At Second Street, leave the piers and bear right to find the area least changed from the halcyon years of 1939 to 1940.

At Avenue F, cross the street and go into the parklike area on your right.

Go beyond the grassy mall to follow the walk through old pepper, olive, and palm trees. The Navy buoy is a decorative signal to indicate Bachelor Officers Quarters. At B Street, go back to Second Street, then go into the chapel grounds to see the stained glass.

When you have enjoyed the calm simplicity of the chapel, bear left again on Avenue A to conclude this walk with a visit to the museum for a look at the salty artifacts and at Lowell Nesbitt's huge mural of the *Navy and Marine Corps in the Pacific: Past, Present and Future,* believed to be the largest mural in the United States. It covers 6,600 square feet.

43

Continental Ways
in Berkeley

Some Berkeleyans, unable or unwilling to live in Paris, have been creating a continental little neighborhood of their own in the vicinity of Shattuck and Vine.

You may not see the typical Gallic shrug of the shoulders there, but one who goes to browse will find a real *charcuterie,* a *patisserie,* some remarkable boutiques and restaurants, and best of all, a place to linger in a "sidewalk" cafe in the sky.

Since the West Coast frequently is the front runner in trends, this may well be what lies in store for the nation's Main Streets tomorrow. Why not? It is very pleasant, indeed.

To see for yourself, cross the Bay Bridge and take the University Avenue offramp into Berkeley. Follow University to Shattuck, bear left to the vicinity of Cedar Street and park where you can. Two corners have long been dominated by the old parent Co-Op and its satellites, the Co-Op hardware and nursery. Once you are on foot, the new ambience of the street is immediately apparent, beginning with the well-planted boulevard strip in the center of the street where once the Key System interurban tracks ran. If you are on the east side of Shattuck, peek into the outdoor garden court of 1517 to observe Chez Panisse restaurant and *voila!* A Parisian mood.

Cross at the corner and skirting the Co-Op parking lot, look for the hand-carved sign of the Pig by the Tail Charcuterie. To set off the sausages, baguettes of French bread come in here daily. A few steps along is another fine hand-carved sign for The Cheese Board, but you may glimpse a tremendous wheel of cheese or two bicycles in the window, first. Notice the sign

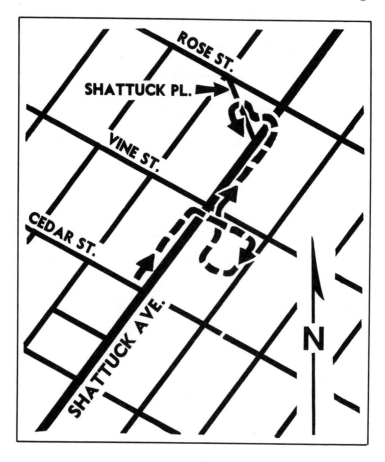

announcing a 10 percent discount for people over 60, 15 percent for those over 70.

The next French touch is the Berkeley Fish Company, with nets and creels behind the counter, live fish in the window, and fresh fish for sale daily. Its neighbor, the Produce Center, arranges vegetables as charmingly as flowers. Women shopping along this block often come with string bags, as in Paris, and refuse paper wrappings.

Cross Shattuck at Vine and walk uphill past the Birkenstock Shoe Store, On Edge Trimmings, Northside Tennis Shop, and the Bike Shop, a trendy juxtaposition of boutiques. The Juice Bar Collective has all of four tables, three stools, and a bench. Honeybear Toys is so sophisticated the miniature Victorian furniture includes a pull-chain toilet and an antique chamber pot. It also has six-foot velvet hobby horses, kids' books in foreign languages, and a fine collection of posters, including one of a turtle roller-skating that says, "If it feels good, do it." The adjacent (and adjoining) gift shop offers an extravaganza of macramé. Look for the pottery aquarium that looks like an old deep-sea diver's helmet amid this jute jubilee.

Beyond it, Aura Antiques must be entered through the Payless Cleaner's door. Peet's Spices holds down the corner at Walnut Street, with an aroma so rich it is a turn-on just to pass it. Bear right and the tremendous leather sign at the Golden Calf Custom Leather looks as though a giant had lost his sandal. When you reach the Green Growcery, which touts "bashful beautiful cyclamen," turn into Walnut Square, which is somewhat like Ghirardelli Square by way of Handmade House. I especially liked Above and Beyond Kite Shop, with its triwinged Fokker and its ghostly clipper-ship kites, Far and Few dress shop, and Zasaku Japanese Crafts.

Up on the deck takes you above the prole struggle to the "sidewalk" cafe.

Look in on The Magic Horse bookstore, which seems to intermingle Tibetan and children's books. Stop in at Papyrus for distinctive paper products, imported greeting cards, postcards, etc. At Bite the Cookie, sweets are the forte. Go all the way to the end to find the Hand Loomed Fabric Store, which also has ethnic dress patterns by Alexandra Jacopetti.

When you finally get your cappuccino, there is the pleasure of seeing San Francisco and Mount Tamalpais, framed by glinting water above the roofs of Berkeley.

Go out the exit to the right of the stairs to return to Vine Street. Cross it at Shattuck and continue north to 1481 to visit Cocolat, where the Rum Truffles, the mousse meringue, the Queen of Sheba, and the Chocolate Whiskey Cake can be bought by the slice.

If you think you have already passed Bing Wong's laundry once, relax. There are several along the street.

When you perceive that Shattuck is taking a turn, reverse your direction and start back to make your own discoveries. That's half the fun of browsing, *n'est-ce pas?*

44

Short Walk, Long Pier

"Lady, where does a walk begin?"

He was leaning against the railing of the Berkeley Fishing Pier, a lanky boy of ten or twelve. Long streaks marked the rump pocket of his jeans where he wiped his bait knife. Was it a taunt? A put on? Did he want to know where all walks begin or just this one? I looked at him carefully.

The eyes had that serene faraway look that comes to the genuine fisherman, as if they had absorbed some depth of the water, so I took him at his word.

"Ideally a walk begins when you open the front door and let your foot pass the lintel. That's the way it was for hundreds of years before men and motorcars messed up the world. Now a walk, like a little vacation, which it is, begins when you enter a place, preferably natural and unchanged, but at least beguiling, where your senses and reflexes begin another kind of life."

He was with it instantly. "I never thought of a pier as a walk before."

Neither do most people. Yet the long (3,000 feet) Berkeley Fishing Pier at the foot of University Avenue is one of the best water walks in the Bay Area. Long abandoned, part of it has been rescued from the shipworm, rebuilt, reinforced, and furnished by the Berkeley Recreation and Parks Department with attractive street furniture, running water, fish-cleaning sinks, windshelter benches, and privies. From the Pier the ocean view through the Golden Gate can be spectacular, especially at sundown.

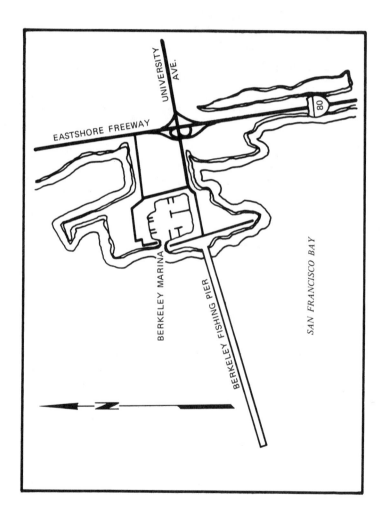

Ocean View, appropriately enough, was the name of the community that preceded Berkeley on this shore in the 1860s. It began along the waterfront between Strawberry and Codornices creeks, on what was once part of the vast Rancho San Antonio, a land grant to Don Luis Peralta in 1820. He later divided it and deeded it to his four sons. Domingo received this part. By 1873, the end of University Avenue, about where Spenger's is located, was known as Jacob's Landing. Four ferryboats came and went here daily.

A gristmill stood at the foot of what is now Hearst Avenue, laying the curse of industrial usage on the tideflats early on. Soon it attracted a starch and wheat processing plant in the estuary of Strawberry Creek, using its clean water to wash grain. Surrounding small holdings and truck farms have left their owner's names on the land as streets—Ashby, Blake, Colby, McGee, Shattuck, and Woolsey, to name six. When these farmers lived here, you could walk from the Indian trail that became the county road and is now San Pablo Avenue to the water in a matter of minutes. Today it is a matter of life and death. A torrent of machinery writhes and twists through the Eastshore Freeway like a river on the rampage.

If you have no wheels, one way to reach this walk is via AC Transit Line 51 M bus, which uses the pier approach as the end of the line. Farsighted citizens have suggested a pedestrian overpass from nearby Aquatic Park as one way to make it more accessible to young fishermen.

At the outset, notice the tremendous contemporary sundial, a gift from Berkeley's Japanese sister city, Sakai. The gnomen is large enough so small fry often use it as a slide.

Continue past and look for steps going up on the little building at the entrance to the pier. Climb it for an overview of the adjacent 800-berth Berkeley Marina and "Great Field," a tremendous prairielike place ecologists describe as a biological recovery area. Originally a dump, it was covered with six feet of topsoil some years ago and now shelters wildlife, shorebirds, and at some seasons, kite flyers. The University of California Yacht Club uses the lagoon on the south side, bounded by the present dump and a natural shoreline park.

The unusual structure on the marina edge is the harbor-master's building. Solomon Grundy Restaurant occupies the Samoan-style pavilion north of the pier, H's Lordships Restaurant the one south of it.

When you have spotted the University of California campanile, turn your eyes west instead and enjoy a baywide panorama. Then descend the opposite side of this observation tower and begin your peregrination to the pier's end. What could be simpler than a walk along a fishing pier? Yet like the 24 hours James Joyce recorded in Dublin, so many impressions crowd in that a walker can make a million choices. Try, for sighs, the magic in a shoreline, this meeting of land and water where two geographies, one a wet world of fishes, the other the freehold of birds, meet. Or the mystery of what lives underfoot here, where a live flounder may be beneath you, all unknown. Or for that matter, the curious fact that only men are concerned with beginnings and ends. For in the mind of bird, fish, or beast, eternity is ever present.

"Lady, where does a walk begin?"

In the mind, son, in the mind. . . .

45

Berkeley's
Watery Scene

As with weather, everybody talks about our deteriorating environment, but thus far nobody has done much about improving it. A singular exception in the Bay Area is the "habitat" on the Berkeley Marina, the creation of landscape architects Zach Stewart and Dan Osborne.

Convinced that man has both the knowledge and technology to repair the damage he has wrought in the ecology, Stewart and Osborne set out to demonstrate how it could be done in an eight-acre waterside park. The result is potentially so good, "habitat," a word meaning "the natural abode of plant or animal," is bound to start popping up in the language frequently.

To see this habitat, come for a water-edge walk in the Berkeley Marina. Begin by transporting yourself to the free fishing pier at the western end of University Avenue. The AC Transit Line 51 M bus stops right there. Disembark and look about. As enticing as the 3,000-foot stroll over the water on the fishing pier is, save this for last and walk east instead, across Marina Boulevard to the little hill on your right.

A path leads uphill between the newly planted cypress on either side. Go up and over the ridge. You become aware that this is no ordinary park of stereotyped conception when the path peters out, leaving a feeling of natural wildness. In "captive landscapes," paths seldom dwindle to nothing as they do in unspoiled countryside. Notice the swale between the hillocks on either side. It is a marshy meadow with dune grasses, rushes, and when I was there, wild bathing ducks. A little rivulet runs from the pond to the bay. A sprinkler head assures that it will not dry up.

When you have surveyed the landscape from this aspect, retrace your steps to the corner and walk east on University Avenue extension in the direction of the houseboats, and the marina office, a handsome building designed by McCue, Boone, & Tomsick. Soon you will be abreast of a little building

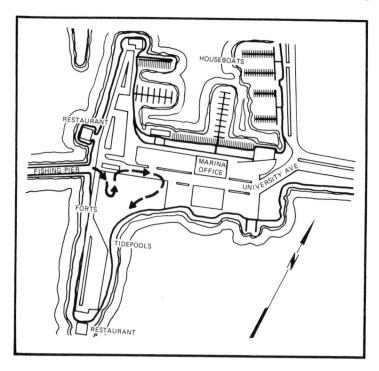

for sanitary facilities snuggled in behind a dune. Turn right here into the park again and follow the broad compacted earth trail.

As you walk, you will become aware of a sandy beach at the shoreline and beyond it rocky tidepools. Follow your natural urge to leave the trail and explore, for to be free is part of the design for use by man. From the sand, look back at the hills and you will discover that they seem to form a horseshoe of dune, spacious and unconfined, just as one might find in an area untouched by man. As the plantings of native trees, shrubs, grasses, weeds, and sedges grow, the park is changing year by year to become ever more natural, shaping itself with wind, weather, and water. Park superintendent Paul Sutterly estimates the cost for the habitat is about one-fourth that of a "cliche" park.

Go over to the rocks near the two "forts," contrived of old pier pilings salvaged from offshore debris. Notice how earth has been tamped down between the rocks. Next step is "hydroseeding" with native plant seeds, a method used to halt erosion in which a truck with tank and nozzle sprays a slurry mixture of fertilizer, seeds, and soilbinder into the crevices. Result: instant grass cover.

As you walk around, birdwatching, beachcombing, butterfly or beetle hunting, observe how unrestrained the outward views are, partly because dune mounds shut off the mechanical world. As one child exclaimed on his first visit, "Here I feel like I am somewhere."

When you have explored the park, return to the fishing pier. If you still have wind left for walking, this pier (see page 169) is one of the great all-time water walks of the bay.

46

Where It Began

In the beginning there was Ocean View, and then there was Berkeley. The story of the first University of California trustees naming Berkeley for the bishop who wrote "Westward the course of empire takes its way" had such popular appeal, most people believe it was also the beginning of the town itself. Not so.

For almost 15 years before that, the thriving community of Ocean View had stood at the mouth of Strawberry Creek between the waterfront and San Pablo Avenue.

Early maps show two wharves extending into the bay from First Street, one at the end of University, the other at the end of Bristol, soon to be renamed Hearst. In 1855, a mill using the water power was thriftily grinding to flour grain that nearby farmers brought from their sunny fields. Many a farmer also brought in pigs, sheep, or calves for slaughtering on the shore nearby.

In the classic nonplanned pattern, these necessaries soon attracted related enterprises. Munro Fraser's 1883 *History of Alameda County* lists among others the Pioneer Starch Works,

Hoffburg Brewery, Wentworth Boot and Shoe, and Standard Soap Works, which shipped its fine castile across the bay to San Francisco by the Berkeley ferry steamer, a vessel it owned. So workers could walk to the job, factory owners often arranged to build houses nearby.

The vestiges of this bucolic little transitional industrial town, soon to be overwhelmed by its more intellectual neighbor growing uphill, are still to be found on the land. The walker with an eye for architecture and anthropology can find them clinging like wisps of straw on corduroy, as he strolls in old Ocean View.

To make this walk, transport yourself to the corner of Ninth Street and Hearst Avenue, one block north of University Avenue and two blocks west of San Pablo Avenue. (Bus routes 51, 58, 65, 73, G, and H, all come close.) Here in front of the charming Church of the Good Shepherd, which dates from 1878, pause to get your bearings, examine the louvered steeple, and coincidentally listen for the cooing of pigeons from a loft nearby. Placards indicate that both Episcopal and Presbyterian services are held here. Fine stands of calla lillies, daffodils, and camellias may be as old as the church itself.

Walk west to discover on either side of the next block, modest but attractive "workingmen's Victorians" with nice fish-scale shingles interspersed with more contemporary homes. At the corner of Eighth, pause for a good look at the controversial St. Procopius Church, built in 1879 as Westminster Presbyterian Church and now somewhat Roman Catholic. A gaggle of small dogs seems to live in the yard behind an arch which says, "For we are laborers together with God 1 Corinthians, 3:91."

Look left on Eighth to see an entire block of workers' houses, but continue on Hearst to Seventh for a look at a classical "mom and pop" grocery building, designed in the 1870s so the proprietors could live over the store. Still in use, it is now a tortilla factory as well as *groceria*.

Continue on to Sixth to see one of many weeping willows in the neighborhood, indicators of Strawberry Creek's drainage basin, now out of sight below the earth.

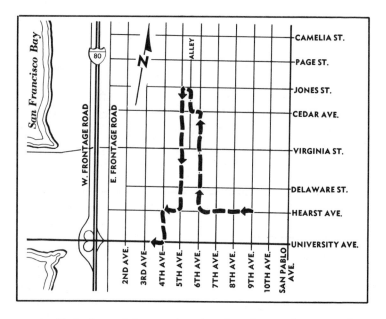

At Sixth, bear right, passing the site of a confrontation between the owner of the second oldest house in Berkeley and the
redevelopment agency. Fire department units dragged the
owner off the roof when he refused to leave. Other members of
the Ocean View Committee have since lain down in front of
bulldozers to demonstrate their concern for their community.
Attitudes on the part of government have now changed, "although Ocean View is still treated like a stepsister," according
to property owner Richard Katz.

At Virginia, look past the big willow tree and the handsome
two-story house to locate a functioning windmill at midblock,
last of many that once stood in Ocean View. An old farmhouse
stands across the street from it.

At Cedar, observe the nice Turkish arches outlined in green
at 1522 Sixth, but walk half a block west on Cedar to locate a
genuine three-block-long alley, possibly the only one in Berkeley. Turn right on it and you are soon abreast of a redwood
barn, circa 1870, complete with skyhook. A hundred feet fur-

ther is a concrete-floored shed, once the workshop of a piano tuner. Like the adjacent house, it was restored by Richard Katz. The odd sign another 100 feet along the alley "Avenida de las Investigaciones Filosoficas" commemorates Harris Hagar for his genial wine-drinking and philosophizing, cracker-barrel style. At Jones, bear left by the picket fence, noting to the west the biggest weeping willow of all. At Fifth, bear left, by the brown-shingled building, recently restored, as are many others on this street. A cancer research project operated by the Ariquipa Foundation is in one. Farallones Institute has classes in another. The little green shiplap house, number 1519, was occupied for 60 years by Herman Furman.

Press on between alternating small industrial buildings and modest homes to 1808 Fifth, built in 1878. Berkeley's town council originally met here. The house on the corner beyond has a yard full of stovewood for sale, but the goats that used to browse here are gone.

At Hearst, bear right, noting the beautiful bronze eagle by the parcel-post station, and the remarkable teeter-totter on wheels. At Fourth, bear left to reach Spenger's Fish Grotto, whose fish used to come in at the dock three blocks west. In 1876, its parking lot was Willow Grove Park, complete with pavilion and picnic area. Merrymakers often came by train to the fine old Southern Pacific railroad station, still standing under the freeway.

If the enticements of Spenger's don't lure you in, end your walk by the station. Buses stop there, even as the horse cars did in 1874.

47

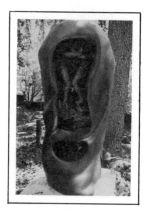

A Walk
Into the Past

Perspective, in these difficult times, is where you find it. The scholarly walker could well find it on a quiet street in Berkeley, where the history of western Jewry has been gathered into an archive called the Judah L. Magnes Memorial Museum. Nearby, one will also find glimpses of a spacious, gracious past, anachronistically encapsulated within a few short blocks.

To set out for this walk, use the charming old Claremont Hotel as a landmark (or the Berkeley Tennis Club on most street maps) and transport yourself east from San Francisco via the Bay Bridge and Highway 24, as Ashby Avenue is also known. At Piedmont and Ashby, bear right one block to Russell Street, and right again to park where you can near 2911 Russell, the address of the museum.

Once located, take a good look at the four-story, slate-roofed building of clinkered brick built in 1908 for Jeremiah Thaddeus Burke, attorney for the Southern Pacific Railroad and cousin to the founder of Miss Burke's School for Girls in San Francisco. But save the museum visit for a dramatic climax to this expedition.

Walk along its front wall, past the orchard and the villa-like building constructed for Mme. Newton Woodworth on what was once the Burke tennis courts. The living room of this house, now occupied by the museum director, boasts a stagelike corner balcony from which Mme. Gabrielle Woodworth, an opera singer, could practice. Notice the zucchini and lettuce interplanted with the ornamentals on the hedge that fronts the brick wall.

At Pine Path, turn right and start uphill. In a few short steps you pass a Tudor-style house on the left and are among pine trees. Climb a few more steps along this little lane, like an English path among hedgerows, and if the season is right, you are alongside a cascade of heavenly blue morning glories. All too soon, this little lane brings one out on Avalon Court. Immediately there is a change of character, for every house visible at this point in the street seems Mediterranean, even to the bougainvillea and geraniums tumbling in profusion over sunny facades.

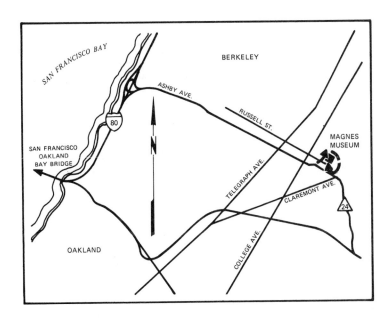

Bear right. As you walk, the distinctive roof of the Claremont Hotel is visible. When you reach a contemporary house, look right through the breezeway for a sensational view of beautiful downtown Oakland. Pass house number 2934 and turn right (parallel to Oak Knoll Terrace). Here another quaintly turn-of-the-century path passes through hedgerows. These are of ivy and rose.

At the brick pillars turn right. You will again be on Russell Street walking under great arching trees as venerable as the houses they shield from traffic noise.

When you reach the museum, go in. Come along at the right time and a string quartet may be playing in the garden. Or the lively burble of an art opening may surge from the first floor galleries out into the patio. The permanent collections are impressive, and chronicle the travail and triumphs of Jews through the ages. Numismatists should go upstairs to see the "Coin of the Return," minted after the Babylonian exile and possibly the oldest coin in existence. There are also six rooms of ceremonial art.

Ketubas, or wedding certificates, from many countries dot the hallway walls, all beautifully ornamented. Menorahs, Dutch oil-burning candle lamps, Torah pointers, spice boxes, textiles, wedding gowns, and artifacts of Judaism from around the world trace long years of transience.

Climb one more level to find an unusual shingled interior that houses the Western Jewish History Center, an historical archive with many original documents and papers. Then go all the way to the basement level to find a comfortable research library. Go out through the side door into a half-acre of grounds to find beyond a classic traffic turnaround, a rose garden and carriage house occupied by a lecture, film, and social hall, and by an artist-in-residence.

48

See Me, Feel Me, Touch Me

"Fair the terrace that o'erlooks/ Curving bay and sheltered nooks;/ Groves that break the western blasts/ Steepled distance fringed with masts,/ and the Gate that fronts our home/ with its bars of cold sea foam," wrote Bret Harte in 1867 for the ground breaking at the California School for the Blind and the Deaf, the first state institution to come to Berkeley. These rhapsodic lines were placed in the school's cornerstone.

I went for a walk in the vicinity to seek out the view that had prompted the poet and see how it had fared since he immortalized it.

Typical of Berkeley, what I found was the unique combination of open space, distant vistas, comfortable homes, tree-lined streets, and secret footpaths that make the scholarly city so livable. There were also some remarkable surprises for a walker.

To discover them, put on your loafers and seek out the corner of College Avenue and Dwight Way, served by AC Transit buses 51, 58, and 65. Shudder your way past the "ponderous, poured-in-place concrete building in the Brutalist style of the 60s," as Gebhardt et al. describe Newman Center in their recent *Guide to Architecture in San Francisco and Northern California*. For relief, hurry toward 2727 Dwight Way to find a house built in 1891 and remodeled by Willis Polk into a Berkeley brown shingle around 1910.

Cross by the deodar at the intersection minipark and bear right beside a handsome stone wall on Warring Street, probably named for Professor Warring Wilkinson, an early principal of the School for the Blind and the Deaf—now divided into two schools on adjoining campuses. Brown-shingled houses across the street were among those that determined the Berkeley

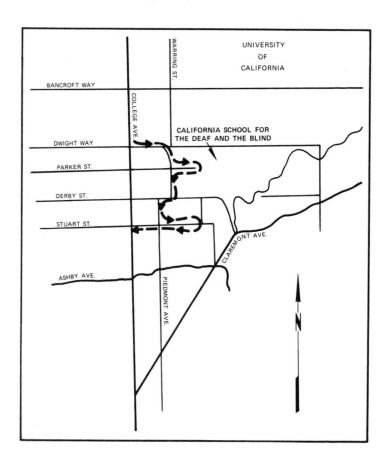

neighborhood pattern. Architectural historian Fillmore Eisenmayer recalls walking past number 2516 as a child especially to hear the beautiful music that emanated from it during the lifetime of Alexander Raab, a piano teacher much loved among Berkeley musicians.

Soon the wall opens into a double wrought-iron picket fence revealing the parklike grounds of the School for the Deaf. At Parker Street, bear left into the campus past a redwood grove and fruit trees toward the Strauss clocktower, known for its Seth Thomas works.

The green hills of Berkeley make a reassuring backdrop beyond the red-tiled roofs of the school as you climb the gentle ramp of the walkway. At the flagpole, bear left into the arcade, then right to a small court to discover *The Bear Hunt,* a striking statuary group by Douglas Tilden, one of the school's most distinguished alumni.

Pause here for a moment and as a contemplative exercise try to imagine yourself blind. What a delight the birdsong and flower odors would be. Now imagine yourself deaf and discover the pleasures of the textures, gardens, and hillside. Notice on the statuary the patina on the baby bears' noses and the lower Indian's hands, left by thousands of children feeling them down through the years.

Continue into the inner court and playing field. Cross from the pergola, whose sign says "Self Trust is the First Secret of Success," toward the huge carved eagle, then bear right and walk through another court to find yourself at a second flagpole parallel to the first. Stop here to look west and find Bret Harte's "steepled distance fringed with masts."

Then return to Warring Street and bear left to Derby Street, passing houses whose streetside gardens have long been a pleasure to deaf children. Notice the lawn of California poppies, the Japanese garden, the birch trees. Old gnarled trunks also show hand shine where generations of blind children have caressed them.

On Derby, bear right one block, passing at 2814–2816, a pair of neighborly houses designed by Julia Morgan to face each other, rather than the street. On Piedmont bear left. In another block you reach the Emerson School, where a venerable lepto-spermum tree seems to be leaning like an inebriate on the fence.

Bear left on Garber. Immediately past the school's smaller play yard, it dead-ends for cars, but steps and a winding way lead the walker uphill to one of Berkeley's choice neighborhoods, Elmwood. At the crest, woods open out near a house whose tower indicates the architect was Henry Gutterson. Stroll down to the traffic barriers beside another minipark and turn right on Oak Knoll and right again on Avalon.

Walk past Mediterranean houses, whose views are of Oakland and the bay, to the Avalon cul-de-sac. Near the curb number 2901 and a storm drain by Phoenix Iron Works, an unidentified public path leads downhill, sometimes to the music of the carillon in the University of California campanile.

At a half turn, it becomes steps which emerge a few moments later and lower at Palm Court. Among the trees, there are no longer palms, alas, continue on Stuart for two blocks to end this walk on College Avenue, again with public transportation easily accessible.

49

A Walk
Out of Parrish

Try to imagine a Maxfield Parrish come to life. That's Orchard Lane. Winding gently uphill, with steps bordered by
Italianate balustrades, curving garden benches at just the right
places for lovers to linger, unexpected turns, enticing vistas, and
elegant buildings barely visible behind lush shrubbery, Orchard
Lane is a romantic dream fulfilled.

This paragon of secret pathways lies, not in the imagina-
tion, but in Berkeley. Uphill and slightly southwest of the Uni-
versity of California stadium, it rambles through part of the
Berkeley hills that architects and historians sometimes call
"Morgan country," for the celebrated woman architect, Julia
Morgan.

The walker who looks for it may not find Orchard Lane on
the map, nor its tributary, Mosswood Lane, yet both have been
on the land and well used for more than 60 years. To walk them
is to return for an hour to a happier, more romantic time of
innocence.

Transport yourself to International House at the corner of

Bancroft Way and Piedmont Avenue in Berkeley. (AC Transit buses 51 and 58 stop one block away on College Avenue.)

Facing International House, bear right toward what is now the Sigma Phi fraternity house. Originally the Thorsen House, designed by Greene and Greene, it is so choice that it is House Number One on Berkeley Architectural Heritage Walking Tour Number One. Bear left, uphill, on Bancroft Way without crossing the street for the best perspective on this extraordinary brown-shingled building with its second-floor bridge.

At Warring Street, Bancroft becomes a walkway barred to cars. The center handrail is to divide pedestrian traffic during sporting events at the stadium, soon visible on your left. You will come out at the complex intersection of Prospect Street, Canyon Road, Panoramic Way, and the stadium parking lot. Cross there, angling to the right, away from the parking lot, to pick up on Panoramic a length of brick sidewalk laid in a herringbone pattern. Walk 50 feet uphill on it and stop by the white fireplug. Lo! Orchard Lane.

It begins in concrete steps between two houses, looking for all the world like a private entrance. Public it is, however.

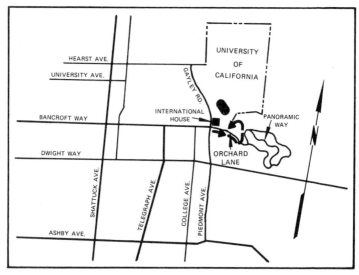

The house on the south side, 11 Panoramic Way, was designed around 1910 by Julia Morgan, famous for creating San Simeon. On the left, or north, Number 1 Orchard Lane was designed by architect Walter Steilberg, for many years employed in her firm, for himself.

Although Steilberg worked out the engineering to cope with underground streams, credit for the elaborate stairway design should go to art dealer Robert Atkins, who had a gallery at Powell and Sutter streets for many years. Mason McDuffle had the lane, which crosses loops of Panoramic Way twice, constructed in 1910. Start up the steps of Orchard Lane and prepare to lose yourself in enchantment.

At the junction with Mosswood Lane, bear right, around that enticing curve. At Panoramic, go around the street divider to pick up the next lap of the lane beside the house whose steps say "entrance to 101." Go up those steps, bear left, and notice how the ambience has changed from tanglewood to flowery Mediterranean, with informal pots of flowers on the steps, a potting shed, tile rooftops, and, if you pause to look back, a spectacular view of San Francisco near the weigela.

Pause by Number 19 to see the campanile through the roses, a favorite place for Fillmore Eisenmayer, who grew up here, to sketch. At Arden Road, go left, past the hammock that looks like a ship afloat in a sea of trumpet vine, to find a dead end whose street sign says Arden Path and Arden Steps.

Take the steps down, bear left at Mosswood Street and walk through treetops to the telephone pole numbered 45. Here, beside a country mailbox, Mosswood Lane slips in as a narrow footpath, to pass a split rail fence before it widens out by a lane of a dozen tall redwood trees.

Notice, by 4 Mosswood Lane the steps leading to a rooftop patio, and across from it, some of the formal lane balustrade incorporated into a terrace. Once past the gnarled tree roots in the path, you are back on Orchard Lane, having made an irregular loop.

Go down one flight, bearing ever right to return to your starting place. If you can't quite believe it, walk it all over again.

50

The Berkeley That
Only A Few Know

Paths and little parks are among the amenities that keep
Berkeley uniquely livable. Berryman Path near Codornices
Creek and the surrounding Live Oak Park are fine examples.
The walk through them is one of those reassuring strolls that
leaves the walker with renewed hope, a fine outing for com-
posing resolutions for the New Year or dropping off the cares
of the old.

To make this walk, transport yourself to Shattuck Avenue
and Berryman Street (AC Transit bus 33 and the F bus are
handy). The neighborhood is comfortable and rustic. A good
example is the Shedd house at 1319 Shattuck, built as a cottage
in 1870 and enlarged into a mansion around 1910.

Notice the volleyball, basketball, and tennis courts off it
and the tremendous wisteria tree by the Live Oak clubhouse,
then glance down Berryman Street to spot a house designed by
Julia Morgan (the one with the pink woodwork), and on the
opposite side of the street, the pretty Church of St. Mary Magda-
lene. Then seek out the beautifully carved wooden sign with an
acorn finial that indicates Live Oak Park. Berryman Path takes

off uphill by the theater beyond it, paralleling the handsome line of globe-topped street lamps.

Enticing as the creekside trees and bridge in the valley on your left may seem, for the moment ignore them and start uphill. The brick theater building you pass was the work of architect Robert Ratcliff, completed in 1956 and used largely by local groups.

As you near Walnut Street, look on your right for the workroom of the Live Oak Acorns, a group of physically handicapped adults, many of them senior citizens, who have met here regularly since 1957 in a program sponsored by the Recreation and Parks Department that offers 15 separate activities.

Go under the big oak tree to emerge at Walnut Street. Cross it and walk into the second section of Live Oak Park to find Berryman Path continuing uphill. Digress here toward the left for a special treat, to visit the Berkeley Art Center, approached by a footbridge over Codornices Creek. Also designed by Ratcliff, it was a gift from the Rotary Club and opened in 1966. It is free, and open on Sunday from 11 A.M. to 5 P.M.

When you have marveled at the shells, bells, velvet, beads, bronze, feathers, and mica, turn past the azaleas, the outdoor barbecue, and minitheater to Berryman Path and continue uphill. En route, one passes a typically erudite Berkeley graffito in orange spray paint: "Let those who do not support the revolution do *nothing* against it." *Nothing* has been edited and replaced with *everything*.

At Oxford Street, detour to the right about 50 feet to find at 1300 Oxford Street, "The Cedars," the 1868 home of pioneer Napoleon Bonaparte Byrne. After freeing his slaves, Byrne brought ox teams, a drove of cattle, his wife, and four children overland from New Madrid, Missouri, in 1869 to take up farming here. Many of the trees along the creek were planted by him.

Return to cross the bridge and take Berryman Path uphill again through a tunnel of fine trees past the gardens of several old Berkeley brown-shingled homes, built before the fire of 1923. Behind one is what architectural historian Fillmore Eisenmayer calls a "brownie" cottage. Bear left on Spruce Street

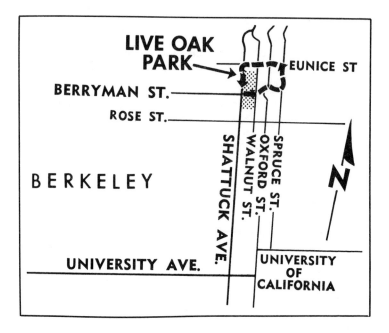

to get a better look at the cottage, which has a stained-glass window in the V of its gable.

As we came along the row of brown-shingled homes here, the clickety clack of a typewriter made counterpoint to a practicing saxophone, typical Berkeley street music. Notice the cut-leaf maple tree whose color in fall is enhanced by the red door behind it.

At Eunice Street, bear left by the livid peach and Krishna blue Ramona-style apartments, a reminder that this area was first developed by the Berkeley Villa association. Developers of the 1880s customarily included footpaths in their plans.

Look for two of the handsomest houses in Berkeley, one an original Julia Morgan design at 2209 Eunice, somewhat changed by additions, the other at 2201, designed by Olive Violett Rogers Wilson. When you reach Walnut Street, cross to the northerly side; in the fall the red pyracanthas are in full berry. As they ferment, migrating robins often hold a bash here getting drunk on the berries.

Continue on Eunice to Shattuck Avenue, then bear left to observe the Flagg house at 1201, a Maybeck built in 1901 and hidden in the pines. Across the street, 1208 and 1210 also have a Maybeck influence. In a few more steps you will be back at the boundary of Live Oak Park.

To conclude this loop walk, walk toward the big blooming magnolia, then toward the dawn redwood, which looks like a caricature by Disney. A plaque announces that it was the gift of the Berkeley Boys. From the tree, bear right to cross Codornices Creek via the footbridge, ending this walk on the soothing note of water music.

51

A Walk Through Maybeck Country

Rose Walk, the block-long stairway designed by architect Bernard Maybeck in 1913, has been described as "North Berkeley's perfectly planned environment compressed into one block." It is also the gateway to "Maybeck Country," a heavy concentration of homes created by California's most famous architect when he lived in the neighborhood himself. Climbing Rose Walk is a little like being Jack on the Beanstalk, for as one goes higher, the enchantment seems to increase.

To experience it, transport yourself to Berkeley and seek out Euclid Avenue, north of Cedar Street. Rose Walk begins just south of Codornices Park, on the uphill side of the street.

Go up the steps, which were built through neighborhood contributions, noting how Maybeck united balustrades, benches, lamps, planters, patios, and entryways into a composition at once lyrical and Mediterranean.

As you climb, observe how adroitly the community spaces have been situated to share sunshine. After Berkeley's devastating fire of 1923, architect Henry Gutterson was hired by Mr.

and Mrs. Frank Gray to design the one- and two-family houses on the north side. Wisely, he consulted Maybeck in the siting. When the steps end, bear left at LeRoy. The corner house across Rose Street at LeRoy was designed by Professor John Galen Howard for himself. Julia Morgan, whose best known work is San Simeon, added a library in 1927.

Follow Rose Street uphill to woodsy Greenwood Terrace and bear right, or south. William Wurster, long dean of the University of California School of Architecture, and his wife, Catherine Bauer Wurster, a great outdoorswoman and environmentalist, inspired this imaginative use of the old Warren Gregory property and made their home at number 1459 Greenwood Terrace.

Greenwood Common on the downhill side of the street has a square lawn shared in common with a dozen houses that surround it. The tree-lined lane on the south border ends at a spectacular viewpoint. Architects whose work surrounds the common read like a "Who's Who" of Bay Area architects and include Joseph Esherick, R. M. Schindler, Henry Hill, John Funk, W. S. Wellington, Howard Moise, Donald Olsen, Roger Lee, and Harwell H. Harris, as well as Wurster and Howard.

According to *A Guide to Architecture in San Francisco and Northern California* by Gebhardt et al., Maybeck designed 1476 Greenwood Terrace in 1908, while 1486 is John Galen Howard's "essay in the Maybeckian Craftsman mode."

Cross Buena Vista Way and start uphill, noting number 2626, designed by Michael Goodman for Charlotte and the late Joseph Henry Jackson, once the *Chronicle's* literary editor. At La Loma, walking on the west side of the street, make a 1,000-foot digression downhill from Buena Vista Way.

Stop and look across the street to 1515 La Loma, to see one of the most unusual of Maybeck houses, the Pompeian villa Maybeck designed for geologist Andrew Lawson, discoverer of the San Andreas Fault. Lawson was also godfather to the Golden Gate Bridge, for it was he who reassured engineer Joseph Strauss that it could be built. Sculptor Nancy Genn and her family now live in the villa.

"Maybeck dandled me on his knee when I was a toddler" Nancy Genn told me. "He was a short, merry-eyed man with a prophet's beard who always wore a knitted tam o'shanter. He said he designed for the man in the street because that was who would buy his houses after the first owner sold."

Today the cult of Maybeck appreciators is so keen that Maybeck-designed houses, known for their cathedral ceilings and warm wooden details, pass from owner to owner almost secretively with the man on the street rarely getting a chance to buy one.

Return uphill to the corner of La Loma and Buena Vista Way, then bear right uphill on Buena Vista. Look behind the

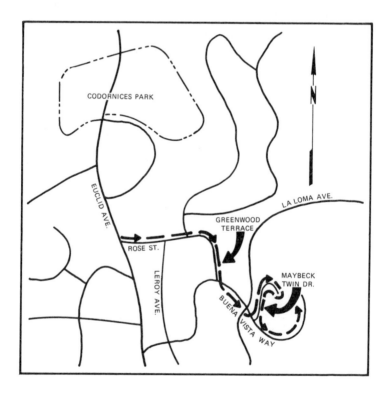

trees to glimpse 2711 Buena Vista, the pink "sack house." After the Berkeley fire of 1923 destroyed his own seven-level home here, Maybeck dipped burlap sacks in a frothy cement mixture and hung them like shingles on a framework to demonstrate a rapid rebuilding technique.

The Pompeian villa and 2704 Buena Vista are Maybeck houses that survived the fire. Other Maybeck houses on Buena Vista include 2730, 2733, 2751, and 2780. Residents in the latter can see the University of California campanile from their kitchen windows.

At Maybeck Twin Drive, named for the architect, veer north from Buena Vista. The walker who goes to its end may encounter Maybeck's daughter-in-law, Jacomina, gardening along here, as I did one time while walking through here with the late great educator Alexander Miecklejohn, and more recently with a University of California Extension class on an architectural walk. Persist to the end and you will find yourself looking up at Samuel Hume's place, inspired by a cloister in Toulouse and designed by John Hudson Thomas.

Continue instead along Buena Vista and you will reach another stronghold of rugged individuality, the Greek-inspired home of the Charles Boyntons, identifiable by its Corinthian columns, and known as the "Temple of the Winds." The Boynton family encouraged Greek dancing on the lawn and hoped to make Berkeley known as the Athens of the West. Early health food fans, they offered visitors nuts and dried fruits, possibly the origin of the name "Nut Hill" for the area.

Retrace your steps back to Rose Walk and bear right, or north, on Euclid to reach Codornices Playground. From the playground, take the tunnel under Euclid and you will arrive in 100 paces at Berkeley's Rose Garden.

No, the walk didn't take its name from the garden, but from Rose Avenue, which is shown on Berkeley maps as early as 1876. Until 1933 this was a gully filled with poison oak and blackberry brambles. A Works Project Administration project created the terracing, but Maybeck fans will recognize his influence in the 220-foot-long redwood pergola.

52

A Garden of Roses

"O gather me the rose, the rose, while yet in flower we find it," cried poet W. E. Henley, speaking for thousands of poets who have yearned unceasingly after beauty.

When the yearning to look at a rose, really look at a rose, gets imperative, it's time for a trip to Berkeley, home of one of the more riotous aggregations of roses, as well as of students. The famous Berkeley Rose Garden by any other name would be Codornices Park. The walk around it is a sensual experience.

Begin this walk in Codornices Playground, on the east side of Euclid, north of Bayview Place. This is a little pocket canyon in which Codornices (Spanish for quail) and Strawberry creeks join, just north of Berryman Reservoir.

If you have children, let them explore the unusual slide before seeking out the tunnel (beyond the ball diamond) that leads under Euclid to the Rose Garden.

From the cool gloom of the tunnel, one emerges near tennis courts, usually into bright sunlight, for Berkeley is in one of the

Bay Area's warm "banana belts." Bear left, or south, and in a few steps you are alongside the workshed of gardeners who tend the 4,500 rose bushes in the amphitheater of roses.

They also answer questions. One of the commonest is "Do you sell roses?" The answer is "No, but we'll be happy to give you the addresses of dealers who stock the varieties we have here."

Gravity, curiosity, and good planning by landscape architect V. M. Dean will pull you naturally toward the rose beds. Shortly, the walker will find himself on a landing under a redwood pergola which defines a 221-foot upper rim of the theater. Within the pergola is a stone drinking fountain, the gift in 1937 of Jane Doyle. There are also benches at convenient places. Another plaque near the center walk indicates construction by the Works Progress Administration.

The garden was begun in 1933, on fill that covered a poison oak brambled valley, and finished in 1937. Although the plaques don't say so, it was initially under the guidance of Dr. C. V. Covell of Oakland, a well-known rose specialist. Members of the East Bay Counties Rose Societies pitched in to give hundreds of hours of volunteer time, and professional rose growers gave rock bottom prices.

The tradition is carried on in the All-American Rose Society annual winners that are planted as a demonstration and supplied by rose growers from all over the United States. Walk down three terraces below the pergola to see "Roman Holiday," a floribunda, and "Bewitched," a big pink hybrid tea rose, both from Howards, Inc., and other winners.

Others are nearby. To find last year's prize selections, look in the area south of the amphitheater in a natural dell. Early in the year it is glorious with rhododendrons.

On its way to the bay, Codornices Creek emerges briefly in a little waterfall that has been dammed on occasion to form a mirror pool. One such occasion in the past, according to the park superintendent, was an annual Rose Day.

When you have decided with Gertrude Stein that "a rose is

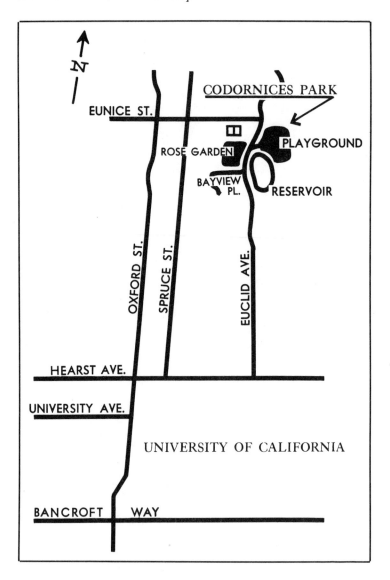

a rose is a rose'' after all, walk back uphill to the highest point of the garden, to find on a smog-free day that the viewpoint offers all the splendid panorama of the San Francisco skyline, fronted by bay and bridges. Behind you will be Euclid Avenue, just across from the starting point in Codornices Playground.

53

"Holy Hill"

The time will come when this, our Holy Church
Shall melt away in ever-widening walls and be for all
*   mankind.*
And in its place shall rise another church, whose
*   covenant word shall be the act of love.*
*   Not Credo then*
But Amo shall be the watchword through its gate.

In these words from his *Liber Amoris,* the poet Henry Bernard Carpenter phrased the dream of men of goodwill down through the ages.

The dream has often been far from reality in the past. As George Bernard Shaw said when asked if he thought Christianity worked, "I don't know. It hasn't been tried."

Over on Holy Hill in Berkeley, it looks as if it is being tried under a blanket word of ecumenism. About 15 years ago, several graduate schools of theology pooled their resources to become the Graduate Theological Union, which now calls itself "the most ecumenically inclusive center for the theological education in the world." Included are Baptist, Episcopal, Franciscan, Jesuit, Dominican, Lutheran, Methodist, Disciples of Christ, Presbyterian, Congregational, Unitarian, and Jewish schools, all of whom share a faculty library, an urban-black studies center, and an unusual Palestine Museum.

Holy Hill, otherwise known as "Daley's Scenic Park," is one of the oldest of Berkeley's hill communities, once the home of such movers and shakers as Benjamin Ide Wheeler, Phoebe Apperson Hearst, and John Galen Howard.

Much of the original character and some of the important architecture of this historic neighborhood still stand intact, a little wearily perhaps, awaiting fate in the form of rescue by rediscovery or oblivion by redevelopment.

The walk around Daley's Scenic Park is good anytime. I like it best in the autumn, when fallen leaves of Berkeley's great street trees give that bittersweet hint of melancholy that goes with fall.

To enjoy it, transport yourself to the corner of Euclid and Le Conte streets, just north of the university campus.

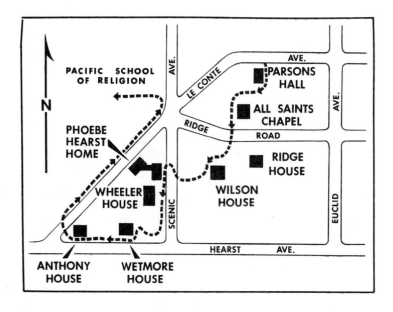

Walk east on Le Conte with the line of palms and campanile on your left. Parsons Hall is the handsome ivy-covered building built in 1965 to the designs of Skidmore, Owings, and Merrill. If the gate is open, cut through the central court, go up the steps and discover that you are on a roof garden. From it, look uphill to the colonnade of Boynton House on "Nut Hill," named for the "orgies of nuts and fruits" served there to neighbors, among them Isadora Duncan. Then walk to the railing to see a pond with schools of goldfish surrounded by plum trees and pond lilies.

Return to the walk, go up more steps and stop short of All Saints Chapel, church of the Episcopal divinity school, one of many birds of a feather flocking together under the blanket name of Graduate Theological Union. Bear left through the tree-shaded cloister and under the arches to emerge by an olive tree and bench near Ridge Road.

Across from it is Ridge House, a student residence originally built in 1906 by John Galen Howard for his fellow professor, Adolf Miller of the school of political economy. In the 1930s it was remodeled and lived in by yet another professor, William Wurster.

Cross Ridge Road to Scenic Way. Cross again and bear right. The gray stucco house at 1860 Scenic was designed by Ernest Coxhead in 1900 as reception center for the adjacent 2368 Le Conte, both built for Phoebe Apperson Hearst. According to neighborhood oral history, devoted students climbed to the rooftops to wet down the buildings and save them from Berkeley's disastrous fire of 1923.

Then go left to see the home next door of university president Benjamin Ide Wheeler. When President Theodore Roosevelt visited Wheeler, school children festooned what is now Hearst Avenue with ivy and geraniums.

Strawberry Creek is the water you hear murmuring at the corner of Scenic Way and Hearst. The pergola on the right "is a ruins," to quote Fillmore Eisenmayer, "but it is nice." The only remaining portion of a prefire home of Robert Wetmore, it was replaced by the half-timbered house at 2323 Hearst, designed for Wetmore by architect Walter Steilberg.

At the corner of Hearst and Le Conte, you reach the Anthony House, built in 1939 as an "Ile de France Moderne," the first streamlined style to be built in Berkeley. As you climb Le Conte, notice the stylish little French apartment house, now called Kofoid Hall. Green oriental tiles are a trademark of architect Steilberg. The house at 2357 is reputed to be a design of Bernard Maybeck.

At the confluence of Le Conte with Ridge Road and Scenic Way, walk to your left into the Pacific School of Religion open mall, designed like an English village common. The Pacific School is the oldest seminary in the complex. Interdenominational, it was founded in 1866. Mrs. Hearst's servants once lived in a cottage on this stunning eminence. Parallel to the benches, go into the library, if it is open, to see the unusual Palestine Museum.

If not, walk to the head of this serene oasis for a stupendous view of San Francisco.

54

A Jog Away From the City

"Into the heart of the hills winds a canyon, not large and imposing, but very beautiful. It is called by some, after the policy of the University of California, through whose domain it runs, 'Co-ed Canyon,' by others, from the abundance of charming blossoms and luscious fruit found upon its rugged sides, 'Strawberry Canyon,'" wrote W. E. Hutchinson in a charming book published in 1915 called *Byways Around San Francisco Bay*, which came to me as a gift from a reader not long ago.

"Trees, gnarled and twisted, reach out their arms across the little brook that sings merrily at the bottom. Far into the hills it pushes its winding way, and one must needs scramble over many a fallen tree and mossy rock in following its beautiful path.

"One cannot see very far ahead, but at each succeeding turn in the trail, new wonders open before us. . . ."

After 62 years, if Hutchinson were to walk Strawberry Canyon today, he could still find the brook singing, gnarled trees, and new wonders at each turn in the trail, for the central portion has been retained in as natural a state as possible. Designated as a University of California ecology study area, in addition to being an outdoor classroom, it offers an unexpectedly bucolic ramble through wildwood surrounded by urban bustle.

To make this walk, transport yourself to the Berkeley campus, preferably by public transportation. (On weekdays the free Humphrey Go-BART shuttle bus takes you to the trailhead.) On your own wheels, park as close as possible to the upper edge of Memorial Stadium.

To reach the stadium, leave Highway 80 at the University Avenue offramp. Turn left off University at Oxford Street to Hearst Avenue, right six blocks on Hearst to Gayley Road, right on Gayley past the Hearst Greek Theater, left on Stadium Rimway. Pray for a parking place near Centennial Drive (which old grads will recall as North Canyon Road). Once parked, start walking uphill on Centennial, which now has a walking trail, nicely delineated by a low wall to protect pedestrians.

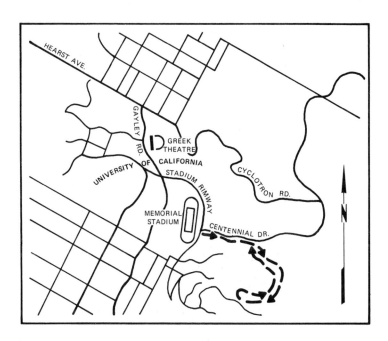

The route takes the walker along the campus tennis courts and swimming pools reserved for faculty, staff, and students.

When you reach the stile, a simple pair of steps over curbing, continue inside the barrier and you soon find yourself in a minuscule parking area. From it, more steps and a path dip through a teacup of land to emerge uphill beside a gravel road, barricaded to motor traffic. This is the trailhead. A sign identifies it as an ecology study area.

Round the curve and in 50 paces you are in the country. Fillmore Eisenmayer, who first conducted me on this trail, finds the road winding across the stone bridge beyond the first noble old tree reminiscent of 19th-century landscaping paintings. There is the murmur of water as one climbs and the glint of it in terraced ponds, glimpsed through trees.

As you climb, Grizzly Peak peaks through the trees, but instead of the Big C undergraduates used to guard before football games, which Hutchinson saw, today the walker glimpses more recent landmarks—the Lawrence Hall of Science, the radiation lab, the cyclotron, and greenhouses of the nearby botanical gardens.

Climb higher and Mount Tamalpais surprises one between madrones. At another curve, pines make a dense Rumpelstiltskin forest. Finally the view widens out to reveal the North Bay and much of Marin on the horizon with the campanile in the middle distance.

As you are going up the gentle incline, sometimes only the thump-thump of passing joggers reminds you that this pristine land actually is within Berkeley.

55

A Science Hall
That Won't Say No

"Hands off!" Remember those stifling commands when you were pint-sized? No matter where you went, just about the time you spotted something really interesting, it was "Move on! Move on!" Find something you were aching to examine—not to keep mind you, just look at, or feel, or smell—there always seemed to be a pair of grownup eagle eyes with grownup authority to match saying, "Don't touch!"

It's just the opposite over in Berkeley on a wonderful hill where the attitude is, "Hands on. Sit down and stay as long as you like. And touch all you please."

This paragon of places is the Lawrence Hall of Science, where to quote one of their own leaflets, more than 150,000 people, young and old, have explored "the world of 'hands on' biology, physics, astronomy, computer science and mathematics." They realize that direct experience is the first step in understanding.

Anyone who has looked up into the Berkeley hills since the eucalyptus freeze of 1972 has been stunned to find a low building, formerly obscured by trees, sprawling across one of the upper crests. This is the Lawrence Hall of Science, open to the public for a modest fee and full of sophisticated equipment.

In odd contrast, the surrounding open space supports a host of wildlife, including black-tailed deer that come down to a pond to drink, gray foxes, bobcats, kestrels, the shy Swainson's thrush, and cliff swallows that return as regularly as those at Capistrano. To walk in and around it is to enjoy many an unlikely juxtaposition.

To make this walk via public transportation, go to Berkeley via the AC Transit's F bus to the northeast corner of Shattuck and Center streets. On weekdays (check on weekends), the free shuttle bus named Humphrey Go-BART hauls walkers up to the Hall.

If you are using your own wheels, cross the Bay Bridge and take the Eastshore Freeway north to Berkeley's University Avenue offramp. Follow University to Oxford. Skirting the University of California campus, bear left to Hearst, right to Gayley Road, and continue uphill on it, taking Rim Way and finally Centennial Drive past the University Botanical Gardens to the Lawrence Hall of Science.

Park at the lot on your right, then cross the road and cross the bridge to enter the many-sided plaza. Typical of many Berkeley hillside buildings, Lawrence Hall of Science has its main entrance on the top floor with other levels below.

At the outset, walk around the plaza to enjoy the sensational views and orient yourself to the terrain. If the day is clear, look for the Farallones beyond the Golden Gate Bridge.

Blackberry Canyon will be on your right. Strawberry Canyon on your left. Their streams join below and flow together through the campus. In the middle ground, Albany Hill, Point Isobel, and the Berkeley Marina are outlined by the bay, with San Francisco and Marin across the water.

When you have enjoyed the view, take a good look at the eight-sided building. It was designed by architects Anshen and Allen, who won the contract in a national competition. The hall opened in 1968, honoring Ernest Orlando Lawrence, inventor of the cyclotron, and the first Nobel laureate at the University of

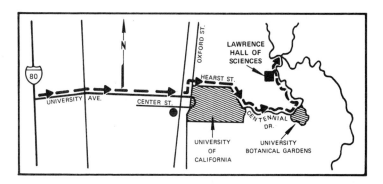

California. Go in to discover that it houses a museum, research center, and science curricula development center.

The breathtaking stabile in the center of the hall represents the smallest and largest items in the universe—a silver nucleus superimposed on the Crab Nebula. Walk to your right and begin making your way around the room to the hologram in a standing case.

The next area is designed for under-ten-year-olds. Near it is a space whose games are for preschoolers. Go through the far door, where there are more "hands on" experiments and again start circling toward the right. This area contains temporary exhibits on "beauty in nature."

You have now reached the main exhibit halls. On one hand is the William K. Holt Space Science Hall, on the other the Edwin W. Pauley Nuclear Science Hall, and in between the Lawrence Memorial Hall. Bear right if you want to try focusing a big telescope. There are so many features to discover here, I will leave you to find your own special interest as you continue around the building.

One no one will want to miss is the Discovery Corner, a shop where one can find the Corrugahorn, a wind instrument created by physicist Frank Crawford. It sounds like an automobile horn of the 1920s.

Another is the lower laboratory level, where there is a computer that draws Snoopy, any number of labs, a cafeteria, a

TV studio, and best of all, several auditoriums. Film buffs can drop in on a continually changing film program on weekends and holidays. For information call 642-5132.

The capper to this walk is the path that swings below the building—it goes across the meadow to a pond, climbs to the lawn, descends again past the eucalyptus forest, and goes past a beehive under a bridge.

If the building gives you a feeling of *déjà vu* from this aspect on the lowest east level, it may be because the movie "Colossus" was made here.

56

Where to See
the Wildflowers

An ideal Easter walk, surging with the hope and rebirth which the day celebrates, is through California's largest Native Plant Botanical Garden, a 6½-acre sanctuary for wildflowers in Berkeley's Tilden Park.

There is no convenient public transportation, unfortunately. So transport yourself to Grizzly Peak Boulevard and Shasta Gate. Follow Shasta Road to the point where it meets with Wildcat Canyon Road and South Park Drive. The garden, well marked, fills the adjacent part of Wildcat Canyon.

Most botanical gardens are arranged by plant family groups. Tilden's, in contrast, is in geographic sections. Go through the front gate, bear left around the gardener's shack, then right on the flagstone path. Two California fan palms, the trees that gave Palm Springs its name, introduce the Sierra Madre Desert in microcosm.

By the time you have walked through all seven major sections laid out on either wall of the canyon, you will have made a simulated 1,000-mile botanical journey through California from the Arizona border to Oregon. There are also areas in which the flora of less extensive regions has been duplicated. One of particular interest to San Franciscans has the flora of San Bruno Mountain.

Cross a creek and you are in the Channel Island section, heralded by a big island bush poppy on the left, and a switch to narrower gravel paths. A perky fox sparrow hopped out from under it as Charlotte McGregor, a knowledgeable East Bay naturalist, and I followed the trail. Overhead in an ironwood tree, a scrub jay called, another of the 25 kinds of birds resident in the garden all year.

Pause to look down at the panorama of all sections revealed here. The 100-foot-tall redwoods visible on the opposite ridge were planted in 1940, shortly after Director James B. Roof founded the garden. The spiky Santa Lucia firs nearer at hand, the Monterey and San Luis Obispo cypress, put out insect-free seeds that are traded, sold, and shipped all over the world. Members of the California Native Plant Society have helped locate many of the rare varieties.

Follow the little path downhill to your right and digress into the Franciscan section to see the same San Bruno Mountain vegetation that surrounded Portola and his party of explorers on their expedition to San Francisco Bay 200 years ago. Then, from the adjacent Santa Lucia section, swing back along the creek to see golden and coast currants, fuchsia, flowering gooseberry in bloom, and alders, willows, and hazel. Little areas blocked off with frail twine and post fencing indicate newly seeded places, while plastic tents over dry region plants protect them from too much water in rainy seasons. It takes much gardener's magic to grow native plants from varying areas in a single microclimate.

Bear left, go over the wooden bridge, then up a few steps to cross the main stone bridge over Wildcat Creek. Midway on the bridge pause and look back to see the wonderful cascade of San Luis ceanothus that sprawls over the bank. The big spiky flower pompons are yucca from Tassajara. There is also a spectacular California barberry by the bridge.

The seabluff on the far shore presents a miniature Point Reyes cliff. When you have examined it, climb to the Juniper Lodge building, which divides a south Sierran from a north Sier-

ran meadow. A potting shed nearby is a place for visitors to duck out of the rain. Lodgepole pines, white firs, red firs, and manzanita border the south meadow. Walk up steps and go behind the building to find white-bark pine and other timberline plants.

Bear left to reach the redwood section, divided by a charming zigzag split rail fence made from Ponderosa and Jeffrey pines. The steps uphill lead through wild ginger and strawberry to a bed of red trilliums, and near a pond another bed of white trilliums. Swing back left and make another side expedition to see a little pond where the Pitkin lily of Sonoma County, the leopard lily of Tiburon, and later in the season, Volmer's and Bolander's lilies bloom.

Then follow that chain-link fence (it's there to keep off deer, not student activists) to observe many sprawling ceanothus varieties. Walk on the grassy meadow to find the pine mountain ceanothus, now being used by the highway department for erosion control.

Bear left again and go down to cross the creek into a Shasta Cascade section. On this bridge, look under the roadway to see a pleasant waterfall. Then swing through the foothill section to loop back to the entrance. You will have passed on this loop 150 carefully cultivated wildlings, many in bloom. If you really dig it, plan to come back in May when most of the plants in bloom are white, in June when reds and yellows prevail, or for that matter, anytime. There is always something rare to see at the Tilden Botanical Gardens.

57

Something for Everyone

Charles Lee Tilden Regional Park is a 2,065-acre chunk of the East Bay ridgelands that offers something for everyone.

One of the three oldest parks in the East Bay Regional Park system, and named for the man who founded the system, it has freshwater swimming with lifeguard protection at Lake Anza, an 18-hole golf course, a little farm where children may pet the animals, a carousel built by H. Spelman of New York in 1911, a vast garden of California native plants, a miniature steam railway on which to ride, a miniature airplane field, a public reception room, and an ecological interpretation center—to name nine of its main attractions.

For the walker, there is a lofty loop of trails that offers superb vistas that sometimes include both the Golden Gate and the snow-covered peaks of the Sierra.

To make this walk, pack a knapsack lunch and canteen, don your lug-soled boots, and transport yourself to the Brazilian building (it's a clubhouse) on Central Park Drive, slightly northeast of Shasta Road intersection. Trail maps are available at the information booth. This is also a bus stop on the AC Transit

Regional Parks Special Summer service, which operates during vacation times seven days a week.

Look for the large green lawn south of the parking lot. Go through a scattering of trees at its corner and walk downhill on the grass diagonally to the fence of the California Native Plant Botanical Garden, then bear right, following the fence around to the entrance of the garden. The glimpse over the stone wall by the waterfall is so enticing, plant fanciers may defect from the walk here to enjoy the flora within.

At the triangle formed by South Park Drive, Wildcat Canyon Road, and Shasta Road, stand with your back to the garden gate and look to your left across the road for a black and white 25-mile speed limit sign. An unmarked footpath goes uphill six feet west of the sign. Cross the road and go up this path about 150 paces through meadow grasses and coyote brush. Here you will reach a broad trail, also unmarked.

Bear right on it and a few hundred yards further it will dip down toward the paved South Park Drive. Go through the motor barrier, parallel the road for a hundred feet, broach the second motor barrier, and begin climbing at a gentle grade. You are now on the Big Springs Trail.

Abreast of an old shale quarry whose hopper still stands, you will be above Big Springs Campground, visible below. The trail soon passes from the slightly wooded area through meadowlands studded in summer with wild buckwheat in bloom and the sticky monkey flower.

The next fork meets the Sea View Trail, renowned for its fine views. Bear left on it. At the first curve, pause for the panorama of San Francisco Bay and Mount Tamalpais. The reforestation underway on the next ridge west will have redwood plantings.

Round one more curve and if the day is fair, you can see Mount Diablo, Mount St. Helena, and the Sierras on the horizon. Vollmer Peak, also known as Bald Peak, is south. At 1,913 feet, it is the high point of the southern part of Tilden Park.

In the middle distance to the east, Briones is the higher of the two reservoirs visible below, San Pablo the lower, and often studded with sailboats and fishermen in rowboats. East Bay

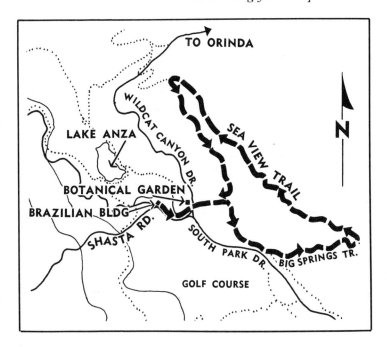

Municipal Utilities District has recently opened it to wider recreational use. Carquinez Straits and the Delta are sometimes visible beyond.

Horsemen, joggers, and dog walkers all regularly traverse this ridge. If you see a pair of hikers picking up litter along the trail, they will probably be Professor and Mrs. Alfred Childs, both associated with the University of California, who live nearby. Park planner Harry Reeves, another accomplished walker, was out on the trail with his young son Wesley when I came up and pointed out red-tailed and marsh hawks far below us.

Diane and Ken Hunter of the Bay Chapter of the Sierra Club, who introduced me to this superb trail, say John Muir himself might well have walked this ridge en route to his Martinez home. Park historians record that Captain Pedro Fages and Father Juan Crespi of Monterey passed through Wildcat Canyon below in 1772. Juan Bautista de Anza came along four years later and is commemorated in the lake visible a little below to the north.

Since there isn't a trail marker to be found on it, getting back can be tricky. On the next fork, just below the last group of·pines, go downhill. (If you reach a paved road you have gone too far on Sea View Trail.) On the unnamed downhill road, continue straight ahead. Go under the telephone wires. About 200 feet beyond, past the brushy draw—when the entrance to the botanical garden is revealed across the road below—look for the downhill path. Slip into it and lo! a quick drop delivers you back at the start, handy again to the Brazilian Building lawn and the bus stop parking lot.

58

The Walking Schtick

For wonderful winter woodland walking, few places can surpass Tilden Park, just east of Berkeley. It is nearby, easily accessible, has good parking, and offers the illusion that one has left the wicked world behind.

At the northern end near Wildcat Canyon and Jewel Lake, there is also a richly varied series of short trails. One of them is the Sylvan Trail, a logical selection on an icy morning for trying out walking sticks.

Walking sticks are once again in fashion, if the demand for them is an indication. The presentation of a gold-headed stick to the outstanding graduate yearly at the University of California Medical School made news, although the tradition is one of long standing. Novelist Richard Brautigan, to name but one pacesetter, has recently been sporting a briar crombie formerly used by John McLaren. The prize blackthorn stick in my own collection, the gift of a reader of my newspaper column, once belonged to the Scottish music hall comedian, Sir Harry Lauder.

On this excursion, I took this fond companion of many

walks, a stout stick with crooked handle that looks like it has crossed legs. It proved to be as effective as an alpenstock.

The Sylvan Trail winds around a gentle slope and passes through exposures sure to be alternately sunny and shady. A light snowfall on the trail also gave a footprint record of recent activity along the way of foxes, racoons, deer, rabbits, squirrels, and a hawk who had lost a feather while breakfasting on quail. Snow is a rarity in the Bay Area, of course, but the keen-eyed walker can often read such signs of wildlife on this trail in the early morning in the damp of the rainy season or the dust of summer if he's out early.

To make this walk, go into Tilden Park near the northeast border of Berkeley where it meets Kensington at Canon Drive. Spruce Street, Grizzly Peak Boulevard, and Wildcat Canyon Road all meet Canon at one fork by a reservoir that at first glance seems to be open. Closer inspection proves that instead there is a cosmetic sheet of water that imitates a pond on the reservoir surface. Drive downhill on Canon Drive, turn left at the foot by the pony rides, and drive as far as you can (it will be Indian Camp) and park.

Go through the stone pillars beyond the parking circle, pass the little silt pond, and turn right uphill abreast of the red barn that distinguishes the little farm here.

Within a few paces one reaches a large map under glass and a display of fine animal photos selected by ranger-naturalist Lou Testa. The site across from it is now an environmental study center.

Continue past the farm, bearing left, and soon one reaches a small lodge. The Sylvan Trail, whose wooden signs bear three carved trees, takes up beyond it to the left, downhill. Follow the Jewel Lake Trail, indicated by a blue duck, for a while to see the wonderful new, long serpentine low bridge that wanders through the marshy swamp.

When you reach the flume, cross the bridge, turn right,and start uphill on Sylvan Trail. If it is icy, as it was when I walked it, a walking stick can be as helpful as cleated Vibram soles on your boots, as this veers up the southern foothill wall of Wildcat

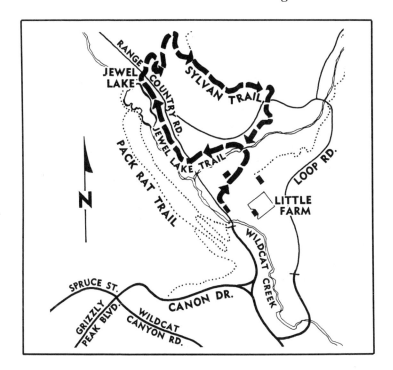

Canyon. When the trail peels off to the right, follow it through the eucalyptus grove.

Soon you will hit the Equestrian Trail, a broad dirt road. Bear right on it to return to the Range Country Road if you like, or cross it to make a complete loop, returning to the lodge.

The short three-fourths of a mile on Sylvan Trail is so convenient one can do it in an hour. If you're game for more, try the Pack Rat that goes uphill a little past the weir at the northerly end of Jewel Lake.

PART FIVE

FURTHER
NORTH

59

A Garden of
Earthly Delights

"Who loves a garden still his Eden keeps," wrote Amos Bronson Alcott a hundred years ago. It could well be engraved over the gate at 70 Rincon Road in Kensington, for this is the entrance to the 10-acre Blake Estate, one of the best-kept (semipublic) secret gardens in the Bay Area. A living workshop for the Department of Landscape Architecture of the University of California, it is an Eden indeed. If you have been looking for a tranquil spot to visit, this is it.

To make this walk, transport yourself from San Francisco across the Bay Bridge and north on the Eastshore Freeway to Gilman Avenue, Berkeley. From Gilman, take San Pablo to Marin, up Marin to The Circle, and then go north on Arlington Avenue. At the Arlington Community Church in Kensington, which stands in a yoke formed by Rincon Road and Arlington Avenue, bear left downhill to 70 Rincon Road. (AC Transit bus 7 stops nearby.)

Within the lower parking lot, walk downhill to its lowest border to find steps that will bring you out at a road. Cross it to find a sunny seating area, designed and built by students. Pause here a moment to orient yourself. Landmarks are the greenhouses, restrooms, and superintendent Walter Vodden's offices to the south, while the Blake House stands to the north.

Designer of the surrounding gardens was Mabel Symmes, one of the earliest students of landscape design at the University of California, who created it in 1925 on a bare hillside for her sister, Mrs. Anson Blake. The four miles to the Berkeley campus was considered far away when the Blakes purchased their site in 1922. Receptions, weddings, and garden parties are often held on the lawn in front of the sunny conversation pit.

From this outdoor seating area, walk to the left of the broad lawn and step down beside the square pool. *Michelia doltsopa,* a choice magnolia, and *Ilex paraguayensis,* whose leaves are used for the South American drink maté, are two of the more unusual plants nearby. More than 2,500 rare species adorn the garden.

For a sensational framed view of the Golden Gate, walk west from the lily pool to an overlook above Australian hollow. Then return to the pool and walk north through the arches of the handsome arbor, surprisingly made of PVC (polyvinyl chloride) pipe, and like many of the garden innovations, contrived by students.

Cross the driveway toward the house and go through the gate. Designed by Bliss and Faville for the Blakes, both house and garden were deeded to the university in 1957, with the Blakes' retaining lifetime occupancy. Now it is the university president's official residence, and is occupied by Dr. and Mrs. David Saxon and their family. Walkers are required to respect the privacy of the house and stay off the patio, steps, and immediate approaches.

Notice on your right the formal garden and grotto, fronted by a long pool lined with a double row of magnolias. Built in 1926, it reminds architectural historian Fillmore Eisenmayer, who introduced me to this walk, of Villa Tusculana at Frascati, Italy.

Take a few steps toward the grotto to discover on the right

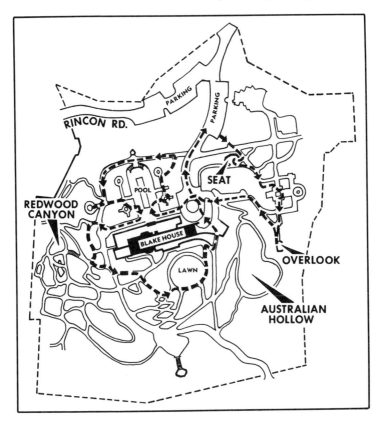

the yellow, or morning, garden with its Chinese sundancer in ceramic. Walk around to his far side and look across the pool to see that he faces a partner.

Then stroll up to the highest bench on the sunny south side through yellow flowers to find to the right a pine-needle path. Follow it, releasing pungent piny odors with every step, up around to the left and across to the top of the grotto. Pause to look down. Formal though it is, the grotto and pool system have a practical purpose. Miss Symmes thriftily used it to drain a little spring uphill.

If you hear bells as you come along this way, they belong

to the Carmelite monastery, whose Mediterranean pink buildings are barely visible through the trees.

Soon after passing the Canary Island pines and a big hawthorne, you will find the pagoda pool on your right, whose water comes from the long pool facing the grotto before it goes down into the canyon below to nourish its redwood trees. Notice the frogs on its eaves. Then bear left from the main path into the pink, or evening, garden.

Senior nursery technician William R. Jones, who showed me around the garden, likes the strong sculptural form of the evergreen pear tree here. From it, look uphill to a round pond, then downhill to see a second sundancer, before coming out near the house. Bear right, away from the house, beside the big spiky spear lily, or *Doryanthes aplemeri,* just coming into bloom. The vine on the corner of the house is the kiwi, sometimes called the Chinese gooseberry. It bears well here.

Take the path to your right at the end of the house to reach the redwood canyon. Agile walkers may want to go down to explore it and discover the grove of hoheria trees whose wind shelter fostered the redwoods.

The less spry should bear left on the path skirting the rim of the canyon to under the copper beech tree, *Vagus sylvatica,* and overshoot the next set of steps to reach a dead-end overlook to the rhododendron dell below. After you have enjoyed it, return to the steps near the bayberry tree, *Myrica californica,* whose deliciously scented leaves are often used in candle making. Go up the five steps, then up four more to the next footpath, and bear left to a big sunny circle of saint-john's-wort for another great vista, this one framing Mount Tamalpais.

Cross the western exposure of the house well downhill from it on the path that encircles the lower lawn. Wise siting of the building across the ledge shelters delicate plants in the formal garden behind. You can spot a children's swinging tire here. Bear left and go up toward the stone wall, but bear right, shy of the house, to come out on a driveway. Go left, up the driveway to reach the parking lot and complete this loop walk.

If it isn't Eden, it is Eden enough.

60

An Island on Land

In the counties that touch on San Francisco Bay, Albany Hill, an island surrounded by flatland, rather than water, is unique.

To thousands of homeowners who inhabit that vast amphitheater of higher Coast Range hills ringing the East Bay, it is the graceful tree-festooned middle-distance landmark. To equally many fanciers of the sport of kings, looking up from the deadly monotony of the freeway, its bank of highrise apartments is the signal to anticipate the Golden Gate Fields turnoff.

The precedent is classic. For Albany Hill, the El Cerrito or "little hill" of the Spaniards, was the Contra Costa landfall for which pioneer boatmen headed. As the Indians did before them.

It is not such a little hill as one would expect. It is also wilder. Walkers who would care to explore it will find that here, totally surrounded by sprawling urbanity, is a little bit of country that has miraculously escaped most of man's worst efforts.

To make this walk, get out your Vibram-soled walking boots, transport yourself east across the Bay Bridge, then north beyond Berkeley to the Pierce Street offramp into Albany. Turn immediately uphill on Washington and park in the 800 block. Look for Number 843, the mission-style house of artist Catherine Webb, who has lived here since 1932. Immediately beyond are the Sunset Steps, long used to accommodate the faithful who come to celebrate on this hill Easter mornings. Start up them.

As you climb, the Berkeley Marina, Yerba Buena Island, and the Bay Bridge come into view. The Chamberlain House, first to be built on the hill, is the yellow one you pass on the left.

The steps stop at Hillside. Bear left and follow it to its end. Pause at 839 Hillside, built by the builder of the racetrack so he could watch from his home.

Number 833, which looks like a back alley, leads to an elegant house owned by a former mayor of Albany. Notice the odd conservatory on Number 827, which looks as if it should be in Rio. For fun, try counting the number of materials used in the two bastard chalets just beyond.

Land on which the freeway below now stands was a farm until 1933. The offshore fill is the profitable Albany dump. Native oysters once thrived there.

At the dead end of Hillside, the woods go off to the left, following the path through the grass. Bunch grasses, sunflowers, two kinds of eucalyptus, and other wildlings were in bloom here when Mrs. Webb showed me this trail.

Above an outcropping of sandstone, which crumbles when exposed, one passes the only badly defaced part of the hill. There is bluestone bedrock 30 feet below, which was quarried in 1942. Later, this section of the hill served as a police gun practice range. Curve round the hill to your right, staying in the trees above the highrise apartments.

Parallel to the big barny White Front building, pick up a dirt road bearing left. You are skirting El Cerrito Creek, a boundary of Rancho San Antonio, granted to Luis Peralta in 1820 for his

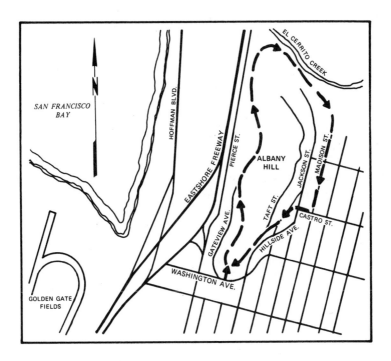

'long service as a soldier of Spain. The Peraltas and their northern neighbors, the Castros, loaded hides and tallow on small boats here. Indians would then paddle them across the bay to San Francisco. Holes in the hill rock left by Indian squaws who made acorn meal here can still be found further along this trail.

For a long time one could look right to spot old concrete foundations, all that was left of a powder company operated by Judson Dynamite and Powder Company in 1898. It blew up after changing from powder to nitroglycerine, killing the plant superintendent. Later calcimine, the water paint that decorated much of the Panama-Pacific Exposition, was made and tinted here.

Walk a few more steps and look uphill. Suddenly you are on the north side of the hill below an oak forest. Birds sing. The "Slaughter on Tenth Avenue" noise of the freeway has receded.

Wild roses bloom. Children slide down the grassy slope on cardboard in the time-honored country way. Elders, alders, blackberries, and filberts grow nearby.

Near the end of the old sluiceway across the creek, bear right, uphill, via a path. (Don't take the Devil's Trail that goes straight up, but the left fork that is gradual.)

The brick building on your left, beyond the chain-link fence, is the Albany School for the Blind. Blind students, whose hearing often becomes hyperacute to compensate for their sight loss, derive a great sense of peace from the shelter of the hill.

To circle back to your car, turn right uphill on Castro Street. Go uphill on Hillside, noticing, if you will, the country mailbox bearing the name Herb Rubin. Designed by George Homsey of Esherick and Homsey, it has been included in many architectural texts for its subtle integration into the site.

After swinging past two unlikely Polynesian lodge structures, look downhill for big redwoods, which stand on a spring. When you reach 846 Hillside, go down. You are back at Sunset Steps.

61

The View From
the Contra Costa

The lively little community of Point Richmond, an island of ecological sensitivity in the Contra Costa half-morass of industry, has scored another victory. Nicholl Nob, the lovely bare landmark hill that overlooks the area, has become a park.

So are the two smaller hills immediately south of it. All three are contiguous with Keller's Beach, one of the rare new waterfront parks on the bay.

To promote it, the Contra Costa Shoreline Park Committee has published a *Picnic-in-the-Point-Park Cookbook* available at the Chamber of Commerce, 416—11th Street, Richmond, 94804, for $2, postage free. It is a charming book, full of good recipes, and best of all for the Californiana buffs, a series of remembered picnics and some suggested ones, including a moon-viewing picnic on Nicholl Nob.

Day or night, the sweeping views from Nicholl Nob make for very pleasurable walking. If you'd like a sampler, try this walk Louise Hammond and Marlys L. Reynolds of the committee suggest.

Begin, as we did, at the corner of Park Place and West

Richmond Avenue, the end of the line for the AC Transit's trans-bay "L" bus and focal point of the excellent little downtown section of Point Richmond. Look for the shop called International Down Home Joy, which creates in stained glass. From it, walk northwest one block to Washington Avenue, turn left uphill to Crest, then left again on Crest, past friendly houses, as far as the street goes. Soon Crest is in open grassland.

It terminates at the macadam road up Nicholl Nob. Follow this macadam road, which is closed to cars, but not to walkers, round its gentle spiral to the top. You arrive at a fine shore view of the contra costa, unimpeded in all directions.

As we climbed, Louise reminisced about local history. The point was once part of the great Rancho San Pablo owned by Don Francisco Maria Castro who ran cattle on "El Potrero" until the property was broken up in a court battle. A shrewd old country Irishman, John Nicholl, was awarded the 152 acres that included the Nob underfoot. It was also he who induced the Santa Fe Railroad to buy land here for its western terminal.

Two odd footnotes to the age of speed occurred here. Around 1905 an early-day Icarus, one Mr. Botts, who had patented a steam-driven flying machine, had his hangar headquarters in a shed on Nicholl Nob. While Botts was gathering funds for an air expedition to the North Pole, a storm destroyed shed, machine, and all. The celebrated demon racing-car driver Barney Oldfield made the other, with a wild preprandial ride up the hill to visit a local lionizing lady.

More exciting to the park committee was a picnic episode that happened to them. They arrived "laden with ice buckets of champagne, baskets of glasses wrapped in cocktail napkins and a big platter of hors d'oeuvres" only to find surveyors from the East Bay Municipal Utilities District about to locate a tremenduous water tank at the peak's eastern vista point.

This was exactly the time at which the committee was proposing its project to the East Bay Regional Park district, which subsequently has taken an option on the land. Happily, the water tank location was abandoned by EBMUD.

Look south to locate Ferry Point, still used by the Santa Fe for barging freight cars to San Francisco. If ferryboats ever re-

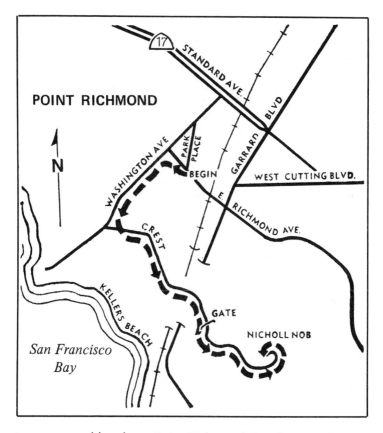

turn, one could make at Point Richmond the classic walk from the water to the nearest high vista point that was the highlight of thousands of Bay Area Sunday excursions in the halcyon pre-motorcar days when the world was fresh and the air clean.

Keller's Beach is the nice curve of sand visible below, a little west by north of the nob. Park plans include beach from Keller's to the Ferry Point. The young-in-legs can "run the course" as Louise Hammond's children used to do from the Nob via a grassy path to Keller's Beach.

More sedate types can picnic on the Nob then take a shortcut path downhill on the north side to return to Crest Avenue.

62

Island That No One Knows

Ask the average San Franciscan where Brooks Island is and he'll give you a vague evasive answer. Yet Brooks Island has been on bay maps under that name since 1850, is four times the size of Alcatraz, has had 121 years of widely varied activity on its grassy hill and shores since the Gold Rush, contains shell mounds that reveal Indian culture for 4,000 years, is distinguished by shell, shingle, sandy, and rocky beaches, and last year became another link in the East Bay Regional Park system.

It stands offshore from the Richmond inner harbor, about six minutes away by shallow draft motorboat. Brooks Island is visible from the Eastshore Freeway, near El Cerrito.

It is leased to an affluent coterie of businessmen who call it the Sheep Island Gun Club. The walk around it, unfortunately, is one not open to the public at the moment. It will be available, however. For information, write to the East Bay Regional Park District, 11500 Skyline Boulevard, Oakland, California 94617.

Come in imagination with me to anticipate what you will

see on the island Canizares' Plano del Puerto de San Francisco called Isla de Carmen in 1776.

As the boat pulls out into Richmond's Sante Fe Channel, leaving behind the welter of industrial buildings, oil tanks, and railroad tracks on a shoreline man has marred ruthlessly, the maritime excitement of a passing freighter or sugar boat, seen from the bug's-eye view of a chip on the water, may be the first hint of many delightful contrasts in this excursion.

Park officials plan to work out a system of regular transportation to the island.

Within a few minutes, one pulls into a floating dock, takes a few steps onto shore and, time out of mind, is back in the halcyon natural world that preceded the Industrial Revolution the world is now finding increasingly revolting.

Off to the right loop several small sandy coves and beyond them a long sandspit. From the dock a road winds uphill and out of sight. Bear left instead along the landward shore and soon you reach the shell mounds. Archeologist George Coles of Contra Costa College says they date to the California Middle Horizon period. Indians lived here on shellfish from around

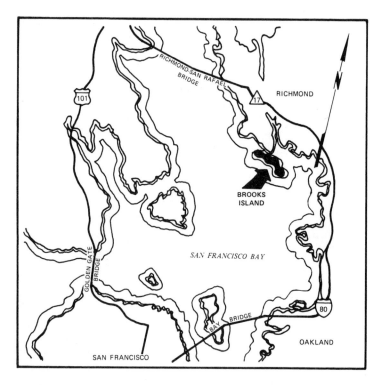

2,000 B. C. until around the time of Christ. From the evidence in the middens, a second culture, about 100 years long, followed, then a hiatus of about 800 years when the island was apparently uninhabited. Difference in tools, beads, and other artifacts supply the record.

Continue walking along the shore and you will reach an unlikely, out-of-character habitation, a mobile home, used by the caretaker and gun club members. The pilings offshore are remains of the California Yacht Club whose clubhouse sat here between 1907 and 1920, and of a fishing operation conducted by Luccas Gargurevich in the nineteenth century. Further along as the shore grows rocky, I found the little rare native rock oyster growing.

Take the road that goes uphill past the trailer, to examine the summit of the hill, a grassy knoll whose surprises include springs and a few fenced compounds where game birds have been confined, mostly pheasants imported for that purpose, although this is one of the few known places where Canada geese breed in the Bay Area.

It is also the location of an odd mouse war in which field mice, planted for observation by University of California zoologist William Z. Lidicker, Jr. overcame a resident population of house mice who had escaped from a ranch that once stood on the island. There are no indigenous mammals.

From the crest, the bay views are stupendous, unimpeded in all directions. Since this lies in the banana belt, the fog probes south of the island, a visible finger in the distance.

Look down and there is the remains of a quarry operated in 1892 by A. T. Arrowsmith, of the Bay Rock Company. Prisoners from San Quentin did much of the work at that time. Later quarrying supplied rock for Treasure Island.

Listen awhile and marshbirds call below beside a reedy pond. Walk out to the point and bear right and there is a gentle path that trends downward, then follows a shingle beach to a sunny picnic cove.

To return, keep walking around the shoreline. Nobody gets lost on an island, although Brooks has both a hidden treasure story and an ugly murder mystery, both resolved long since, in its past.

Score One
for the Parks

As late as 1957, of Contra Costa County's 75 miles of shoreline the score could have been chalked up on the tally board as "74½ miles for industry—½ mile for the ladies of Point Richmond." That half mile was Keller's Beach, dedicated just ten years ago.

After successfully negotiating what East Bay Regional Parks general manager Dick Trudeau described as "an unbelievable horde of hurdles," the score for public access to the Contra Costa shore has risen to six miles.

Part of it goes along the Santa Fe tracks in the new 171-acre George Miller, Jr. Regional Shoreline Park. Fishermen, joggers, picnickers, kite flyers, beachcombers, sunbathers, wildflower fanciers, railroad buffs, and hikers are already finding it a godsend.

To explore this cove yourself, take the AC Transit L bus from the Transbay Terminal at First and Mission streets. Ride it to the end of the line, alongside the newly refurbished Point Richmond Natatorium, a classic indoor swimming pool, known to hundreds of kids, including those who trained under swim coach George Miller, Jr., as "The Richmond Plunge."

Via your own wheels, take the Eastshore Freeway and Hoffman Boulevard (State Highway 17) toward the Richmond-San Rafael Bridge, turning south off Standard Avenue into Point Richmond on South Garrard Boulevard with the stoplight. Take South Garrard Boulevard through the tunnel, and park beyond Western Avenue.

From the plunge, walk under Nicholl Nob through the tunnel that was built to serve commuters on the San Francisco ferry. The construction on the natatorium lawn bodes well for swimmers. It is the renewal of a 90-foot-deep well which originally supplied the pool and still has an unending supply of good water.

Once through the tunnel, the bay, the San Francisco skyline, the Tiburon peninsula, and Mount Tamalpais may make you gasp at the contrast. When you can take your eyes away from this stunning panorama, observe that you are at the corner of Western and South Garrard. As the Keller's Beach sign on your immediate right indicates, it is now part of George Miller, Jr. Regional Shoreline Park, which stretches off along the shore as far as that distant shudder of blue and white petrochemical tanks.

As enticing as the newly landscaped park's undulating paths seem, for the moment forbear them. Instead bear right into Keller's Beach, crossing above the Santa Fe tracks. Bear left at each of the next three junctions of paths. In a few hundred feet you will find yourself between the water and the tracks.

Continue south and at the third telephone pole, look back to see that the tracks disappear into a tunnel under Nicholl Nob, much like the one for walkers and motorcars. At the fourth pole, look east. When park construction is completed, a footbridge will arch gracefully from the berm of earth on the far side across the tracks to the point on which you are now standing.

The crest of Nicholl Nob, the higher hill in the little ridge that enfolds this cove, was purchased by Lucretia and Capt. Tom Edwards to save it from development long ago. Like most

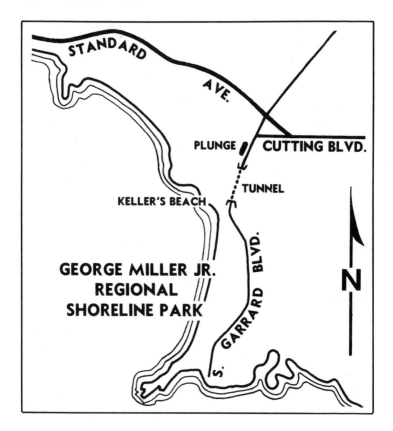

of the other ridgeland abutting, it has become part of the regional park.

The wharf visible on Ferry Point as you continue south is still in use by Santa Fe for shuttling railroad cars from China Basin in San Francisco. At the fence line, notice the big diked area in front of the tanks. When the soil is stabilized this is to be a lagoon with water pumped by an offshore windmill. The big warehouse is destined to become a museum for the Pacific Locomotive Association's Castro Point Railway, appropriately enough since Pullman cars were long manufactured in Point Richmond.

As you turn back from the barrier, the pier visible north toward Red Rock and the Richmond Bridge is Standard Oil's Long Wharf, often abloom with tankers. Retrace your steps to the corner of Western and South Garrard, noting the handsome trees and sunny sand trap of Keller's Beach as you pass. Treeless a scant 11 years ago, this was full of old tires, tin cans, and other debris.

Bear right on South Garrard to the end of the white fence and take the first walkway sloping downwards. Follow it as it meanders through poppies, rabbit-tail grass, red maids, and young trees struggling to survive. It is worth the effort to discover picnic tables, barbecue pits, kite-flying areas, and other amenities.

From South Garrard, mountain goats can make it to the top of Nicholl Nob for a 360-degree view, including the other 69 miles of Contra Costa's industrial shoreline.

64

Offshore Brothers

In the halcyon days of convenient water transportation, seasoned regulars aboard the overnight ferry to Sacramento used to anticipate eagerly the glimpse of several islands that cluster off the Richmond shore—Red Rock and the Brothers.

Because of differences in county liquor laws, the bar didn't open until the boat had rounded Red Rock. The goal of thirsty passengers, in an early manifestation of TGIF (Thank God It's Friday), would be to cue the dash from the afterrail to the saloon in time to hold a glass aloft triumphantly as the ferry passed East Brother Light.

Today, hundreds of motorists crossing the bay's least-loved bridge, that humpbacked platform between San Quentin and Point Richmond, zoom by Red Rock with barely a glance. It's a different story when they catch the glimpse of East Brother Island. Instant intrigued curiosity.

With her tidy white gingerbread buildings, East Brother Island is a sleeping princess disguised as a Kate Greenaway milkmaid set down among a welter of thuggish industrial installations.

The National Register of Historic Places has acknowledged its uniqueness with a listing, thanks largely to the tennis shoe underground, a conservation-minded group of Point Richmond people. Their publication *Save Our Lighthouse,* Tiny Tennis Shoes Book No. 2, helped save the buildings from routine destruction as the Coast Guard no longer needed them after automation of the light and foghorn in 1969.

A use for the Victorian buildings on the island will, it is hoped, provide maintenance for them. Contra Costa County Department of Education is currently exploring the island as a study area for wind and water.

The walk around East Brother Island is a delightful one, and unique, but until the princess awakens and it becomes open to the public, it is one to do from a distance, through binoculars only. Or vicariously.

A heavy current rips in and out through the San Pablo Strait, the place where San Francisco Bay joins San Pablo Bay, where the two Brother Islands stand just off Point San Pablo. The distance is not far, but imagine yourself pulling against the tide in a rowboat as lighthouse keepers of the Lighthouse Service, forerunner of the Coast Guard, did, as they came and went in 1874.

Today, an offshore pier anchored on some jutting rocks is connected to the island by a gangway. Coast Guard electronic technicians, making routine checks of the power terminal, say it takes skill to land in the swift channel.

Once ashore, one is immediately at a small low building that houses machinery for both the small electric horn that has replaced the old diaphone's bee-oh fog signal with a pure tone of 400-frequency vibration, and for the light, which flashes once every five seconds during foggy weather.

Beyond the power shack is a large cemented court surrounding an odd little pondlike place. When the lighthouse was inhabited, this was the rainwater catcher. Rainfall was stored for cleaning and bathing. In later years, a supply ship brought drinking water to the great round tank nearby.

On the opposite side of the little island, the lighthouse itself, a four-story tower attached to the residence, its windows

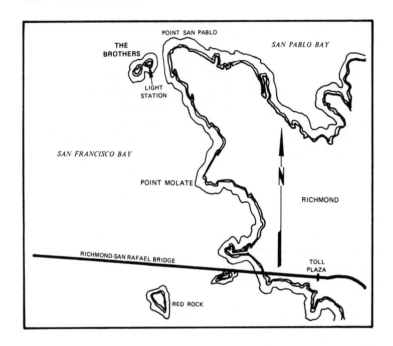

shuttered, has an expectant air. No single historic rescue placed the island on the historic places list—indeed, it prevented the necessity for rescues. The inside is modest, like the island itself an unsung hero. Without fuss, it did its job well, like the men who manned it.

West Brother, incidentally, bare as a basking whale, was once a pasture for the lighthousekeeper's goat.

65

Where Wine Flowed

The idea of "wine country" conjures up images of rolling hills planted to vineyard, old brick buildings nurturing Virginia creeper, snug little villages, and picnics under stately trees. A deep-water port and a sandy beach scarcely seem in character with the image.

Yet once the largest winery of all was located on a Contra Costa County shore, shipped thousands of gallons of wine to France, and entertained tourists who came by excursion ferries to sample its products, enjoy its wine garden, and stay at its resort hotel.

This was Winehaven, the California Wine Association enterprise at Point Molate, just north of the Richmond Bridge. Point Molate now has a shoreline beach park. If you thought the Point Richmond hills were one vast industrial wasteland of oil tanks, consider a walk of exploration and discover this rare bayshore oasis.

To make this walk, approach the Richmond-San Rafael Bridge from the East Bay side. Take the Point Molate exit, the last turnoff on the right. It bumps along to become Western

Drive near the bridge toll station, about the place where one passes the unsightly quarry that has been supplying fill for BART. Large tanks to accommodate oil from Alaska are destined to be built here when the hill is leveled.

Look to the waterside as you pass the bridge pediments to locate tracks of the Castro Point Railroad and Terminal Company. The Pacific Locomotive Association of San Francisco operates a museum train here which makes a 15-minute run along the shore around 10 A.M. on the first Sunday of each month. Oftener in summers. Once the Richmond Belt Line connected with an electric trolley at a three-track transfer near the ferry landing at Winehaven. Train buffs hope regular excursions will go as far as Point San Pablo Yacht Harbor and Fritzie Kauffman's Galley soon.

Soon one reaches the gate for Point Molate Naval Fuel Depot, which has occupied the old Winehaven buildings and company town since 1941. At the gate, bear left down to the beach and park there. Like Black Point on Fort Mason and many other park areas of military installations, Point Molate Beach is open from 6 A.M. until 6 P.M.

As you walk along the beach, whose approach boasts newly planted trees, try to imagine the great Winehaven tankers, Four Sisters and Seven Brothers, steaming out with their cargoes of wine. Winery workers lived aboard the City of Stockton, a riverboat anchored here. Others occupied the trim little houses that front on Point Molate's main stem. The topmost house, once the wine maker's, is usually occupied by the commanding officer and his family. Commander Richard Moore, former director of the Fuel Depot, was much admired by Contra Costa County citizens for his cooperation with the school system. He helped in establishing a shorelife study laboratory within one of the big castellated Winehaven buildings. One day the entire 48 acres of depot will be available to the town of Point Richmond.

Boats serving a Chinese shrimp camp, and a sardine fleet of purse seiners could also once have been seen from this beach as they came in and out of Point San Pablo. Four of the bay's remaining shrimp boats still operate out of this harbor.

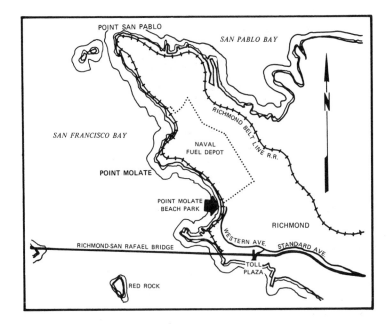

At $4 per pound, their catches are sold for bait, rather than people-food. Point Orient, the Standard Oil dock, is immediately north of Point Molate.

When you have explored the sand, linger awhile at the water's edge to look for ghost shrimp, grass shrimp, and other still-water life. Students from Contra Costa high schools, who rotate through the Winehaven science lab have filled many large aquariums with their finds here.

If they had come along one decisive day during Prohibition, the stupidity that did Winehaven in, they might also have caught drunken striped bass floating on the surface. Bungs were knocked out of vats and 240,000 gallons of wine once drained into the bay here.

66

A Place
Time Forgot

One of the pleasures of a walker is to happen upon an unexpected cranny that Time seems to have forgotten. Such a place is Alvarado Park, the mouth of Wildcat Canyon in Richmond at the northernmost end of that long ridge boulevard called the Arlington.

Like a shell imbedded in plastic, an almost invisible protective cloak, perhaps of civic indifference, seems to envelope some shards of Yesterday at Alvarado. The walker who explores it will find the remnant of a former dancing casino, a spring where water was once bottled, an Indian shell mound, fine old buckeye trees sheltering brookside grinding holes, waterfalls, little bridges, and a trail that leads away to open hills beyond.

To make this walk, transport yourself to Contra Costa County to the complicated junction of Arlington Boulevard, Park Avenue, McBryde Avenue, Marin Avenue, and Wildcat Canyon Road. The Arlington bus number 7 goes directly there from Arlington Circle, Berkeley.

On arrival, the walker will find a San Pablo city limit sign on one corner, a Richmond city limit sign on another. Between the two is a funky old commercial-looking sign designed to be lighted from within that says Alvarado Park, Skateland. Don't be put off by the look of it. Instead follow the walk it heralds down a lane marked by stone walls and old pylons of rock that once were surmounted by light fixtures, a vestige of Works Project Administration improvement of the park. In a moment, the road crosses Wildcat Creek, burbling happily when there has been rain.

Soon one reaches a broad paved area. If you come by car, park here. Then return to the entrance marked by an attractive ramada or shelter of logs that has served its time as ticket booth and refreshment stand. A beautifully shaped, many-trunked buckeye tree stands on one side of it. On the other is an ugly green corrugated metal building, much defaced with graffiti. Go past it to find under another patriarchal buckeye the stones where Indian ladies once ground acorn meal. Rushing of waterfalls will urge you to look further. Steps about 20 feet to the right lead down to Camp Creek picnic area below. The Wolf Spring, where Alvarado Springs Water was bottled for sale long ago, is further upstream.

When you have explored the area, climb back up to the central plaza and, skirting the lot again, walk along the perimeter until you are abreast of a bridge. Cross it and bear right to find near the creekside several picnic tables sitting on the shell mound commemorated in the name, Camp Shell. Artifacts from it enhance many collections.

Once again return to the central plaza. Your eye will be drawn to the big yellow half-shingled barnlike building. In trolleycar days, pleasure seekers from San Francisco would come first by ferry, then by streetcar to dance here. Many of them also dined at Chateau Boquet, the big white building visible outside the park on the cliff above Camp Shell. Now housing a philosophical group that calls itself Astrologos, in the past the Chateau also contained a nursing home, a speakeasy, a gambling hall, and ladies of the evening.

In one classical confrontation, Richmond resident Ethel Kerns recalls that a group of ministers disguised with mustachios and beards once went to the Chateau to gather informa-

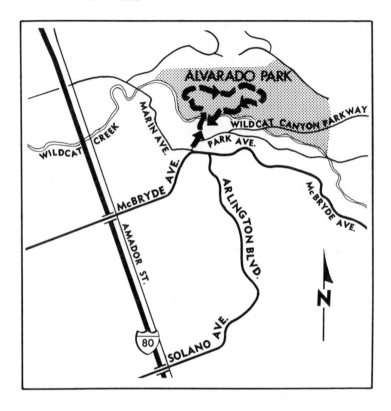

tion about it until the proprietor commented "Enjoying yourself, Reverend" to one. Subsequently a raid by the district attorney put the Chateau out of the entertainment business.

Walk up the steps near the round barbecue pit to find a rapid change of character in the park. Within 300 yards it switches from urban to rural. Continue uphill beyond the trees and you will soon be on the ridge in open pastureland, little changed from the time when this land was Rancho San Pablo and the canyon was called Arroyo Grande. Grand Canyon seemed pretentious to later residents who renamed the park for Governor Juan B. Alvarado, who was married to an heir to the rancho.

To explore a series of a dozen small camp and picnic sites, bear consistently right, skirting above the big pavilion (which now no longer has dancing or rollerskating, but park rangers' offices and a repair shop in it). The network of trails skirts Wildcat Creek on one side, ultimately passing under Wildcat Canyon Road to reach a little footbridge. Cross it and bear right to make a loop that will bring you back to the heart of this fine old park, geographically the beginning of the East Bay Regional Park system.

67

A Point to Ponder

Point Pinole Regional Shoreline, an unspoiled 1,014-acre peninsula in Contra Costa County surrounded by industrial Richmond, has three and a half miles that front on San Pablo Bay and a flavor of the West that was. It is the west of grassy meadows where cattle grazed, meadowlarks sang, butterflies fluttered over wildflowers, and crabs scuttled along the shore.

For me, it also has a soupçon of the chili-peppery No-Law-West-of-the-Pecos flavoring that goes with a trigger-happy guard. The first time I tried to walk around Point Pinole, some time ago, he discouraged me with a shotgun and two shots into a nearby bank. The second time, reassured by two lawyers that California shorelines are public below the mean high-tide line, I went at dead low tide, made it safely around the point while the guard hovered near a chain-link fence, and emerged with no more serious problem than marsh mud up over my boot tops.

Now that it is a park, I have recently gone back to see the land above the cliffs and explore its trails. East Bay Regional

Parks manager Richard C. Trudeau was right when he described it as "the crown jewel of the park system." Already a favorite with walkers and bikers, now that the pier on the point is completed, it has become the prime spot for all East Bay fishermen.

To enjoy it, transport yourself to Richmond. The Richmond-San Rafael Bridge continuation is Standard Avenue. From it go left on Garrard, right on Pennsylvania Avenue, left on 13th (which becomes Rumrill), left again on Brookside Drive to Giant Highway and right on Giant past the golf course to the park entrance. It is well marked. If your choice of routes is via the East Bay bridge, take Highway 80. Just north of Richmond go off on the Hilltop Drive exit, west to San Pablo Avenue. Go north to Atlas Road, west to Giant Highway and south to the parking lot.

Once parked, head toward the pair of Johnnies-on-the-spot, as park people like to call their portable privies. Then follow the trail north along the fence line to reach an old concrete overpass. Come along at the right time and an Amtrak train may pass underneath you.

Once you have crossed the tracks, the ambience changes immediately. Old eucalyptus sigh, birds flit in lively flocks, and paths seem to beckon one off into the woods. For the present, resist the side paths and hew left to the paved Meadow Road until you reach a major junction, again marked by a pair of privies. Take a sharp left on the paved Giant Road and go about 100 yards until you are parallel with the end of the eucalyptus grove on your right.

Leave the road and skirt the eucalyptus to find at the shoreline a broad sandy beach, rich with driftwood, the shells of Washington clams and rock oysters.

The beach may well have been the landing place for an 1812 Spanish survey party.

After you explore the beach, climb uphill to the higher beach path that follows the cliff and head north. Part of this trail follows the route of a battery-operated narrow gauge railway that once ran on wooden rails to cut down the possibility of sparks that might ignite explosives manufactured here. At several points, you will pass old munitions storage batteries and factory sites, distinguishable by their earthworks, still standing though the buildings are gone. One nearest the point has been pressed into use as a sun trap. It's great for picnicking on chilly days.

The new pier construction allows fishermen to get out to deep water. After you've gone out on it, follow the fence line back to the shore to reach Chinese Cove.

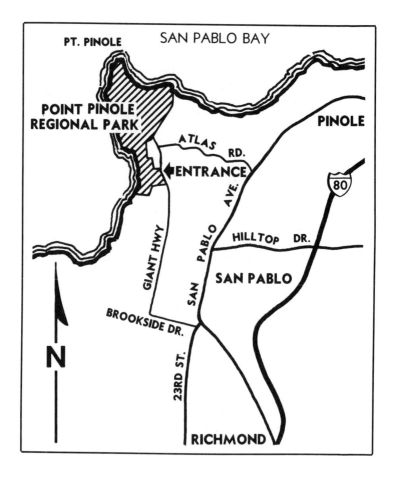

Shoreline views are so great, that if the tide is right, you may want to retrace your steps back via the beach itself.

As you walk, you pass driftwood coves, both salicornia and sardinia marshes unchanged for a hundred years, defunct oyster beds, cliff overhangs, the remnants of earthen bulwarks used at different times by the Safety Nitro, the Giant, and the Atlas powder companies. The latter two have left their names on the land on nearby roads.

The first name is the result of a classic story and revised government safety regulations. In 1866, the first shipment of Alfred Nobel's invention, nitroglycerine in clay, arrived in San Francisco with instructions on the barrels, "Do not hammer." A curious wharfside employee, disregarding the instructions after a look at the seemingly innocuous material, did just that and blew himself and a dock to kingdom come.

Duckblinds, illegal fill areas visible across the water to the left, McNear's Quarry, Point San Pedro, and Peacock Gap across the bay come into sight. After one rounds the point proper, a quarrying operation at Hamilton Airbase reveals its shoreline scars. Nearer at hand there are old deep-water piers and a succession of pier pilings, some festooned with shaggy clumps of baling wire shoved over the cliff above at high tide.

Look underfoot for the blue clay once used in the powder manufacture, for peat, which floats in from the Sacramento Delta area carpeting the shore, often in alternation with fragile Washington clam shells. Egrets and blue heron feed in large numbers near the pickleweed offshore. For a shorter, one-half mile route back to your wheels, stick to the paved bicycle trail, Meadow Road.

PART SIX

CARQUINEZ STRAITS

68

The Waterfront That
Was Born Again

"Discover Vallejo!" the invitation proposed.

Remembering Robert Louis Stevenson's immortal description: "South Vallejo is typical of many California towns. It was a blunder", I resisted. Vallejo is also the place that twice tried to become a state capital and once to become the county seat, all with a hilarious lack of success.

"We have a new waterfront park," my enticer persisted. Back to *The Silverado Squatters* for a second look. "A long pier, a number of drinking saloons, a hotel of great size, marshy pools where the frogs keep up their croaking . . . these are the marks of South Vallejo. Yet there was a tall building beside the pier, labeled the Star Flour Mills; and sea-going, full-rigged ships lay close along shore, waiting for their cargo. . . ."

A peg-legged seafarer, recognizable for the archetype of Long John Silver, lurched into mind. "Those old saloons might be colorful," I ventured.

"Gone, that's where the waterfront park is."

Full-rigged ships are also gone, almost everywhere. Pleading the cause for the human dimension, I parried with "Frogs?"

"Probably not, but we have a new town square with a great deal of contemporary sculpture."

Ships and frogs naturally occur in environs that can be a pleasure for walkers. For different reasons, this can also be true of sculpture.

"I'll come," I said. I went and I'm glad, I think. I was treated to a pleasant walk.

Vallejo, 30 miles north of San Francisco in Solano County, is best known as the home of Mare Island Naval Shipyard and the California Maritime Academy, two factors that have helped its population grow to 80,000. Its waterfront park is beautifully situated across the Mare Island Strait (which is also the lower end of the Napa River) from the Isla de la Yegua.

Yegua is Spanish for mare, and there are several stories on how the island got its name. One is that General Mariano Vallejo, for whom the town is named, lost his favorite mare there when she swam across the channel to join a band of elk. Another is that Victor Castro once pastured his mares on the island to protect them from raiding Indians who fancied horsemeat. Today Mare Island is a hive of naval activity and off limits to anyone who does not have business on it, mares included.

Marina Vista, the redeveloped downtown heart that was formerly notorious lower Georgia and Virginia streets is immediately northeast of the seawall park. Together the two are an example of what government means when it talks of "interweaving a freeway into the fabric of a city." The freeway isn't there yet, but the gulch to accommodate it is.

To enjoy this walk, head first for York and Sacramento streets where a historical marker in a Civic Center parking lot nearly dusts off Vallejo's abortive tenure as state capital. The hill that once stood here has been leveled, but there is sufficient rise to survey Mare Island and the new Marina Vista complex.

When you have your bearings, browse among the handsome new buildings and artifacts of Town Square, a plaza at the foot of Georgia Street. Notice especially the tremendous log wind chimes called *The Structure* by Stefan Novak, the stainless steel and acrylic piece *Triad* by Freda Koblick, and the bronze *Genius* by Carl Milles.

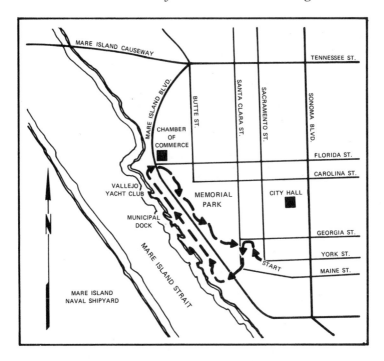

Then walk downward to Santa Clara Street to cross to the U.S.S. Independence Park on the seawall, also enriched by a sculptural wall set with historical bas-reliefs and a line of flags.

Follow the seawall north past a yacht basin to find the terminal of the little Mare Island ferry. For a contrast of past and present, continue along the waterfront past the two yacht clubs. Then cross the freeway scar at Florida Street (near the Chamber of Commerce building) to pick up a meandering walk that will lead you back, past apartments and playgrounds, through Memorial Park to make a complete loop.

69

John Muir's House

"Making your way through the mazes of the Coast Range to the summit of any of the inner peaks or passes opposite San Francisco, in the clear springtime, the grandest and most telling of all California landscapes is outspread before you," wrote John Muir, founder of the Sierra Club, and the patriarch of the conservation movement.

He is credited with establishing the U.S. Forest Service, at least five national parks and monuments, and inspiring many more.

He may well have written this excerpt from *The Mountains of California* at his spacious home on a fruit farm in the Alhambra Valley, two miles south of Martinez. The book, his first, was published in 1894, four years after he moved there.

"At your feet lies the great Central Valley glowing in the sunshine, extending north and south farther than the eye can reach, one smooth flowing, lake-like bed of fertile soil."

He also described the mighty Sierra visible beyond, its foothills, gold fields, and the nearer Coast Range "rising as a grand green barrier against the ocean . . . composed of innumerable forest-crowned spurs, ridges and rolling hill-waves which enclose a multitude of smaller valleys; some looking out through long forest vistas to the sea; others with but few trees to the Central Valley; while a thousand others yet smaller are embosomed and concealed in mild, round browed hills, each with its own climate, soil and productions."

Muir's own home, now the John Muir National Historic Site, stands on just such a "round browed hill" and is open to the public for a modest sum. It includes a guided tour of the house. From its second-floor study windows, one can almost be John Muir for a moment, and envision him tearing upstairs to the windowed cupola for another lofty look at the sunset over the gentle surrounding landscape he loved.

Walkers who make the stroll about the 8.7-acre grounds and go through the Victorian adaptation of a Georgian house, will find several surprises, among them a growing collection of

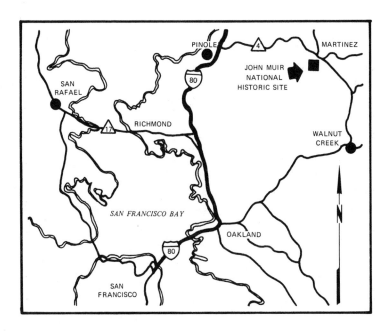

Mr. and Mrs. John Muir and daughters.

Muiriana, orchard trees in bloom, a newly recreated vineyard, lively little Franklin Creek, and the well-preserved Vicente Martinez adobe, a gem of Monterey architecture constructed when this was part of Rancho Las Juntas.

To make this walk, transport yourself about 20 miles north of the Bay Bridge along the Eastshore Freeway, Interstate Highway 80. Just beyond Pinole, look for the cutoff of State Highway 4, the Franklin Canyon Road, renamed ironically, the John Muir Parkway. After taking the ferry from San Francisco, John Muir often walked to his home. Walking is prohibited on the "Parkway" that bears his name.

The Muir house will appear on the north side of the road surrounded by a morass of interchange for the Alhambra-Pleasant Hill Road and downtown Martinez. Bear left on this, then turn into the long low pink visitors' center on the west side of the road. Be prepared to wait for the tour, which starts with a slide show.

When you go through the Muir house, remember that this was built by Dr. John Strentzel, Muir's father-in-law, a fancier of horticultural exotica. One of Muir's own daughters, Helen, was a train buff and often put out ripe cherries for the crew of the Santa Fe trains that passed the place.

Look north from the second-floor windows of John Muir's den for an excellent view of ugly electric power transformers, oil tanks, used-car lots, gas stations, pizza restaurants, and even a "Muir Motel." Real John Muir fans will stifle the gorge that rises in their throats and regard it as an object lesson, sympathizing with the young ecologists who have been known to "walk for survival" between Sacramento and Los Angeles. Most of that route is equally slurbanized.

When you have walked through the house, go downhill toward the little vineyard to find the creek and beyond it the Martinez adobe. These, at least, are little changed.

70

Call on Crockett!

Crockett, the Bay Area prototype of everyone's home town, hasn't changed much since 1927. It was then that Time, like other hasty travelers, followed Highway 40 across the new Carquinez Bridge leaving Crockett, population 5,000, half-forgotten below by the waterside.

If passing motorists notice Crockett at all, it is usually to comment on the tremendous California and Hawaiian sugar refinery, which has a 3,000-foot deep-water frontage on Carquinez Strait, or on Dowrelio's party-boat and fishing pier. A twin to the 1927 bridge was built in 1958 and the refinery is visible from both, the fishing pier from one.

Few passersby suspect that just a few hundred feet from the highway awaits a journey into 40-years-ago. It is best made on foot. To enjoy this stroll, turn off into Crockett and park your car on Pomona Street. If you come by bus, the stop is very near. Walk east on Pomona. Ignore the cross-street signs. For some inexplicable reason, Fifth Avenue is followed by First.

Four blocks will take you through the Valona district, a

name given to the Southern Pacific railroad stop soon after it was built here in 1877, largely because Crockett's or the Chicken Ranch, as it was then known, seemed inglorious. In another block you will be passing between the spacious grounds of the John Swett Union High School and the Carquinez Grammar School.

At Rolph Avenue, named for George M. Rolph, longtime president of C & H Sugar and a brother of "Sunny Jim," walk north toward the refinery and the water. This is Crolona. Alexander Park is the bosky dell on your right, the high-school athletic field on the left. The rooftop barely visible amid trees beyond the field is the Old Homestead, built by Thomas Edwards, Sr., in 1867. Edwards received part of the Rancho Canada del Hambre y las Bolsas (which means Valley of Hunger and Pockets) as a legal fee. The name refers to Mexican troops who ran out of food while camping here, and to the pocketlike land formations. Pioneer Edwards named the settlement for his lifelong friend, Judge J. B. Crockett. Hay scows often tied up within 50 feet of the dwelling. Now registered as State Historical Landmark No. 731, Edwards's home is a women's club.

The old brown-shingled building you pass is the Crockett Club for Men. Across the street from it, at the corner of Winslow and Rolph, is the Crockett telephone office with its manually operated board, 12 positions, and nine girls in headsets, one of three such boards still in use in the state. People still remember the old, spry, bright-eyed lady who sometimes could be seen coming to visit the office after her retirement. She was operator Annie O'Brien, who came to work here in 1907 when Crockett had a magneto board. Much of its activity was devoted to switching railroad cars. Miss Annie had one of the last single-digit numbers in the state. She could recall when the present switchboard was installed in 1923. Emergency calls during the flu epidemic of World War I, the time Port Chicago blew up, and the Big Strike of '38 have been all in her day's work.

Rithet Park, a sunken garden once known as "The Mudhole," is across Winslow Street. Loring, the main shopping area, almost a ghost street, is across the park.

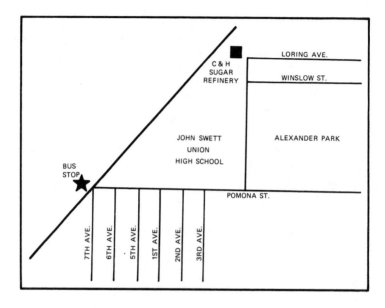

Since 1897, when the antecedents of the C & H refinery purchased Starrs Flour Mill and the Edwards Ranch, the lusty "Scowtown" described by Frank Norris in *The Octopus,* has shrunken. The "trade wind that filled the air with the nimble taint of salt" is sweeter.

To walk through the sugar refinery, which often operates on weekends, cross Rolph Avenue to Crockett Community Center. The department of community relations conducts daily tours, has an office here, and can also arrange to take visitors through the Old Homestead. (Children below seventh grade are not taken in large groups.) For any group of more than ten, it's a good idea to call to make arrangements, or write a letter. Of course, if you want to be newfangled, you can telephone.

71

A Walk at the
Old Coal Mines

Two musical voices in history mingle unheard in the northeast foothills of Mount Diablo. Think of the refrain "Waitin' on the Levee" as played on a steam calliope, a rousing rinky-tink tune that conjures up a paddlewheel riverboat. For counterpoint, consider a Welsh work song, sung high and clear with that poignancy that made *How Green Was My Valley* memorable.

Coal is the tie that binds them. For it was coal that powered the big sidewheel steamers on the Sacramento River in the 1870s. This coal was dug by Welsh miners on the slopes above Antioch in Contra Costa County.

As unlikely as it may seem, the coal pits have been transformed into picnic places.

To create the new Coal Mines Area Regional Park, 1,123 acres of land encompassing the sites of the once-thriving mining towns of Nortonville, Somersville, Stewartsville, and Judsonville have been purchased.

The park district has opened the land formally to the public. The townsites are linked by a narrow county road that runs

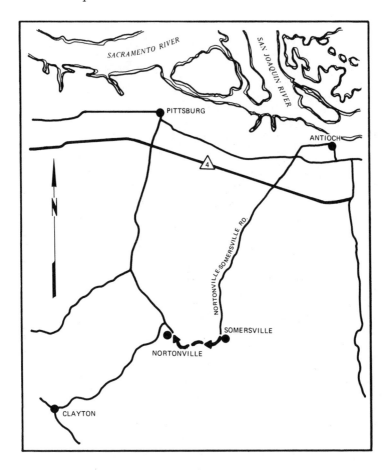

through the area. It is too washed out for cars, but provides a good trail for walkers.

In spring, when the land is green and glorious with water and wildflowers, is the best time to explore the two miles from Somersville to Nortonville. En route, the trail passes the historic Rose Park Cemetery, long known for its somber Italian cypress trees.

The easy way to Antioch from the Bay Bridge is Highway 24 to Walnut Creek, 680 north to Route 4, then to Pittsburg.

Between Pittsburg and Antioch, take Somersville Road up into the hills until you have passed the last three clusters of ranch buildings.

Park when you reach an area on the left bare of vegetation and black with many years of mine tailings. This is the site where coal was discovered in 1855 by George W. Hawxhurst. By prearrangement with the East Bay Regional Park District, one can go through a sand mine, although abandoned coal mine tunnels are too dangerous to admit the public.

Notice the ailanthus, or tree of heaven, grove along the road, intermingled with blue oaks. Then look uphill and to your right above the canyon to locate the old cemetery by its five columns of cypress. With this as a landmark, begin walking uphill on the road.

When you reach the cemetery, currently fenced and locked to prevent further vandalism, look down at the land below. Through the 1880s a community of 300 houses, hotel, shops, and schoolhouse existed in this area.

At that time, there were five mines at Somersville and many more in the nearby towns. A campaign was waged to rename Mount Diablo "Coal Hill" or "Black Diamond Mountain."

The miners were gone before 1900, following anthracite discoveries in Washington and Oregon that pulled the rug out from under the bituminous, or "soft," coal mines here. Sandmining was profitable until World War II.

Return to the road and climb to the crest of the ridge. Visible to the west from this point at the bottom of the hill is the tailing dump that marks the site of Nortonville.

As you walk down to Nortonville, watch on the left for a species of manzanita, *arctostaphyloe,* which is at its southernmost limit of natural distribution.

Look underfoot in the road for coal fragments before retracing your steps to complete this country ramble.

72

Port Costa
Lives in Yesterday

Port Costa, population 275, once the greatest grain port in the world, is back on the maps after an absence of almost 37 years. Reason: the ingenuity and enterprise of a young ex-beer-truck driver named Bill Rich, who bought "a hotel, a warehouse, a sandstone-faced building and 7 vacant lots" all empty, and turned a ghost town into a thriving community of 30 or more unusual shops.

If the easy lazy country ways of doing things appeal to you, if you like to watch the trains and boats pass on the end of a street, if mousing about in the artifacts of yesterday gives you a charge, then a walk around Port Costa, 38 miles north of San Francisco via Highway 80, is for you.

To make this walk, take the Crockett turnoff as you approach the Carquinez Straits Bridge, then follow the Straits three miles east. When you reach Canyon Lake Drive, you are on Main Street. Park beyond the school and walk toward the water. As you walk, notice the pleasant cottages ranked on either side of the street against a background of fulvous hills.

The stroll along this street of elms, which the community

pitches in to trim and spray annually, is like a visit to the pre-technology small-town America of Booth Tarkington and Sinclair Lewis, although it was Frank Norris, in *The Octopus,* who wrote about it. His grain monopoly villain was smothered in the wheat he had cornered as it was loaded on a ship docked at the piers that once fringed the shore here.

Keep walking and in another block you reach the business district, thronged on weekends with collectors of all sorts. Notice the "timid salesperson" sign in Sasha's Antiques, the old and new jewelry at Ann Olmstead's, the pioneer boutique in the village, the general merchandise store, and the activity of renovating an old western-style building whose upstairs porch juts over the sidewalk. This is to be called "The Wheat Dock" and many of the dealers inside have national reputations among antiquarians. A few steps further will take you to the Warehouse Cafe of Bill Rich. Go inside to discover an unusual restaurant, lunch counter, bar, and upstairs an O-shaped alley of unusual shops, all delightful and unrevealed here so the walker can have the joy of making his own discoveries. Don't miss the artistic spoof on fossils.

When you have explored it, go outside and walk toward the water a few paces to discover the post office whose small boxes are on the street for walk-up outdoor service. Then cross Canyon Lake Drive to see the Burlington Hotel, both camp and quaint. As you cross, look west toward the water to locate a white tower on the shore. Between 1880 and 1891 hundreds of ships loaded grain at George W. McNear's Port Costa Warehouse and Dock Company and at the adjacent docks built by five other exporters at his suggestion. As the "Big Six," they once dominated the world grain market.

Start back up the street on the west side and you pass the Bull Valley Inn, originated by Bill Rich at a time when he drove a beer truck during the day, then changed shirts to become the chef in the evening. Maître d' is Angelo Coppa, who doubles as the village barber and is known for his wardrobe of dinner jackets.

Some Sundays, there is music by Canyon Lake, where the reservoir dam is pressed into service as an amphitheater.

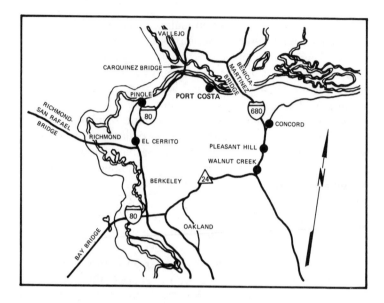

Donald Pippin chooses the music, which has included an all-Mozart concert, an afternoon of baroque, the music of Russia today, and of Bartok. Tickets are a reasonable $2.50.

To reach the lake, take Reservoir Road left when you reach the school. After passing four or five houses, you will be surrounded by hilly fields on the left and a eucalyptus grove on the right. Go into the grove after you round the curve, cross a footbridge over the spillway and there, fronted by an old-time circus wagon ticket booth is the improvised Port Costa Outdoor Theatre.

If you don't find the antidote to mechanization in Port Costa, then you're not a full-fledged technophobe.

73

Tubbs Island

Lower Tubbs Island is one of the few places on the margins of San Francisco Bay that a coastal Miwok Indian, time-warped out of a thousand years ago, might recognize as home if he returned today.

Tubbs Island is a salt marsh, scintillant in spring and fall with thousands of migrating birds, and as far removed from the crass commerciality of the recent season as one could find. If you yearn for a breath of fresh air, an intimacy with land unspoiled by man, a renewal of the spirit, come today for a walk around the Tubbs Island border dike.

Supply yourself with binoculars, a good birdwatching field guide, your most waterproof footgear, a lunch, and a pleasant companion. Then take Route 101 north, turning east just beyond Ignacio on Route 37, the Black Point cutoff. On Route 37 go east about 8 miles to the major three-way Sears Point intersection. Go past the Sonoma-Napa turnoff. Immediately beyond this junction runs Tolay Creek, named for an Indian chief whose tribal territory this once was. Cross the creek by the small

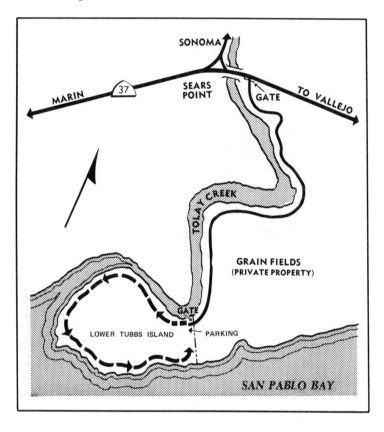

bridge and 50 yards east there is a ranch-style double gate which is identified by small yellow and green Nature Conservancy signs on either post.

Drive in (sports cars beware; the road is deeply rutted), closing the gate behind you, and follow the road bordering Tolay Creek through grain fields on the one hand and pickleweed marsh on the other until you reach another gate and two modest buildings. Then park and prepare for a delightful waterside walk.

It is possible to walk to the right or left and loop back from either direction to this same spot. When I made the walk with artist Gordon Baldwin, we started in the direction of the barn and house, stopping first to register in the barn office. There is birding literature here and a fine wall map of the area.

Past the house, head down the broad levee trail, again following Tolay Creek. Within a few steps as we walked, godwits, dowitchers, plovers, avocets, willets, and sandpipers by the hundreds rose flashing like confetti in the air. Heavy pheasants, tame as chickens and released by a neighboring gun club, started before us every hundred feet or so. Once we saw a rare white-tailed kite and a black-crowned night heron. Osprey flew amazingly close overhead. An owl landed nearby, heavy as a dirigible. Huey Johnson, director of the State Natural Resources Agency, has also reported sighting the California clapper rail and the salt marsh harvest mouse, both endangered species.

Ninety percent of the surviving canvasback ducks using the Pacific Flyway winter off Tubbs. Bitterns, grebes, egrets, and the elegant tern are also visitors.

The trail peels off at one point to cross the creek. It returns to the starting point on the opposite shore. Ignore this shortcut for the most unusual treat of the walk and continue around the island. Soon you will be on the shore of San Pablo Bay, one of the few places where a walker can enjoy this body of water.

If a young man packing his child on his back comes along as you walk, he may be the caretaker of the property. Stop in the house at the reception center when you complete the loop. Then, if your excursion has left you hopeful and possessed with a burning desire to protect more shore lands before it is too late, contributions should be addressed to San Francisco Bay Project, The Nature Conservancy, c/o Wells Fargo Bank, P.O. Box 26657, San Francisco, 94126.

74

Nice Towns
Finish Last

Benicia is a comic-opera town that ranks with the all-time losers, a Fibber McGee's closet of a town, bursting with yesterday's artifacts, crammed with undiscovered nostalgia.

Once named Francisca when men of vision knew that a town that carried the name of the bay would develop into an international port, she lost out to San Francisco. Once thought the ideal location for a state capital because of her strategic location on Carquinez Straits between a great river and a great bay, she was, briefly, but lost out to Sacramento.

Her other losses sound like the letter Mabel wrote Paw about the barn burning, the one that ends "so Maw ran off with the hired man." Most recent of them is the loss of the great Benicia Arsenal, raison d'etre for her existence for more than a hundred years.

For a walker in search of diversion, Benicia makes for pleasant exploring. From San Francisco, drive across the Bay Bridge, take Highway 80 north past the Carquinez Bridge, then east to Benicia via 680.

Once in Benicia, begin this walk near the old Southern Pacific Railroad Station at the foot of First Street. Here, thousands of early travelers from the East took a train ferry across Carquinez Straits to Port Costa.

Start up First Street, as the soldiers long assigned to the arsenal did. Instead of the bawdy houses that existed here not too long ago, the walker will find a welter of antique shops.

Go into Washington House Cafe at the corner of West D Street to see its vintage zerolene pump lights, guaranteed to remind old-timers of days when they had to "get out and get under." For those deep into the nostalgia mystique, there is a treasure lode along First Street that includes the House of Clocks and some 20 other emporiums for those whose blastoff is the castoff.

More historically minded walkers can continue to G Street for scholarly fare at the Benicia Capitol building, now a state

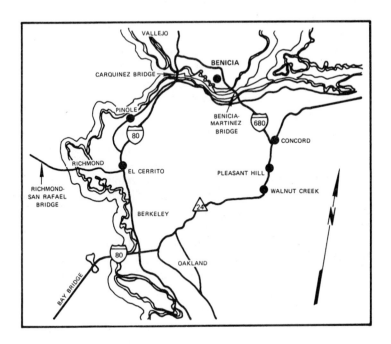

park. Governor John Bigler was inaugurated here in 1854 to the music of the San Francisco Blues, a crack military outfit.

Benicians considered it treasonous that he took the capital subsequently to Sacramento. There are those who still claim this was the reason Lake Bigler's name was later changed to Lake Tahoe.

The stately Georgian building with its Doric columns served for a while as the Solano County seat. In yet another of Benicia's losses, even this administrative function was later usurped by little Fairfield.

When you have explored the building, the handsome grounds, discovered the picnic tables between the barn and the old Fisher House, donated recently to the park system by the sisters Catherine and Raphaelita Hanlon, continue along First Street to J Street. On the west side is the first Masonic Hall (but not lodge) in California and on the east, St. Paul's Episcopal Church, whose rectory, a classic New England saltbox built in 1790, was shipped prefabricated around the Horn. John Muir held a pew in the church.

Also in the environs on East L Street is the mate to General Mariano Vallejo's home "Lachryma Montis" in Sonoma. It was one of three such prefab houses brought to the Bay Area from Boston by Captain John Walsh, in 1849.

For those interested in romance, Concepción Arguello, whose ill-fated lover, Rezanov, never returned though she waited for him to her death, is buried in St. Dominic's Cemetery across East Fifth Street beyond M Street.

For those more interested in the regimental barracks and quarters, the Benicia Arsenal, now an industrial park, is at the watery end of M Street. Maritime buffs may want to seek out the old Pacific Mail Docks, now the Yuba Construction Company, east of the site of the Benicia-Martinez auto ferry.

Poke about as you please, for the most delicious of all discoveries are the ones you make yourself. This one pickle barrel of a town is loaded with such surprises.

75

Chinatown
in the Delta

The unlikely town of Locke is a little bit of San Francisco's Chinatown, contrived in wood instead of brick, and set down on a delta riverbank.

It is unique, even in the fascinating waterworld of the hundred-odd islands that make up the delta country, that complex alluvial fan of the Sacramento-San Joaquin rivers that supplies San Francisco Bay with water. If you've never seen it, and few people have because the maps are so confusing, consider a walk in Locke.

To make this walk, fishermen should pack a rod or reel, for striped bass run in the delta. Cross the Bay Bridge and head north along Highway 80 to cut east on Highway 4, the Franklin Canyon Road, at Pinole. A little beyond Antioch, pick up Highway 160 heading northeasterly, but instead of crossing the bridge over the Sacramento River into Rio Vista, continue on to Walnut Grove, passing Isleton, the town that was flooded in 1972 by a break in the dike. Unfortunately no heroic Hans Brinker saved the day and receding water scars are obvious there.

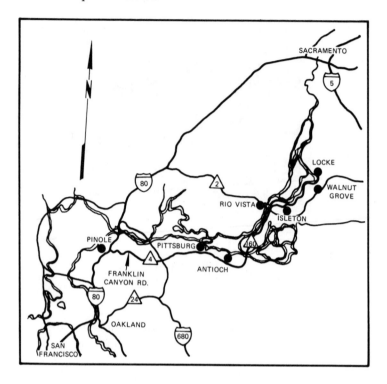

Walnut Grove is where the going becomes confusing. The reason is Georgiana Slough. Some maps show Walnut Grove and Locke, which is six-tenths of a mile north, on one side of the slough, some on the other. Some even show Locke and Walnut Grove on opposite sides of the Sacramento River. They are both on the same side. To find Locke, go to Walnut Grove. Then keep going north on Highway 160 for less than a mile.

The landmark is a long wooden river warehouse on the Southern Pacific tracks beside the levee. Now called The Boathouse, and used for pleasure boat storage, it was originally used in the transfer of fruit and vegetables from boats to trains. The fine freight elevator that once hoisted produce now lifts small boats in and out of the water for fishermen who berth their motor craft here. If your immediate reaction is, "Why shut off this fine river view with a long wall of building?" reflect a moment. The warehouse is older than the town of Locke.

Park as soon as you spot the corner restaurant called The Tules, easily distinguished by three outside tables on its little front patio and a nearby pagoda telephone booth. The brass historical society plaque on one wall gives some of the background of Locke: "Founded in 1912 by Tin Sin Chan on this site, this unique Chinese community grew rapidly after a fire destroyed the Chinese Section of Walnut Grove in 1915 . . ." it begins and goes on to describe Locke in its heyday.

It must have been quite a town, with nine groceries, six restaurants, a theater, hotel, bakery, school, church, lodge, and post office on the record. Who knows how many cribs, fan tan rooms, bars, and dream-smoke purveyors were in the back alleys?

After you have gone in to size up The Tules, which has a classic Western frontier-cum-Cantonese ambience although its present owner is a Caucasian named Logan McCall, walk down the sloping wooden sidewalk that fronts the River Road, passing potted agaves and chrysanthemums until you reach the old theater arch, whose side stairs lead enticingly down like the many little lanes of Hong Kong, or indeed of San Francisco's Chinatown. File them in mind for later and continue walking north.

Another set of steps soon jaunts downward, offering more beguiling glimpses of another world behind the houses, and another little street beyond the one visible at the foot of the stairs.

The grocery, too, has inviting stairs, but continue to the end of the block, where you reach Locke Road, a name, grocer Tom King says "was imposed on us by the county." Then bear right half a block to discover Locke's main street, called, interestingly enough, Main Street. Walk past the school and along one side of the street roofed by second floor porches as a shield against the hot sun of summer. Old men linger here on hard benches or pause to show off the fish they have caught poke-poling.

Notice the overreaching five-digit house numbers on this

block-long street as you pass, the lines of washing and sometimes of vegetables or fish drying in the wind. If some of these buildings look empty, look again at them, for the population of Locke is 1,002 and there is nothing for rent. Go into the grocery to find the kind of goodies San Francisco's Grant Avenue shops offer, then browse along the little street that goes a block or two inland to discover charming little gardens. For an anomaly of delta cuisine, stop in Al-the-Wop's, where peanut butter and jam stand on the bar and many patrons dress their steaks with the former.

Ping Lee, known informally as the "mayor of Locke," says the stir of dismay that followed the death in 1971 of Miss Alice Locke—lest the Locke estate banish the little community—has subsided. "There seems to be no threat now except from possible development," he says and he should know. It was his father who founded the town.

When you have explored Locke to your heart's content, take a look at Walnut Grove. Again like San Francisco's Chinatown, which spreads ever outwards, Walnut Grove becomes more and more like Locke.

76

A Rare Look at
Mare Island

Mare Island, tantalizingly close to the town of Vallejo, of all the larger bay islands is the most inaccessible. Although bounded by San Pablo Bay to the west, tule marshes to the north, the deep, fast-running Napa River to the east, and the turbulent Carquinez Straits to the south, it is not these that are insuperable. Rather it is the old World War II tune "A slip of a lip might sink a ship" and the attendant secrecy that keeps Mare Island so remote, for it has been a naval shipyard since 1854.

The Island is not open to the general public except for one occasion: the Mare Island Heritage Home Tour, a benefit sponsored by the Officers Wives' Club. If you can latch on to this tour, it may be your only chance to visit Mare Island, which has charms that include a pioneer cemetery, a chapel with signed Tiffany windows, the Bay Area's earliest arboretum, an outdoor museum, and a panoply of historic military buildings.

For information on this event, write the Public Affairs Officer, Naval Support Activities Office, Mare Island, 94592. (It is also possible to tour the island if you come with a group on a

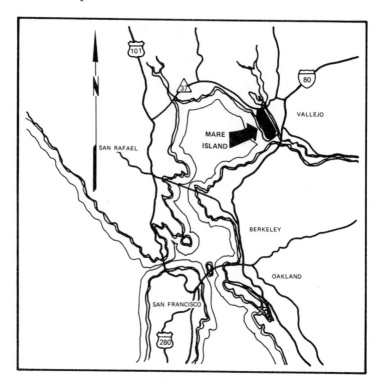

special bus, but for this trip also you must first contact the office mentioned above.)

However, for the walk, transport yourself northeast from San Francisco via Highway 80 across Carquinez Bridge, then swing onto Highway 29. West on Tennessee Street in Vallejo is the route to the causeway and the main gate. On the island, Causeway Street leads to Walnut or Cedar—turn left and park on one or the other as close to Fifth Street as traffic will permit.

Once afoot, head for Alden Park, Walnut at Eighth Street, where an opening ceremony full of naval pomp and ceremony, colors, and music will begin promptly at noon. If the Navy Drill Team in its bicentennial uniforms isn't thrill enough, perhaps the knowledge that bandleader Paul Whiteman began his career in that little white Victorian bandshell will do the job.

This is the north end of Alden Park, named for Commodore James Alden, commander in 1868, who encouraged his far-ranging sea captain friends to bring him specimen trees from all over the world. (Air raid shelters among the trees date from World War II.) Like the seagoing artifacts in the museum around the bandshell, trees are well marked, and guide maps are available for two "tree tours."

The fine old brick office building across Eighth Street, administration building for the shipyard, is Farragut Plaza, renamed in 1954, its hundredth anniversary, for Rear Admiral David "Damn the torpedoes, full speed ahead" Farragut, first commanding officer of the island. For more than a hundred years a giant wisteria adorned the front of the block-long, eagle-adorned plaza building. Look back from its entrance toward Alden Park to see the intertwined trees the children on the island call "The Lovers."

To reach Quarters A, home of the commandant, walk west on Eighth. In 1909 a sentry box topped by a bell stood by the native California sycamore in front of Quarters A.

Houses on the tour range from this, the grandest on the island, through a dozen styles including quonset huts, which officers' families occupy while awaiting something more commodious.

Take the houses on your program in any order you choose. If lines seem to be formidable on Captain's Row, cross the street into Alden Park and continue south through the trees and air raid shelters to Oak Avenue. This is the boundary of the triangle of land on which St. Peter's Chapel stands. Recross Walnut to see the unusual shingles on the chapel and inside, the windows and commemorative plaques dedicated to fallen heroes.

Mare Island takes its name from a shipwrecked white horse belonging to General Mariano Vallejo that found safety here, certainly auspicious karma, but this was name number 2. Don Juan Perez de Ayala sighted the island in 1775 and named it Isla Plana, or Flat Island. The south end, however, is far from flat. To see "The Mesa," hop aboard any of the free military shuttle buses and ride to "The Country" at the south end, where cattle are still pastured.

Several fine old houses, one of adobe brick, a nine-hole golf course, and the pioneer cemetery are on the mesa slopes. Browse the cemetery for a while to find the graves of Russian sailors killed while helping fight a fire in San Francisco.

No one could possibly see all there is to see on 2,247-acre Mare Island in one day, but even the distant glimpses of "off-limits" areas give you the flavor.

To end this walk with the fanfare it deserves, be sure to return to Alden Park by 5 P.M. for the traditional Twilight Parade, almost a pageant of the evolution of the Marine uniform. It will leave you with a strange nostalgia for a long line of ships as well as the shores of Tripoli.

Epilogue

Now that you have walked one or more of these, you should have some idea of what the world was like in that halcyon time B. A. (Before Automobiles).

It is now 77 years since the automobile was let loose on the land. No one, so far as I know, neither anthropologist nor responsible governmental agency, has taken a retrospective look at our culture to assess the changes this seductive monster has wrought. It is time to do it. There has, to be sure, been much talk on how the automobile has changed courting rituals. Mebbe so, as Will Rogers used to drawl, but I wonder if the present day disc jockey has a copy of an early tavern song from the horse and buggy days with the catchy refrain: "But how did Minnie's foot prints land on the dashboard upside down?"

If only for perspective, I would like to have seen with my own eyes the world untracked by highways. Better to have seen it when there were only Indian pathways lacing the state. Or when El Camino Real, the footpath of the padres, was our through road. Alas, I didn't squeak on to this mortal coil soon enough. What I saw as a child was pretty good, though. There were no "freeways sixty lanes wide" as Lawrence Ferlinghetti has described them. The interstate system was simply a glimmer in the mind of some latter-day Caesar then. Roads were mostly dusty wagon tracks cutting sharp corners around somebody's north forty. The wagon itself might be lumbering down the road ahead of you, overloaded with hay and no rear-view mirror.

It wasn't the road one came to see, of course, in the days when motoring was still adventurous and pleasurable. It was the world. The land beyond the land you lived on. It is still there. Try it on foot.

INDEX

MARGOT PATTERSON DOSS was born in the Midwest; she is married to a physician and photographer, Dr. John Whinham Doss, and they have four sons. She is well known in the Bay Area for her column "San Francisco at Your Feet" which she originated seventeen years ago. She still writes a walking column for the San Francisco *Chronicle*; teaches at the extension division of the University of California in San Francisco; appears on local television programs; conducts walking tours for all ages and all manner of groups through all neighborhoods in the city and around the entire Bay Area. She is interested in conservation and serves on numerous boards.

She is a much loved and well-known personality; her projects are many and her vitality boundless.

Her other books include: *San Francisco At Your Feet*; *The Bay Area At Your Feet*; and *Golden Gate Park At Your Feet* (revised edition by Presidio Press, 1978).

NOTES

NOTES